DINNER AT 10:32

DINNER AT 10:32

A NOVEL

MAHYAR A. AMOUZEGAR

UNIVERSITY OF NEW ORLEANS PRESS

Cover illustration by Xuxu Ariya Amoozegar-Montero
Book and cover design by Alex Dimeff

UNIVERSITY OF NEW ORLEANS PRESS
unopress.org

Printed on acid-free paper
First edition

To all our friends from high school, to college, to student housing, to the Kelton Gang, to the Century Club, and beyond...

ACKNOWLEDGEMENT

Ernest Hemingway wrote: "*Writing, at its best, is a lonely life...For a true writer each book should be a new beginning where he tries again for something that is beyond attainment. He should always try for something that has never been done or that others have tried and failed. Then sometimes, with great luck, he will succeed.*"

I have tried with each novel to do something different and perhaps with great luck I may succeed one day. But what has been a constant throughout, is the truism that the final products have gained certain elegance because of the immense support of editors, publishers, reviewers, and friends.

I am grateful to the following: The University of New Orleans (UNO) Press staff who helped transform this novel from many shaky voices into a single solid narrative—Thomas Price (editor), Chelsey Shannon (line-editor), Lauren Garcia (copy-editor), Alex Dimeff (graphic designer), GK Darby (editor), and most of all, Abram Himelstein for managing the entire project. I am also deeply thankful to Xuxu Amoozegar-Montero for the cover illustration. Finally, my many thanks to KaWah Maria Leung (the author *Little Heroes of Bay Street: And How They Stay Strong in an Unhappy Home*), Maria Montero, and Aïda Amoozegar-Montero who provided superb insight and edits throughout the many versions of this manuscript.

PROLOGUE

My grandmother used to say that it's a single moment in your life that defines the path to your future. And every time she said that, my grandfather inevitably would add, "And ours was October 10, 1981, at 10:32."

"Yes, sir," she'd agree immediately.

And then, one or the other, or at times as a duet, they'd tell their story—a sweet tale that provoked a sense of longing that one desperately wanted to be real and duplicable. It was a kind of story that stayed fresh. Like a magical bouquet of flowers, it kept its color and fragrance no matter how many times it was told, and it was told plenty.

I heard the story a dozen times as a child, but I didn't grasp its significance until I was able to connect with it as an adult. It was just a story until one day it transformed itself into a sonnet, and, like all good epics, it required the audience to pause and observe the subtle hints, lest there were hidden meanings.

My grandparents always had a party on October 10th, during which their house was packed with friends, old men and women who had shared decades of life together. My mother was a permanent part of this gathering—after all, she was the direct product of their October 10th decision—and inescapably, I became a fixture at those events as well.

In the beginning, there were many of us, the children and the grandchildren. We called the adults "Aunt" and "Uncle" and referred to each other as cousins. We all knew the story but were always eager to hear it again. It was a simple tale that never changed. The same story every year, as though they had made a promise to only tell one version of it.

When I was a little girl, it was the most romantic, perfect story—a flawless union of two people that created a family that was mine. I believed in that story so much so that it became my obsession; I was always looking for deeper meanings when there were none. But as a teenager, like most other teenagers would, I lost interest in the silly romance of two old people. I challenged them at every turn, annoyed by their zeal for repeating the same lines over and over again, and their insistence that a single moment had made everything possible.

I hadn't found that moment in my own life, even though I desperately searched for it throughout high school and in the early part of college. Yet, I continued to believe in it. But when my boyfriend left me for my college roommate, I realized that nothing in my life depended on a single moment or, for that matter, on a single person.

"What about when you made the decision to call Grandpa? That was a moment as well, right?" I asked my grandmother not for the first time, but this time without hiding my snide tone. "One could also call that the moment, right?"

"Yes, dear, one could, but it wouldn't be true. It didn't change our lives," my grandmother replied in her patient, understanding tone that only added to my frustration.

"But if you'd decided not to call, then what? No you, no Grandpa, no Mom, and certainly no me."

"It doesn't work that way. It's not about going left or right, calling or not calling. Those things don't matter. Those things are just a simple part of life. Those are decisions we make every day. But when everything is right, the day, the time, the mood, the lighting, everything..." She paused to take a deep breath and then exhaled sharply. "When everything is aligned, then you know it in your heart. You feel it in your bones that this is the moment that any decision you make at that point will impact your life forever."

"That's just sentimental bullshit!" I cried out.

That was the first time I had sworn in front of my grandparents, but they seemed not to care—unlike my mother, who would have freaked out about it. I knew I wasn't being fair, but I was angry with them for promising the impossible all my life.

"It may be *sentimental bullshit* to you, young lady, but it's what we believe," my grandfather chimed in without looking up from his newspaper.

Everybody always told me that I was just like my grandfather, tenacious and overly introspective. I never agreed with that assessment. I was my own person and not a reflection of some other. But true or not, it seemed he and I had a kinship that no one else shared. And because of that closeness, we were also comfortably and ferociously combative with each other.

"I still don't believe your silly story," I barked. "Love isn't so simple that it would revolve around a single moment, no matter how magical."

My grandmother replied calmly, "We never said it did, dear. Love is nothing but complicated. It's like a wild beast that can never be tamed, and yet it cannot survive on its own. It needs constant nurturing to endure, and yet it requires an abundance of vigilance, as it can bite back ferociously."

"I've no idea what you're saying—"

"You don't?" my grandfather asked, this time looking straight at me.

"No, I don't. I wasn't asking about love. I was just saying your story is flawed…It is a make-believe. It's…It's…It is just a fantasy."

"Maybe it is, maybe it's not," my grandfather said, shaking his head. "But I don't think you're angry because of our story. You're angry because—"

"Leave her alone, Donte," my grandmother interrupted.

My grandfather looked down.

"What is it, Grandpa? Say what you want to say. Why do you think I'm angry?"

"Nothing…I just wanted to say that you're right. Our story is only real to us. Others, especially you, must treat it like what it is. Just a story. You can't spend your life searching for something you don't believe in."

"I don't do that," I hissed back.

"We know, dear. How about we drop it and have a nice lunch," my grandmother interjected.

"I don't. Really, I don't. I just think you fool yourselves with your October 10th parties and your romantic story. October 10th isn't even your real wedding anniversary. I think you have this fantastic story of love and you've fooled everyone, especially Mom."

My grandmother replied, "We didn't mean to fool anyone. It's just a silly story told by silly old people. No reason to be upset about it. We're thinking about ending it anyway. We're getting too old for parties."

"Speak for yourself, woman. I'm not getting old, and I won't give up our tradition until I die." My grandfather stood up slowly and walked toward us. "Young lady, you can believe it or not. I don't care. Your mother said you broke up with your boyfriend, so we know you're upset, and we understand, but I think you're going too far with this and—"

"Your grandfather lacks prudence," said my grandmother. "You were upset, and your mother was upset. She didn't mean to, but she accidentally let it slip when we were talking and you know—"

"It's private. She had no right. You have no right." I felt ashamed. I didn't want them to know. I didn't want them to see that I had failed.

"I know, dear. We're sorry, and your grandfather is in a lot of trouble. But he's old and has no sense, so please forgive him."

"I don't want to upset you. I'm old and obtuse," Grandpa said. "But your boyfriend was an asshole, and he was no good for you. A month has passed, and it's time to move on. Your *moment* will come. I can promise you that."

It wasn't that I was overly upset about my boyfriend. He was an asshole even before he shacked up with my roommate. I should have dumped him months earlier. But I had been bewitched by my grandparents' story and lived my life in a trance, waiting for that magical moment they had always implicitly promised me. But there was no such thing, and my boyfriend fucking my roommate proved it.

I was okay with that realization; it unshackled me from my grandparents' fairy tale. I wasn't planning to upset them by confronting them so vehemently, but their patient understanding, especially my grandfather's promise of my own moment, was too much.

"Of all people, I'd have thought you two would understand. But all this talk of a magical moment in life is just fucked-up bullshit, isn't it?" I started to cry, not knowing what else to do.

It was like when I was five and some cousin told me there was no Santa Claus, and the more the grownups tried to assure me of his existence, the more I knew it was a big lie. The magic was gone and with it, the power of its fantasy.

My grandmother came over and held me, but I pushed her away hard, not wanting to be contaminated by them anymore.

"You're wrong, dear. We understand full well how you feel. Our lives were not all sweet dreams either," she revealed.

I think she was on the verge of crying as well. I felt ashamed for making them upset, but I also felt that if not them, then at least I needed this dose of reality. She brushed the tears from my face as though I was a little child. She had amazingly soft skin despite her age, and it felt comforting to feel her touch.

Holding my face in her hands, she continued. "We like to tell our story the way we do every year because we made a decision, your grandfather and I—we sort of made a promise without ever saying it out loud—to not look back at all the pain we caused before that beautiful night." She nodded, as if trying to conjure the old memories without letting them infect her. She smiled casually and added, "We chose to start our lives from that moment and forget all about the years before it."

This was the first time that I heard there was a past, let alone a painful one. The story has always been that she called him and he accepted her call. They had a date, and by the end of their dinner, he had confessed his love for her. They were married a year later and had my mother. Sure, they knew each other before that night, but they were just part of a larger group of friends—the same people who came to their house every October. This was the story they had told for fifty years.

I was twenty-two when my grandmother deliberately or accidentally told me there was more to the story. I was too upset to ask about it then, but a few weeks later I cornered her for more information. She refused. I asked their friends, but they all had a variation of the same story. It seemed they had repeated this story for so long that it was the only version they could remember.

My grandfather told me to get on with my life.

I tried to move beyond the pettiness of a devious boyfriend and an untrustworthy roommate. It became patently obvious that I had simply served as a bridge that connected him to her. He wanted her from the beginning but did not have the courage to approach her directly. So I became the conduit that needed to be negotiated several times before he could find the mettle to fully traverse it. My steadfast love gave him that courage. My roommate told me that she had wanted him from the first day, too, but had pulled back out of respect—though her deference to me only held until he found the courage to seduce her. I had served them well. I've often wondered if they had their moment too.

I was ready to give up, but then Nadir, Uncle Nadir to the younger generations, passed away unexpectedly. His death shook everyone around him.

Nadir Gudman was a gentle soul who, unlike the rest of my grandparents' friends, had found contentment long ago and lived life as if each day was more joyous than the day before. Nadir was a large man both in stature and in life, and yet he was humble and sweet in his manner and constitution. He died as he had lived, regally and serenely.

Nadir Gudman passed away while he was sitting in his old, comfortable chair, reading a new book on the history of San Francisco. His wife found him dressed in his suit and tie, with the heavy book on his round stomach and his reading glasses pulled down on his nose. He looked like he was taking a nap and dreaming about something wonderful, as there was still a smile at the corner of his mouth. As the book sat steady on his motionless body, his wife knew at once he had passed away.

My grandparents were very old, as were their friends. Yet, like most of us, they had refused to believe that each of us has an *appointment in Samarra* sooner than we expect. Uncle Nadir's death brought each of them face-to-face with their mortality, and it seemed his absence created a void that none of them had thought could have existed.

Uncle Herman gave the eulogy at Nadir's funeral. He spoke softly and with strange cadence, remembering his friend as if he were thinking out loud. Herman Kennard was a tall man with a full head of white hair. He had dark eyes and an angular face with defined eyebrows that always made him look serious and strong. But that day he looked tiny at the podium, hunched over with his reading glasses perched on his nose, trying to keep his voice steady as he animated their lives off handwritten notes. He kept steady for a long time—his eyes sad and darkened, trying very hard to focus on the crumpled yellow papers—but then the desolation that engulfed him couldn't be contained, and he needed his wife to escort him back to his seat.

Nadir's wife, Aunt Charlotte, had stayed strong throughout and managed to put on a grand reception for her husband in their house with dozens of people attending from across the country. It was a great farewell party for a wonderful husband and father. Nadir had three children and several grandchildren. None of them lived in San Francisco, but they were all there that night.

I was sitting next to the pool, despite the cold San Francisco autumn, when Michael, the eldest of their grandchildren, came and stood next to me. I had not seen him for over five years. When we were little, we went to the same elementary school, but then Michael's parents moved to Chicago. After that our paths only crossed on rare occasions.

I looked up and nodded. He smiled and sat next to me on the lawn chair. We sat there for a moment without saying anything, and I could hear the hum of the conversation from the gallery behind me. It had a steady, hushed tone broken only by an occasional nervous and subdued laughter.

"How are you doing, Michael?"

"Fine, I guess."

"I'm sorry...He was such a sweet man."

"Yes, I'm sorry to see the old man go, but as they say, death and taxes." He chuckled, and although he was not trying to be callous, the use of the cliché was too much for me. I started to cry.

"Oh, I'm so sorry, I didn't mean to...I know you loved him, and he loved you very much. He often talked about you."

Michael spoke in a fatherly but halting tone, and I could not help but think he was a bit jealous that his grandfather cared for me. My mother was the only one of the so-called first generation of children who had stayed in San Francisco while everybody else moved to other cities in and out of the country. Growing up, there was only my mother, my grandparents, their friends, and me. I was one of those old souls who not only did not mind being with elder people, but actually enjoyed it.

"I'm the only one of our generation who stayed around, so it's natural—"

"No, I didn't mean…He really loved you, you know, and that's good," said Michael. He then changed direction. "Last time I spoke to Grandpa, he said that you'd become obsessed with your grandparents' October 10th parties."

"I'm not," I rejoined. I always hated being accused of such things. I never thought of myself as compulsive or neurotic.

"Wow! Don't get angry. He was just saying that you'd been asking and asking. What's the point? That happened, what, fifty years ago?"

It didn't matter to me that the original October 10th had happened a generation ago. And maybe he was right; perhaps that time I was being somewhat obsessive, but I needed to prove it to myself. I wanted proof that life, and more importantly love, did not pivot on single moments.

"I just need to know if I'm here because of one simple decision," I said.

"So it's an existential thing?" He laughed.

"I'm not being self-centered. It isn't just about me."

"Of course not."

"Don't be silly, Michael. Aren't you even a little intrigued by their insistence?"

"No," he replied. Then he asked in all earnest, "Do you want to go out to dinner sometime?"

He made it sound as though he was asking me out on a date, and I felt angry for his nonchalant way,. "I think it's cold to ask me out on a date at your grandfather's funeral."

"So that's a no?"

"Yes, that's a definite *no*."

"What if you would have said yes, and we would have gone on a date and then fallen in love and had children—"

"Don't be an ass."

"But you killed that chance. That person will never be born. So, take that and put it in a pipe and smoke it, lady."

I stood up and walked away from him without another word.

That year's October 10th celebration was subdued, and for the first time in my memory, no one was interested in talking about the past.

They all seemed to be focused on what lay ahead, and after dinner each found an excuse to leave. My grandfather had looked anxious and contemplative all night long and was content to have his friends leave early. Several times during dinner, I had caught him spying on me.

I stayed back to help clean up after they all left, but before I could do anything, my grandfather called me to his study.

He was sitting on the large couch, holding a book on the history of San Francisco in his hand. "He didn't get to finish the book," he said as soon as I came in the room.

"You can finish it for him."

"It's not the same."

"I know."

"He died too soon. We had so many unfinished conversations."

I saw an opening. "Tell me about how you and Grandma met." I was still standing by the door.

He looked up for the first time and shook his head. "Not now."

"Okay," I said and started to walk out.

"Don't leave."

"I want to help—"

"Sit down, please."

I sat next to him. I thought he may have resolved to tell me his story. I could tell that he had resigned to the fact that I would doggedly pursue this and that he urgently wanted his version of the story to be the truth.

But he was still hesitant. "You know the story already."

"But I don't know the real story."

"You'll be disappointed," he said.

"I don't care. I need to know," I insisted.

"And what are you going to do with it?"

"I'm going to write your story."

"I don't think anybody would want to read about our boring lives," he replied.

"I care, Grandpa. Mom cares. We want to know."

"I told your grandmother that we can't tell you our story, but she thinks you deserve the truth." He paused, looking past me as though remembering his conversation with her, and then focused his eyes on me and continued. "She says you deserve the truth, but there is no such thing."

We were silent for a moment. Then he said again, "There is no truth."

"There is yours."

He laughed softly. "Yes, there is my truth, and that may be the problem. I hold it and I may be the only one, though I've always wondered…"

He looked tired, and although he was rambling, I still wanted to know more. Truth or not, I wanted to know a different version of their story.

"I still want to know," I insisted.

"It's not as exciting as you make it, and you'll be disappointed to know that your grandmother is wrong. There is no such thing as the moment. October 10, 1981 was simply another day in our somewhat uneventful lives. There was never one single date, but it was as good as any to celebrate."

"Yes," I urged him on, too excited to sit still in my chair.

"We all take different paths, and mine was a long journey. I needed four distinct events to guide me to her. Do you understand?"

I didn't. I had always thought love came to one without guidance. But I replied, "I think so."

"Do you still want to hear it?"

"I can't wait."

"I'll tell you but with one condition."

He looked up again, and I knew he wanted me to consent first. I nodded.

"I'll tell you what I remember, but you have to promise not to share it with your grandmother."

"Never?"

"Yes."

It was clear that he wanted the promise, and he wanted a genuine one. He was asking for too much, but I needed his story like I have never needed anything else.

"Okay," I offered finally. I wondered if I would be able to stay true.

He looked at me. There was a flicker of doubt, but then it passed. "Then I'll tell you. I will even tell you about the game."

"The game? What's that?"

"You promised, right?"

I nodded again, and he was satisfied. He sat back and closed his eyes for a moment. I could tell the vision of the past rolled in front of his eyes. He took a deep breath, exhaled softly, and then began his story.

AUTUMN 1980

CHAPTER ONE:
THE GREAT THAI RESTAURANT

This is how the story goes, with no real beginning but with a definite end. I could start at any arbitrary moment, to look back or to look ahead. I could even start with when I met Vera Pacient, which would sort of make sense, but perhaps it would give you a better idea of our disordered lives if I start with the party at Charlotte's house. It brought me back from self-exile, and it propelled me to take charge of my life again.

It was Saturday evening, a cold December in 1980—weeks before Reagan took over—and I was on my way to a small dinner party with a few friends. It was a casual dinner, and I had bought two bottles of champagne earlier in the day from a wine shop down on Kearny Street at Clay, right next to The Thai Restaurant. The restaurant was actually named The Thai Restaurant. It used to be called The Great Thai Restaurant, but several years earlier the owner had dropped the adjective without any ceremony.

The wine shop was one of those stores that had every single wine ever bottled and was run by Mr. Stanton, an old man who knew everything there was to know about the wine business.

The store has been closed for many years now.

I went there because I knew Jimmy Wong, who was more or less the manager if there could be such a thing in a small shop. Jimmy gave me huge discounts, plus he let me park in the back, which was even more valuable than the discount. I'm not sure how this whole relationship started, and I won't bore you with the details, but it all came out even in the end.

I drove over before the party and parked in the back lot under the "Tow Away" sign. Jimmy was outside smoking.

"Long time, Donte," Jimmy called out.

"You know how it is." I walked over to shake his hand.

He nearly crushed my fingers. "I heard, man. I thought you and Vera would last forever."

I hadn't told him about the breakup, but Vera had been the one who brought me to the shop in the first place, so she must have told him herself. "Nothing is forever, Jimmy."

I didn't believe it, but I thought this was a good answer. It'd taken me months to appear casual about my failure. I envied people who could, as they say, pick up the pieces and move on. I had unsteady hands, and every piece that slipped through them added more to my vast cache of regrets.

He nodded knowingly and replied, "No shit, buddy." He finally let go of my hand and then said, "Do you need anything special?"

I was tempted to ask if Vera had been there recently, to ask what she had bought, but I checked the urge and replied, "Going to Nadir and Charlotte's house for dinner."

"Something flashy, then?" Jimmy said.

Vera used to insist on bringing champagne instead of wine. She loved champagne and thought no party could start without a few glasses of it. "How about some champagne?"

Jimmy smiled but didn't say anything. He walked into the store and I followed. The store wasn't very busy; just a couple of people were going through the German wine section with Mr. Stanton.

Jimmy grabbed two different bottles. "These are the best we have." He meant the best given my budget but would never say it aloud. He was a great guy.

One of the options was Vera's favorite, the kind she loved to place in the host or hostess's hands like it was a special prize they'd won.

I didn't want to be too obvious, so I shrugged, very casual, and said, "Your pick, but I need two bottles."

He nodded and put two bottles in a brown bag. I gave him some bills, and he put it in the drawer without counting them.

"You running out or you want to have some lunch?" he asked.

"I could eat."

Jimmy put my bag in the large fridge to keep the contents chilled. We went over to The Thai Restaurant. We never discussed any other option. As we walked in, the owner, Mr. Jainukul, greeted us warmly as he did with every regular customer. We didn't need to order either. Mr. Jainukul knew our routine.

When the food was served, we started our usual banter with him, asking him for the thousandth time about the missing "Great" in the name. We all knew why; we'd heard the story before, but our request to hear it again had turned into a silly and not really funny joke.

"Come on, Mr. Jainukul, tell my friend Donte why The Great Thai Restaurant is no longer great," Jimmy insisted.

"It's a secret, boys," Mr. Jainukul cried out, trying to wink with his crooked eye,

"What kind of a secret? Does it have to do with Mrs. Jainukul?" Jimmy said.

We all laughed at the tired joke. Mr. Jainukul had divorced his wife of thirty years to marry a younger woman, but Mrs. Jainukul taught him a good lesson. In the divorce settlement she not only took most of his money, but she also made sure she took the "Great" out of the restaurant's name.

It was silly that we always pushed him to relate the details of the missing Great. That day I wasn't finding the old story very funny.

"Haven't seen you around. I heard about Mrs. Donte," Mr. Jainukul said.

Despite my constant protests, he had always insisted on calling Vera "Mrs. Donte." It used to bother me, but at that moment it was oddly comforting. This was his way of telling us that we were no better than him, that I had failed as well.

"No more Mrs.," Jimmy answered for me.

"Too bad. But then again, she was too good for you." He laughed and winked as though telling me that he understood—we both had made mistakes.

I wasn't sure that he understood, but I didn't want to talk about Vera. Everybody thought they understood, but they were all wrong. How could they know? They all had their own perceptions of how the world should be and their prejudices about what they considered the norm. They all took one look and thought they knew me. Most were wrong.

I could clearly see what Mr. Jainukul was thinking: he didn't really believe Vera was too good for me but rather that I was wrong for her. To him and many others like him, leopards can't lay with panthers.

"What about Jimmy? He hasn't had a proper girlfriend for years," I said. This was my way of getting them off the subject of Vera.

"Watching you guys is enough for me," Jimmy said. "The real question is, what happened to the name of this restaurant?"

Jimmy wasn't going to give up either. This was his way of redirecting the conversation to someone else's misery. It was a circular bashing with no end in sight.

"Neither of you understand anything. You're too young," Mr. Jainukul rejoined somberly. Then, in a more mirthful voice, he added, "Old Mrs. Jainukul thought she could hurt me, but, believe it or not, I don't care. I love the new Mrs. Jainukul with the 'Great' in the name of the restaurant or not."

We both nodded, but I could tell from Jimmy's face that he was with me. We didn't believe Mr. Jainukul for one minute.

"Let's stop this silliness. Let me offer you some great Thai wine. I made it myself," Mr. Jainukul said.

He pointed at the waitress, who seemed to have expected this because she was ready with three glasses and a bottle. It was, in no subtle way, Mr. Jainukul's attempt at getting Jimmy to stock the wine next door. It hadn't worked before, and it definitely wasn't going to work this time because what he served us couldn't possibly be called wine.

We finished eating and drinking Mr. Jainukul's homemade "wine" and left after I paid. I walked with Jimmy back to the wine shop, and after he handed me the bottles of champagne, he clapped me on my shoulder.

"Sorry again, man." And like I wouldn't understand what he meant, he added, "About Vera."

"Don't worry about it." I smiled, hoping he would believe that I was moving on. But then again, I didn't believe it, so why should he? And even if he did, so what? Why should it matter what Jimmy or any other person thought about Vera and me? The sad truth is, it mattered to me.

I took my bottles home and kept them chilled in the freezer. I spent the rest of the afternoon reading the morning paper and lounging about. I dressed and debated about taking a cab but then opted for driving, stopping on the way to buy some flowers. It wasn't necessary to get more than a bottle of wine, but I hadn't seen these guys for a long time. I was nervous.

I searched for a parking place close to Grant and Green. I waited impatiently at the light on Columbus Avenue. I focused on the red, hoping for it to turn green, hoping that I wouldn't have to travel more blocks to find a spot, realizing I should have just taken a cab. Parking was impossible in Nadir's neighborhood, especially around the holidays. But then I glanced over and saw the rows of cannoli in the window of Gina's Bakery.

I hated cannoli, with their odd shape and crispy crust that was hard to bite into or cut properly. The filling was horrible, too, with its strange taste and texture that was neither creamy nor chunky. But Gina's was the place to buy cannoli.

Vera loved them.

Without another thought, I had zoomed several blocks down and parked, forgetting about cabs and cold weather, leaving my jacket in the backseat. I dashed from the car to the bakery.

"A dozen, please." I pointed to the cannoli. I knew it was already too much with the champagne and flowers and now pastries, but I needed these items like a crusader needed his armor. I needed to get through the door and stoke an air of goodwill before the questions about Vera started.

The old man behind the counter arranged rows of cannoli in a white box in a slow, exaggerated fashion, as if he was tucking in little babies for the night.

"I'm double-parked," I lied, hoping he would hurry.

He nodded but didn't change his pace. In this city, everyone was double-parked. Finally, he was finished with the arrangement, but he surveyed the box one last time before closing the lid. Then, in a dramatic fashion, he closed the lid and put the box in an oversized machine that was most likely manufactured the same year Gina's opened its doors. The machine's sole job was to wrap the box tight in a pink plastic string. He pressed a large green button, and after a few loud clangs, the box was tightly wrapped, complete with a small, pretty bow.

"Anything else?" he asked in a low, calm voice as he put the box on the counter.

"No," I said, paying and grabbing the box.

The sun was already stretched across the sky in a lazy, wintery mood, and the dark clouds were impatiently pushing against the hills, awaiting its demise. Strangely, there were seagulls everywhere, so far from the Bay. They all seemed to have awakened at once from the day's slumber, circling the top of St. Matthew's Cathedral, searching for a better shelter. Meanwhile the gentle wind that had started earlier now seemed eager to scamper through the streets. The evening was promising to be frosty. Oblivious to what was to come, I walked hastily toward my destination.

I tucked the flowers, wrapped in crispy paper, closer to my body while balancing the rest of the items in my other hand. I had left my jacket in the car, so my only insulation was the thin paper, which did nothing to break the conspiracy between the cold San Francisco wind and the icy bottles. I increased my pace and headed down toward Grant Avenue, hoping to reach Nadir's house before the rain started.

I was already late and regretting my impetuous shopping. I walked to Grant as quickly as I could, but the cold was getting too much for me to handle. I stopped under the archway of the old church on the corner of Vallejo and Grant and put all my items on the ground, getting a moment of respite from the cold. Then I gathered the packages back up. The box of cannoli in my hands with its little pink bow made me think of Vera more than any other item I carried, more than Vera's favorite chilled champagne and more than, as I suddenly realized, Vera's favorite flowers crinkling in the wax paper. I had gone Vera, three for three.

I felt a great urge to taste a cannoli. Charlotte would throw a fit if she found out that I had eaten before dinner, but I needed the pastry that I despised in my mouth, as if without its bitter taste, I couldn't cross the bridge back to my friends. I had to know if it still tasted the same.

I pulled on the pink bow to unwrap the package, but in my haste, I selected the wrong end and the knot became tighter. I tugged at it harder, but the stubborn string wouldn't give up and my fingers were too numb from the cold to do anything more. Several more tugs only made me more anxious, like the only things that mattered were the crispy shell and sweet ricotta inside the box. If I only had a small knife, I could cut the string away. I searched my pockets for something sharp and was overjoyed to feel my keys. I grabbed the house key and attacked the small box and its string, so innocent-appearing in its delicate pink. I pulled and sawed, but the box only laughed back.

I halted when I heard a footstep behind me.

"Man, do you have a quarter?" A bum shuffled toward me with his hand outstretched.

"No."

"I'm really hungry. How about a dime, then?" he insisted in a patient voice that could only come from years of experience in the art of panhandling. But his tired eyes continuously surveyed the surroundings like an animal that is ready to flee or defend at any moment.

I searched my pockets and gave him a dollar, thereby buying a little bit of grace. I safely tucked my two bottles, the flowers, and the small white box under my arm and headed fast toward the party and a selection of sharp knives.

But I stopped, the little pastries still calling me, daring me to remember the taste of my past.

It was too much, so I turned and yelled, "Hey!"

The man still stood under the archway, smoothing the dollar bill in the palm of his hand. I held the pastry box out, and he started walking toward me, but then I thought that would be too cruel. He didn't deserve my bitter past.

I turned around and took off toward the dinner party. I heard him yell something nasty, but I didn't care.

CHAPTER TWO:
AN INVITATION TO THE PARTY

As I neared Nadir's house, I heard music through a half-opened window—a rhythmic hypnotic sound. I looked up and saw a young couple sitting on the windowsill, sharing a smoke. The woman had long, wavy, almost golden hair that reflected the lights from the interior of the room. She had an angular face filled with small freckles. Her face was hauntingly familiar. So familiar that I thought it was Vera, and seeing her laugh in an easy and unassuming way filled me with a moment of happiness and then dread.

But her hair was all wrong, and, of course, it wasn't Vera. I wasn't even sure why I'd want her to be there. We hadn't spoken to each other for several months now, but her voice still echoed in my head, and, at times, her face was reflected in others'.

The woman saw me looking, and for a moment our eyes linked. She smiled and waved at me, and I rocked back and forth like an old-fashioned doll on a spring. The music stopped, and, as though I had been released from an invisible web, I saw that there were no similarities; it was just my wishful thinking. This was just a stranger waving at me.

I lowered my head as a salute and commenced my journey to Nadir's home, barely a few yards away.

Nadir's house was almost identical to all the other houses on the street, but his had the distinction of having once been occupied by none other than Mark Twain. Not the actual building, of course, but the house that used to be on the same piece of land, a distinction that Nadir Gudman never tired of imparting to his guests. It was a point of pride with him even though he'd never read Twain, not even in high school. This, however, didn't deter him from petitioning the city for an official sign, à la London's blue heritage plaques. The city government patently refused to consider his request, fearing an avalanche of requests by others. Nadir hired a lawyer to sue the city and was planning to start a campaign that included an association of homeowners with famous past occupants. Fortunately, he stopped after three of the five other homeowners also claimed that Mark Twain had lived in their respective houses. When one of the homeowners pointed out that another's house had been built in the fifties, a brawl started that ultimately cost Nadir a painful punch in the stomach.

Then, after Charlotte and Nadir had tried for several years, she became pregnant and convinced Nadir that their four-bedroom flat was too small for their expanding family. They needed to find something larger and closer to the ocean. She forced Nadir to sell the place, which, even without a plaque identifying the house as a former domicile of a famous writer, went within days of posting.

The bright, bold "Sold" sign was still visible on the front gate as I approached the house. I pushed the gate with my body and was glad it gave way without any struggle. I set my packages on the ground and carefully closed the gate behind me. I paused for a moment and looked at the street. The slow rainfall was making it slick and shiny. I loved the smell of rain, but that was not the reason for the pause. It'd been a long time since I had seen my friends. It felt like coming back from a long trip full of experiences that had changed you, but you hoped the others you left behind would stay in a stasis state, knowing full well—at least, if you were honest—that everyone else had changed too.

When Charlotte called to invite me, she pretended that nothing had happened between Vera and me. She didn't ask why I hadn't returned their phone calls or whether I had been away or in town. She didn't ask if I was dating or if I had heard from Vera. She didn't accuse me of hiding from the world. She simply invited me to the dinner party and expected me to show up.

I had been ignoring my friends for months, not wanting to discuss the past or the future. I simply lived in the moment—something I'd never done in my life. It was liberating while it lasted, but it was getting stale and even lonely. My friends did what friends do. They tried to reach out to me and they tried to advise me. I withdrew from them, and they in return allowed me to be me.

But how do you come back? I did it by simply answering Charlotte's nonchalant invitation. I didn't apologize for staying incommunicado far longer than necessary. I did what Charlotte did—I pretended a portion of the past did not exist. I was like a coma patient who suddenly awakens, realizing that time has moved forward and things have changed. He can either pick up his life and move forward or lament about the lost time. I chose the former.

It was easy to come back into the fold through Charlotte. We were playmates before we knew anything about money, social class, family, or love that destroys innocence. We immunized ourselves against such things so that we could stay friends through life's turmoil—and there was much. Career, distance, lovers, and spouses never diminished how we felt for each other—as close as siblings, perhaps even closer, but without all the baggage. We didn't subscribe to the notion that men and women can have close relationships and stay platonic for too long, but with Charlotte and me, it worked (at least somewhat). As she always liked to say, our relationship was *exceptio probat regulam*.

I wanted to know who was invited, though, and she thought it shouldn't matter. I insisted a bit, wanting to tease the answer, so she offered "the usual crowd" as a response. This wasn't satisfactory, but I felt that I was not in any position to argue. I told her that I'd love to go, and that was the truth. I thought enough was enough, and I should get back to my old routines.

A few hours after Charlotte's phone call, Herman Kennard called to tell me that I should most definitely go.

"Why?" I asked.

"Because you've been avoiding everyone, and it's time to be sane again."

"I didn't go crazy, Herman. I needed some time to think."

"I won't debate you on the crazy part, but I don't believe you've done any thinking."

I ignored his comment. "Is Vera invited too?"

There was a pause.

"I don't know," Herman said.

"You don't know, or you don't want to tell?"

"Does it matter?"

Charlotte had offered the same question. Did it matter? I guess I would say yes because I didn't want Vera to be invited. I know it sounds childish, but I wanted our friends to be exclusively mine. After all, they had been just my friends before I met Vera; Vera had come into the mix later. But even then I wanted to see her again, and at the same time, I was too scared to face her.

I had no recourse.

"I guess not," I replied. I didn't want to feel defeated, but it wasn't under my control.

"Good man. Just come early. Don't be late, like you usually are," Herman said.

We ended the conversation on that note, and I sat back to think. Herman was right—I didn't know how to think.

CHAPTER THREE:
THE CLOCK TOWER

As I stood at Charlotte and Nadir's front steps, I felt like a stranger in my own hometown. How should I act? What should I say? I really wanted to go back home, not really ready to meet everyone at once. I couldn't stand their patronizing looks that I'd inevitably get, nor was I ready to deal with Vera if she was there as I was expecting and even hoping. But there was no turning back.

I grabbed the packages, walked up the stairs, and, before putting the bottles down again to ring the bell, realized the door was open. I pushed it with my body, and when it opened, I was face-to-face with Tess, who must have seen me walking down the street.

"Were you debating whether to come up?" she asked.

"No, why?"

"Nothing," Tess said, smirking. "Did you go shopping?" She surveyed the goods in my arms.

Tess Cailean was a tall woman, and she looked even taller in her long baby blue dress that revealed her beautiful collarbone. The dress had an intricate pattern across the front and was laced from the neckline down to its midsection. It was tapered above the hips and around her bosom. Her neck was adorned with a large Moroccan-style silver necklace. Her long, wavy auburn hair was hanging loose on her shoulders. She looked radiant with her green eyes.

It had been a long time since I had seen her, but she was acting uncharacteristically calm, as Charlotte had done. I was expecting her to be more excited, but she just looked at me, waiting. I don't know why, but every time I saw Tess, it was like it was the first. She seemed to put me in a trance. Each time I had to suffocate the emotions that tried to flee from me like a runaway truck.

"Look who's here!" she called out behind her and then looked at me. "Aren't you cold without your jacket?"

I imagined I could hear her thoughts: she was joyful to see me, but she was worried, too, and feared the impending disaster. She had appeared to be calling back to someone specific, a partygoer just inside the house. But who? I needed to know. I stepped up, ready to push past her to see who she had been talking to, but no one was there.

"Hey, Tess, is—"

But before I could finish my sentence, she grabbed the bottles, which until then had been expertly tucked under my arms, and she did it so quickly that it made me drop the flowers while trying to save the pastry box. It didn't faze her. She just gave me a peck on the cheek and left with a rather dramatic turn.

"I know," came a commiserating voice.

Herman stood in the hallway with an amused grin on his face. He walked over and grabbed the flowers from the floor with one hand, then hugged me tight with the other. Herman had a strong, booming voice. I could feel his knotted muscles in his arms as he squeezed. He was wearing a colorful Ecuadorian alpaca sweater that was a tad tight on him, but that brought out the contour of his chiseled body. His hair, as usual, was short and well-groomed, which made his large ears stand out like two radars. He smelled of expensive aftershave.

Herman was mellow and easygoing as much as Tess Cailean was earnest. The old cliché of "opposites attract" was ever-present with those two. He had the look of a fifties leading man—straight, narrow nose, strong eyebrows, a solid chin, and piercing brown eyes. I had known Herman since high school, and though we were not close friends then, our friendship had grown stronger in our adulthood.

"These are for me?" He pointed the flowers like a sword. "You're so sweet. You shouldn't have."

He hugged the flowers and closed his eyes, but then Tess showed up again and grabbed them from him and the box from me.

"You went all out," she said without trying to hide her sarcasm, and she didn't wait for my reply before running away again.

It was classic Tess when she was nervous—lash out and quickly retreat. I knew then that it must have been because Vera was invited to the dinner party. I felt again torn between wanting to see Vera and wanting to have nothing to do with her. Torn between the Vera that I had known in our relationship and the Vera I had yet to meet after it had ended. And all of that in just the first couple minutes of my arrival.

"What do you want to drink, man?" Herman asked as we followed Tess to the kitchen. I expected the whole party to be there, but it was just us and Charlotte's maids, whom I did not recognize. Charlotte couldn't commit to her staff too long, always complaining about them. Or maybe, more likely, she drove them away.

"Whatever you have is fine with me," I said while looking at Tess, who started counting the dishes as if she needed to check the maids' work, all to avoid eye contact with me. "Where's Nadir? Am I one of the first?"

"On the roof," Herman said, pointing to the ceiling and rolling his eyes. "I think he's trying to show off his new telescope. And no, of course you're not one of the first."

"You're late actually. And you know Nadir. Like a child eager to show off his new toy. Now dinner's going to be late too," Tess grumbled, even though she was not the host. "I'm not sure where Charlotte is," she added. She was probably upset at Charlotte for not taking more responsibility for her own dinner party.

The maids were busy with their work, and I was sure they were eager to get rid of Tess so they could do their job. The familiarity of the situation was comforting, like going back to a family reunion.

"Do you know what's on the menu?" Tess asked.

At first I thought she was speaking to me, but then I realized she was talking to the maids. They stared at her as if she was an intruder in their house, which in a way she was.

"What's the difference, love? I'm sure Charlotte can manage with all her hired help." Herman then said to me, "She has an army working here, and yet we have to get our own drinks."

"Doesn't she normally have a cook or chef or something?" I asked.

"No on that front. I think we're getting food from some fancy res-taurant. Meanwhile we need something to drink," Herman said.

Herman surveyed the bottles on the kitchen counter and examined each one carefully. He shook his head with disgust and said, "Just cheap crap."

Charlotte, despite having a large house, refused to keep a proper bar. Or even a liquor cabinet.

"Who's coming to dinner?" I asked.

"Where do they keep their good stuff?" Herman asked the maids, but they shrugged their shoulders again and used the distraction to collect the dishes from Tess.

Herman walked over to the huge pantry, rummaged through some of the cabinets, and came out with a brand new bottle.

"You shouldn't," Tess warned.

"Don't worry, dear wife," Herman said, then opened the bottle of single malt and poured it into two large glasses. He re-corked the bottle and put it back in its original place.

"Nadir will never know." He handed me one of the glasses, raised his, and shouted, "As immortal Ernest might utter, let's utilize this."

They were ignoring my question, so it was obvious that Vera was invited as well. Perhaps she was coming later. Perhaps this was an intervention. Although it was several months too late. I decided to go with the flow for a change.

We walked to the living room and sat close to the fireplace with its beautiful, roaring fire. The heat of the fire was strong, so Herman opened some of the windows to let the cool air in.

"Tess is going to complain," I warned. "She's always so cold." I'm not sure why I said it. Was I telling Herman that I knew her better than he did?

"Yeah, you're telling me," Herman agreed, not taking offense. "We can close it later." He waved his hand dismissively.

We sat between the fireplace and the open windows, where we could smell the salty air. The room was small compared to the others. There were two baby pink Queen Anne chairs facing the fireplace with two complementing couches on each side. The room was painted in light, serene colors, and it looked bright even in overcast weather. There were rows of books in a built-in bookshelf, many tattered from years of use. It was a nice, comfortable room. I had practically lived in this room for almost a month some years earlier.

Herman and I sat next to each other in total silence, simply enjoying the fine Scotch and the beautiful air. That was one great thing about Herman. I didn't have to have a bullshit conversation with him just so we could hear our own voices. We were comfortable sitting around, reading the newspaper or watching a show.

"This is a great Scotch. What is it called?" I said.

"Too-expensive-for-us-to-afford," Herman replied. He was taking small sips and rolling it in his mouth for a long time. He was smiling brightly and then turned serious, remembering what he had to say. "Look, don't freak out. Vera is here." He took a big mouthful of Scotch.

I followed suit without thinking. The bitter liquid burned the inside of my cheeks as I held it in my mouth. I closed my eyes, and Herman waited patiently.

"Why would I freak out?"

I wanted to sound insulted by his implication, but it came out defensive and feeble. I took another sip, which practically emptied my glass. I wanted to throw the glass across the room, but instead I whispered, "Why would I be the one freaking out? Why not Vera?" I gestured to drive the idea home. The glass slipped from my hand and thudded hard on the ground. I was happy that it at least didn't break.

I could see it on Herman's face as he stared at my glass on the floor. I had proven his point.

It was bound to happen, of course. It's the price of having common friends. Vera and I had avoided each other for several months, but we were certain to see each other eventually, and that night was as good as any. I'd been trying to prepare myself since Charlotte had invited me to the party, but hearing that Vera was there, I felt scared.

I loved her. I hated her. I missed her, and I feared that she did not miss me. I wondered how she looked. I wanted her to be miserable, fat, and ugly, but she wouldn't be. I would be the one who had changed instead in my stupid little exile.

"Where's she now?" And then it hit me. "They're all up there pretending to be looking at Nadir's telescope? And it's your job to be down here prepping me?"

"No," Herman replied. "Nadir really is showing off his new tele-scope, but you're right I'm here to prep you because there is more—"

He didn't get a chance to finish as Charlotte came in the room with Tess in tow. She walked over to us as we stood up and gave me her usual quick, precise hug as though we had just seen each other a few days earlier.

"You got a haircut," she said, surveying me, and I absentmindedly ran my fingers through my short hair. "It looks good, makes you look…" she paused. "You look manlier, if you know what I mean."

I didn't but thanked her anyway.

Herman mouthed the word "manly" but didn't say anything.

"It's freezing in here. Close the windows," Tess complained. She hugged her body to reinforce her point.

Herman walked over and closed the windows but still left one ajar.

Charlotte sat back on an oversized couch and pulled out the large hair clip that had held her long black hair in place. Her hair dropped easily around her shoulders like a black silky shroud, hiding the pair of large silver hoop earrings that dangled from her ears. She was wear-ing a black dress with a colorful African pattern with oversized cuffs and a low-cut front that accentuated her olive complexion. Charlotte Adoniram looked like a Mogul princess with her high cheekbones, her narrow nose, and her beautifully arched eyebrows.

Her eyes, a calm, vast sea, surveyed the room for a moment, and then she looked at me and said, "It wasn't my idea."

"I didn't say anything," I replied.

"You can thank Tess and Nadir for this setup. I was perfectly fine with not inviting Vera. They insisted."

"Stop saying setup, Charlotte. I didn't insist," rejoined Tess. "I just said it would be good for them. I like Vera, and it has been way too long, if you ask me. And frankly, you're not helping the situation."

"I like Vera too," Charlotte replied.

We all looked at her as if she was crazy.

"I do!" she said. "I don't know who started this stupid rumor that I didn't like her. She is just fine, and I don't have to be in love with her, do I?"

"Of course not. I just wish you had told me she was coming," I said.

"Yes, I should have, but I was not allowed. I know you're angry with me, but you should know—"

"I'm fine, Charlotte, really," I said. "I'm fine. I'm fine with the whole thing. I'm fine with Vera being here."

"So what you're saying is—that is, if I understood you correctly—is that you're fine?" Herman said.

"I said that, didn't I?"

"I was just making sure you're fine, just in case you weren't." Herman smirked.

"Look, Donte, you know I'm on your side, right?" Charlotte said. "But Vera is here. So say what you need to say to her or say nothing, but either way, it's time for you to move on." Charlotte concluded her thought by wiping her hand, as if that solved everything.

"Let's drop it. I'm fine with her being here."

Charlotte said, "Great. Then it's settled."

I could see she was relieved. I assumed it was because of me, because I said I wasn't upset, but I imagined she was still angry with Vera, or at least I hoped I was reading her correctly. I was happy to have her support, and her anger at Vera made me feel more confident. She hadn't wanted to invite Vera but felt compelled to by Tess more than by Nadir, and that made her angry with herself. She took my words at face value, and I felt the tension leaving the room.

"What are you drinking?" Charlotte said.

She was asking me, but Herman replied, "Umm…just some Scotch."

"I'm going to have some sparkling water. Tess, do you want some?" Charlotte asked as though ordering to an invisible waiter.

Tess immediately jumped up and said she would get it. Charlotte said she would have it with some ice and a twist.

We were silent again, and then, out of nowhere, Herman asked, "Remember the day we climbed the clock tower and drank a whole bottle of cheap whiskey?"

"God, that was such a long time ago. What made you think of that?" Charlotte asked.

He was talking about the last day of school, when Herman, Charlotte, and a few of their friends snuck out and climbed the old tower at school that used to house an enormous clock. For the longest time, it was the tradition for the graduating class to climb the tower, sit in front of the clock, and do what teenagers have always done. The 1906 earthquake had damaged one of the walls. Time and scarcity of funds did the rest. The building became abandoned, its doors and windows covered with heavy wooden boards. The tradition died with the building, and anyone who had a chance to see the inside of that sad place would have agreed.

To get to the tower, one had to cross a tall fence and then climb up a maze of a wrecked staircase with missing steps that dangled like loose teeth in a giant's mouth. For years, students stayed away from the tower, so by the time it was our turn, the tradition was forgotten. That was, until Herman decided to revive it.

I certainly remembered the day; the events are etched in my memory as if on a tombstone. I remembered the day but not the way Herman recalled it. I wasn't with him. Herman had forgotten, or he pretended to forget, that he and I were, at best, acquaintances then. The only reason we knew each other was because of Charlotte. I was at one end of the chain and Herman was at the other. If he was the start of cool, then I was the end of it.

At the time, Charlotte was dating Nadir. Their parents roamed in the same social circle. Nadir was a bit geeky, and they were somewhat of an odd couple, but I thought Nadir was good for Charlotte, especially given her rebellious junior year with her eclectic set of boyfriends. My father was a friend of Charlotte's father because they had met as teenagers in Chile, when their parents were in Santiago for some reason or other. It was really a coincidence because Charlotte's grandparents were supposed to have left a week earlier, but something went wrong with the passenger ship. The foreign land and the kinship among expats temporarily removed the social and economic barriers that would have existed at home, and our parents struck up a friendship that lasted until my father's death.

Herman climbed to the top of the clock tower and was up there drinking, laughing, and making a lot of trouble. He had shouted at me at one point, and I did what I did then, ignored him. It was getting dark, and everyone was leaving. If the kids at the top were left on their own, they would have come down without any incident. But unfortunately, the vice principal, Ms. Shaw, saw them and started shouting at them and then barking at Mack the janitor to do something. Mack, however, wasn't being paid enough to risk his life to climb the stairs of death for some rich kids.

"What do you want me to do, Ms. Shaw?" Mack asked in his haltingly slow voice as if each word required enormous energy.

"Bring them down, Mack. They'll fall," she said.

"How would I do that, Ms. Shaw?" Mack asked, wanting to do something to please her (we all knew he loved her) but at the same time not wanting to get involved with this. "They'll come down on their own if we ignore them."

It had become impossible to ignore the situation, though, as more and more students and even some parents gathered next to the fence. Ms. Shaw was getting frustrated. "Please, Mack, do something."

Mack couldn't ignore Ms. Shaw's pleas and was about to say something when Mr. Loverly, the principal, showed up.

"Christ...What the hell is going on, Mack? Go get the goddamn ladder and force those goddamn kids down. Do you have the key to the gate? How did they cross the fence? Who's up there, Ms. Shaw?"

"I don't know, just some kids," Ms. Shaw replied, her voice breaking with emotion. She loved the students too much to become a principal.

Mack disappeared for a moment and then returned with his long metal ladder. He unlocked the gate and then tried to lock it behind him, but a rush of students pushed through, trying to get a better view. He leaned the ladder next to the tower and started to climb up very slowly, pausing after each step to look down at the adults who were urging him on.

Herman and the others saw what was happening and started to throw food at Mack, and Mack took a step down with each projectile, only to be urged to go back up again by Mr. Loverly, in a not so gentle voice. It was comical, Mack slowly, cautiously going up a step, getting hit with a missile, retreating a step, getting yelled at by Mr. Loverly, and then taking two quick steps while trying to dodge a barrage of food. Students on the ground were laughing and shouting at Mack.

Everything was going fine until Herman and his friends ran out of munitions, and Mack, now angry, climbed up higher and faster. The kids on the tower saw that Mack was serious and started to run around the tower, trying to get through a small opening that led them to the staircase. They all must have piled onto the same landing because the staircase, which was barely standing before, gave way with a thunderous, earth-shattering crash.

There was a deathly silence as fear engulfed everyone outside, and Mack, who apparently was afraid of heights, clung tightly to the ladder.

We stood there for a moment in shock, not knowing what to do, but then everybody ran toward the tower as though released from an invisible hold. A couple of students helped Mack down from the ladder. The door to the clock tower was boarded with heavy planks, but that didn't stop the confused and scared parents and administrators from clawing at it with all their might. The rotten wood gave way with a loud crack, and a cloud of white dust poured out of the building like a ghost. There was no sign of the students, but I could see that the whole staircase had collapsed. Everybody feared the worst and started to scream.

Mack was smart enough to look for a hidden entrance that they had used. He caught them coming out of a small hole behind the tower that was covered with overgrown shrubbery. As soon as they saw Mack, they started running in all directions and trying to hide in the crowd.

The only person who didn't run was Charlotte. She sat on the ground as a narrow stream of blood flowed down from her head. Nadir and I rushed toward Charlotte, but the adults converged on her like buzzards.

Mr. Loverly did not know whether to be angry or relieved that no one was dead. Ms. Shaw was crying and hugging Charlotte, whose injury was rather minor.

"Anybody else hurt, Charlotte?" Ms. Shaw asked as she helped Charlotte get off the ground.

"Who was up there?" Mr. Loverly demanded of Charlotte, but Ms. Shaw gave him a stern look, so he started yelling at the kids who were still gathered around the building.

Two months later, the clock tower was fully demolished, and students found other ways of celebrating their graduation.

That was how it happened, but I knew Herman would alter facts and invent new scenarios. He always did. But I also knew that the reminiscing would keep Vera at bay a few moments longer. It would keep everyone in the room like a secret club, only allowing admittance to those who could remember, even if poorly.

So, I replied, "I remember the clock tower."

"I thought we were all going to die," Herman said. "All of us falling, God knows how many feet, on top of each other with metal and wood crashing all over us, and then, like magic..." Herman paused, still in awe of what had happened so long ago. His eyes were twinkling, remembering the miracle. "We were all right. Not even a scratch." He smiled and sipped from his glass, reliving the memory. "Who was with us, Charlotte?"

He wasn't ready to let go of the story that we had shared so many times and each time with a new role for my character. Time and retelling had enhanced my participation from bystander on the fringe of the action to man near the center.

Herman pointed with his glass, "It was you and Charlotte, of course, and..."

"Julie," Charlotte put in, getting into the nostalgia game.

"Yes, Julie and, ah, that gorgeous babe, Donna. And Jay Jay and..." He paused to think, to remember some of the long-forgotten friends.

I always wondered about what had happened to all those people at my school, the people I was in awe of and admired from afar—the same people who I'd walked among invisibly, surfacing from the oblivion to share a rare moment or two simply because I was Charlotte's friend. The irony of life was that all those amazing people were nowhere to be found, and amongst all the people who used to surround Herman, only the four of us managed to stay together.

"I wasn't there," I said.

I would usually not remind him of my absence in his little adventure, letting him feel good for including me. I think he knew full well that on those days we walked separate paths, but this was perhaps his way of making up for our not-so-friendly encounters.

"Sure you were," confirmed Charlotte. She didn't want to let go either.

"We were up there, drinking some cheap whiskey and throwing junk at the janitor, what was his name? And you, you rascal, you were making out with Donna." Herman wagged his glass at me with a wink. "She was gorgeous, wasn't she?"

"That she was," I said.

I certainly would admit to Donna's beauty but making out with her? I probably would have pissed my pants if she had sat next to me.

Donna was gorgeous in an absolute sense. Her high, strong cheek-bones ended in red, subtle lips. Her nose was straight and, though somewhat pointy, a feature that might have looked out of place on most people, it sat perfectly on her face. She had long black hair, and her eyes were bright and twinkled in the light. She was tall. Her body mimicked classical beauty.

It was a great fantasy even now, so I didn't insist on correcting Herman.

"Now you remember, don't you?" He wagged his glass at me again with a sly smile.

I wondered if he truly believed this fantasy, or was he just being nice?

"She was an amazing girl. Very kind," he murmured as though talking to himself. "Though her parents wouldn't let her see me after graduation." He and I probably shared the same image of Donna, and as such, I could feel his longing heart.

"She was a good girl," Charlotte added. "Where is my sparkling water? I bet you they forgot about it." She stood up and left the room, perhaps tired of our conversation more than anything else.

Herman took a sip from his glass, still focused on his reverie. "Yeah, she called me up a few days later and said her parents thought I was too reckless. Can you believe it, calling me of all people *reckless*?"

The guffaw on his face almost made me believe that he believed himself.

"So she said she couldn't hang around with us anymore." He looked wistful for a moment and took another sip of his drink. "To tell you the truth, I think she was just using them as an excuse."

"Where is she now?" I asked.

"I've no idea. I let her go, but to tell you the truth…" He leaned forward in a conspiratorial manner. "And don't tell Tess this, but I regret like hell not pursuing her more."

I felt a tinge of anger for his feeling of regret. He seemed to have everything but was not appreciating it. He could never understand what it meant to be an outsider. Not ever.

"You're so lucky to have Tess." The words came out a bit harsh. I felt exposed.

We were silent for a moment, trying to expel the somber mood. He succeeded first and slapped me on my leg and said loudly, "That's for goddamn sure. Anyway, I was trying to make a point with this and got a bit sidetracked."

"What was your point?" I asked.

"I don't know, but as I was saying before Charlotte walked in, there is more—"

"What?" I cut him off with a shout and then, feeling stupid, said, "Sorry! Didn't mean to yell."

"As I said, don't freak out, man. Vera is here with a date. Wait, wait." He must have seen me ready to cut him off again, so Herman leaned halfway out of his chair and put his hand out as if he was going to press it to my chest and hold me back. "It was going to happen some-time, right? You knew that, right? So, as your friend, I seriously sug-gest that you stay on your best behavior."

"You don't understand." How could he? And I could never explain it to him.

He leaned back, pulling away from me. "Make me understand. You never wanted to talk about it, and from what I've heard, which was no thanks to you, it seems you're the one who wanted out. So please make me understand."

I sat in silence. I wasn't ready to talk, and even if I were, I knew we wouldn't reach the same conclusion. Herman didn't push his point, knowing full well that he wasn't going to get anywhere.

"This isn't a setup." He underscored each word.

"I didn't say it was, did I?" My tone was nasty.

"Don't be an asshole." He tried to take another sip of his Scotch, but his glass was empty.

"Did you know?" I asked.

"I had my suspicion that she was seeing someone. We just didn't expect her to show up with a date."

"How long have you known?"

"What's the difference, man? Did you seriously think that she would become a nun after you?"

"No, but—"

"But what? Come on."

He was right, but he only knew half of the story. I was sure of it. There was nothing for me to say except, "I'd like to have another, but I fear Nadir would notice."

"No worries. We shall utilize more." Herman stood, taking the excuse to escape the conversation. He disappeared into the kitchen, which was when I noticed he had made sure to take his own glass with him, but mine was still lying on its side on the floor. I picked it up and held it in my lap.

After a few moments I heard Tess objecting to something Herman was doing and, based on her rising level of anger, him ignoring her. Herman came back with two glasses half full. He passed one of the new glasses to me, keeping one for himself, and I sat there, an empty glass in one hand and one with Scotch in the other.

He said, "It's all taken care of. I simply poured some of the cheap Scotch into the good bottle." It sounded perfectly logical to me, so we banged our glasses together and took a large sip.

"Let us utilize this and be merry," Herman said and, in the same tone, "Please don't be hurtful toward her. Can you promise that much?"

"To Ernest," I saluted.

"To Ernest, indeed," he said in a low voice with all mirth drained from it.

"I'll never hurt..." I started to say but stopped. There was nothing to tell Herman, so I corrected myself in my mind. *I'll never again be hurtful to her.* At least I'd learned that much.

Herman replied as though he had read my mind. "Life is full of lessons and we're better for it if we heed them well. You'll be fine and so will she." He moved closer and continued in a low, hushed voice, "I know how you feel. I really do."

It sounded like a secret, but he looked innocent.

After a moment he said, "I just saw this graffiti on a wall on Mission Street. Tell me what you think of it?"

He sat back and closed his eyes, then recited it like he would a poem.

"He is surrounded by love but cannot see/Even when he wakes up in a golden spree/He tells himself to love more/But there is pain in his heart and nothing more."

"Are you talking about me?" I asked, annoyed.

"Why would you think that?" His face was passive and betrayed not a single trace of irony.

"I'll behave if you don't recite anymore poetry, for God's sake."

"Poetry? You have it wrong, my friend. This is the real thing; this is the voice of the street." He laughed heartily.

"Salute," I said.

He raised his glass and I did mine, and we both took a long, satisfying mouthful.

"I hope you boys are enjoying yourselves," Tess cried out. She stood by the door with her hand on her hip in an exaggerated fashion, trying to sound stern.

Tess was straight. No bends. She believed in doing the right thing, and she always did, but there was also that mischievous little girl inside of her who would sometimes, though rarely, come out. She was also in charge; there was no doubt about that.

We both turned around and saluted her in the same exaggerated way. She smiled for a moment and then became very serious again, staring at Herman with her intense eyes. And then, satisfied with what she saw, she turned around to leave.

"Stay and have a drink with us," Herman called after her.

"I'm too busy getting everything done," she replied.

"Thanks for setting me up, Tess." I wasn't going to let it go.

She stopped dead in her tracks. "It's not a setup, as you call it."

"It would've been nice if you'd have warned me."

"Then you wouldn't have come."

"That's true," I said.

"How many times have I tried to get you to meet with Vera, make your peace, and move on?" she asked.

"Once?"

"Once? Once? Are you crazy? Plus, I'm tired of your constant brooding. I think it's time for you and Vera to settle this. I know she does too."

"She does? Are you sure?"

"Don't get ahead of yourself," Herman chimed in. "You need to decide what you want first."

"Herman's right. She's here with a date. You know that, right?" Tess said.

"Yes, I've been briefed by your sergeant."

"Don't get mad, Donte. I didn't know she was bringing a date, but I can't blame her either. You made your intentions very clear and then disappeared…I'm surprised she waited this long," Tess said.

"Don't lecture me, Tess."

"I'm not lecturing, but I think it's time for you to take some responsibility. We're with you, but you have to—"

"You always took her side," I said.

"For God's sake, Donte. There were never any sides. You don't think it hurts us as well? We love you both. Just, for your own sake, try to be nice to her."

"I'm always nice."

She gave a short snort but didn't say anything. She walked closer to me and gave me a hug. That was her remedy for everything, though I needed it then. I could feel every part of her body, and once again I felt jealous of what Herman had and what I could not have.

"Be nice, please," she warned and walked out. Then she walked back in a second later. "And please close that window; it's freezing in here. I'm going to get everybody." She walked out again without waiting for us to reply.

"I'm nice, right?" I asked Herman.

"Almost always." He sipped his Scotch. "But you can be nasty too. You should know that about yourself."

I sat across from him, clinking the empty glass and the now nearly empty second glass against each other, hoping the sound would distract from the silence. I had no idea what he and Tess were talking about. I was like any other person. I had good days and bad ones, but I had never been nasty.

"How's work?" I asked.

CHAPTER FOUR:
A TENTATIVE TRUCE

Tess hadn't been gone long before Charlotte came back into the room with Nadir. She sat down on the couch, and Nadir came over to shake my hand.

"I'm glad you made it. It's been a long time," he said.

Nadir was wonderful. He had a big face with jolly cheeks and a broad smile. At work, he was the all-powerful executive with his expensive suits and intimidating demeanor. At home, he was easygoing and dressed like a lumberjack—denim pants and plaid shirts. He was the unassuming friend who you didn't notice, until he was gone, his absolute role in keeping everyone together. The lynchpin. Later in life, after he retired, he would start wearing a suit and tie at home as if he missed the feeling he had while at work.

"Do you want to go up and look at my new telescope?" he asked, still holding onto my hand. "It's amazing."

"Doesn't it have to be really dark out? Plus, it's rather cloudy right now." I noticed Tess hadn't followed them into the room. Instead, she remained in the doorway, nervously tapping her foot and watching down the hallway where I couldn't see. She was waiting.

Nadir said, "You only need the night sky if you want to look at the stars. Right now, you can see the whole Bay. You want to go up and see?"

"He doesn't want to look at your silly telescope," Charlotte moaned. "Why don't you go open your nice Scotch instead? Give these boys something good to drink."

"No!" Herman shouted a little too quickly. He chuckled. "That is, don't worry. We're going to eat soon, right?"

Tess straightened her back, and I held my breath, ready for Vera to walk in, but instead Rajiv, Charlotte's personal assistant, rushed into the room. He carried a tray of drinks. Sparkling water for Charlotte, which he handed directly to her. Flutes of champagne for the rest of us. Tess rushed over, took a glass, and then returned to her sentry post.

Nadir sipped his champagne. "Oh, this is very good. Vera must have brought this."

No one corrected Nadir, but I could feel several pairs of eyes in the room on me. Maybe they were waiting for me to confess. However, I let the moment pass without comment.

Charlotte took Rajiv by the arm. "Go and bring the bottle of Auchentoshan that Nadir has hidden in the pantry."

And Rajiv rushed back out before Herman or I could protest again. I almost expected him to give Charlotte a little bow before leaving, but he only gave her an affirmative head nod.

Rajiv was Charlotte's personal assistant, driver, servant, and everything in between. Charlotte ran a fashion magazine that attracted many devotees who were willing to follow her around and serve her.

Anat, a friend of Charlotte's, walked into the room, and I saw Tess nod to herself as if she was keeping account of all the people moving in and out.

Anat started to jump up and down as though she was surprised to see me. She wiggled her way across the room and wrapped an arm around my back.

"We've missed you," Anat said. Then she kissed me hard on the lips, something she was known to do.

She tasted like cinnamon and smelled of flowers. I felt the warmth of her body and the softness of her breasts through her thin white blouse as our bodies collided for the momentary kiss. I grabbed her waist, and she leaned on me, putting her head on my shoulder.

"What? You didn't miss me?" Herman protested.

Anat grabbed both of his hands and pulled him toward her. "Of course I did."

Before Anat kissed him, I saw Herman give Tess a little wink. The kiss lingered longer than it should have, and I thought it made Tess uncomfortable. She was back to tapping her foot nervously. I almost pushed Herman away to stop the kiss, but then Tess snickered at his antics and shook her head with a small smile.

Anat stood between us, holding onto our arms and pulling us tightly to her. She was a few years older than the rest of the women at the party, but she didn't look it. She was warm and kind and in the habit of kissing and hugging whenever she met people, no matter if she knew them or not. Her warmth was infectious. You couldn't help but feel a bit better by just saying hello to her. She had the kind of voice that some people might find annoying, but I thought of it as fun and bubbly.

Rajiv returned with a tray of heavy crystal glasses and the bottle of Auchentoshan. He poured two fingers of the Scotch in each. I took a clean glass, my third, and I tried to push the first two under the couch with my foot. But Rajiv saw them and removed them with discretion. Anat refused a glass of Scotch herself, but she kept taking the glasses out of each of our hands and sneaking little sips.

"Please sit down. You all make me tired standing like this," Charlotte ordered, and, with the exception of Tess, we all started moving like little school children. I sat on the couch across from Charlotte and Herman. Anat joined me.

"You know Vera is here, right?" Anat tried to whisper it into my ear as she sat down, but everyone in the room heard her.

"He has been briefed," Herman offered.

"And, just so you know, she's with—" Anat started.

"Yes, I know, Anat. She is with her boyfriend. I'm fine, really, I'm fine."

"The boy is fine. You all heard it," Herman announced.

Anat ignored him and kissed me on the cheek, then said to Charlotte, "This is a fine single malt." She purred as she licked her lips.

"I'm glad you like it," Charlotte replied.

I was glad the conversation had turned away from Vera. I took another sip from my glass; even with Herman's adulteration, it was still a fantastic Scotch.

Herman followed suit and then asked me, "How much does a bottle like this run?"

"How would I know?"

"But you know Jimmy," he offered in earnest.

"So?"

"You always shop at Stanton's, don't you?"

"Again, so? It doesn't mean that I know the price of an Auchentoshan. I haven't even heard of this label before. I just tell Jimmy to get me something good and not too expensive, and he does."

"But—"

"Where's Akron?" I cut him off.

And as if on cue, Akron walked through the door. At first thinking it was going to be Vera's new boyfriend, my heart pounded, but I recognized him almost immediately. Akron was an intense man with a quiet demeanor that made him look even more serious. He came in with a leisurely but deliberate fashion and surveyed the room in a smooth motion.

I tried to extricate myself away from Anat so that I could give Akron a proper handshake, but she clung to my waist like a baby monkey. Akron came over and sat on the edge of the couch next to me as a way of greeting.

Rajiv poured another glass of Auchentoshan and said to Akron, "Would you like a glass of Scotch?"

"Nah, I'll just have a beer," he said.

Rajiv was not happy. He turned to leave the room again, and Herman grabbed the now free glass of Scotch off the tray.

He took a sip and whispered to me, "Even with the cheap stuff mixed in, it's not half bad."

I nodded but didn't say anything as Rajiv got to the door. I thought I couldn't take it anymore, the coming and the going. I couldn't stand to have another person enter the room not knowing if it would be Vera this time. But before Rajiv could exit, Tess jumped to attention, moving out of the doorway and stepping aside.

Vera and her date glided into the room.

I stood up. Everyone went silent, and I felt that time had slowed to a crawl.

Charlotte was sitting back, sipping gingerly from her glass of sparkling water, but her eyes were focused on Vera. I knew she was happy that Vera would finally be out of my life. She had been expecting this outcome for years. Charlotte said Vera was a fine woman, but I knew she also thought it was her job to protect me from Vera's grasp.

Herman, who was still sitting on the other side of Anat, rolled his eyes and glanced away, an expression I'd seen many times in high school whenever he was embarrassed by me. Herman must have been wishing I would grow up. He wanted me to get over my failure and move on. Vera was too good for me anyway. I could almost hear him shouting at me, *Donte, you promised!* But he sat where he was, ultimately not interfering.

Nadir toasted Vera and her date's entrance, happy to see them even though he had just left their presence on the roof moments before. I thought it was time for him to speak out and not be so timid when it came to me. But it was hard to feel anger for Nadir for too long. He'd made this blunder out of his soft nature, his need to be pleasant to everyone, not out of some slight against me. But I hoped, without really believing it to be true, that Nadir would intervene on my behalf if things went too far.

Anat finally focused on her husband, clinging to his waist now that I had walked away. She gave him a loving squeeze. And Akron seemed to be oblivious of the tension in the room. He was in a good place and didn't want anything to affect his mood. Or, he simply didn't care. For a moment, I was jealous of that.

I reached the other side of the room. Despite all the tension and worry, nothing was clearer to me than this: this man was no good for Vera. His mannerisms and affectations appeared artificial and devious. The way he tilted his head so slightly. The way he held his arm perfectly at his side. He was dishonest and opportunistic. If I saw it, then I knew everyone else in the room saw it. We would all break out in laughter at this mismatched couple, at her date pretending to be a good man.

And it was very clear that Vera wasn't happy. Very clear.

"Vera," I cried out. I positioned myself between the rest of the room and her to give her a long, hard, clearly exaggerated hug.

This wasn't what I had planned. I imagined myself all regal and reserved, a personification of someone who was above such petty emotions as envy and narcissism. I imagined myself standing tall and casual—perhaps having a conversation with Herman and becoming so immersed in my discourse that I wouldn't even notice Vera's presence. I'd then look up mid-sentence and notice her and nod to her nonchalantly, telling her with my eyes that I'd be with her as soon as I was done with my conversation. I'd finish my sentence and then walk over to her casually and greet her in a friendly yet somewhat formal manner. She would introduce me to her date, and I'd greet him in the same manner. We'd chat for a while as others would watch in anticipation, but after a few minutes they'd feel relieved and go on with their own conversations. I would of course start to apologize for my past mistakes if there were any, and Vera would stop me mid-sentence and say she was also to be blamed. I'd mildly rebuke her and claim all the blame for myself, and she would try to do the same. After a few minutes, we'd both laugh and hug warmly. We'd say, *Let's forget all our past trouble and just be good friends.*

Maybe it had been too optimistic of a scenario, but Vera and I had loved each other once, so why couldn't we become good friends? Wasn't that something reasonable couples were prone to do? While the scene hadn't played out as I had hoped, at least we were mature enough to hug one another.

But then I realized her body felt stiff between my arms, like the onset of rigor mortis. Her arms remained at her side, one hand still clutched in her boyfriend's, even. Her face fully betrayed her distaste of my action.

"I didn't know you were back," I lied. I forced a laugh. "Everybody else seemed…"

It was not going like I had imagined.

Vera brushed me off, as if pushing a house cat off her lap, and straightened her dress, smiling faintly. She looked at the others, who were watching us with nervous eyes. She pointed to the man beside her, who seemed ambivalent about the strangeness of the situation.

"This is James." Vera pointed again as though to make sure I was looking at the right person.

I gazed at her with all my strength, trying to keep her immobile. I wanted to keep her at the door because once she entered the room fully and embraced our friends, I knew that I would have lost the moment to handle the situation on my own terms. But everything was moving too fast now.

Vera looked at me directly, bringing me out of my thoughts. "This is my boyfriend, James." She spoke softly, but I knew from her look that I had gone too far.

All eyes were glued on me now, and I could feel the collective weight of their judgment. I knew I looked pathetic and desperate, but I still couldn't stop myself.

"Oh, yes. Of course," I croaked. I turned to James sharply, like a toy soldier with my hand outstretched. We shook hands for only a moment and then each took a step back, daring the other to cross the invisible line. I imagined us circling each other, snarling and gnashing our teeth.

I felt Vera jab me in the back, forcing me to utter, "Nice meeting you."

"No," he declared like an orator ready to pounce on a lectern, "it's very nice meeting *you*, Donte. Vera has said so much about *you*."

He said the word as though it tasted bitter in his mouth. He meant each utterance to be a hard slap. *You*—slap! *You*—slap! Like a nineteenth-century gentleman, he had called me to a duel to restore his honor and the honor of his lady.

I could not ignore the invitation. "Well, I've heard nothing—"

Charlotte jumped out of her seat, her drink splashing a little out of her glass. A new woman had walked into the room, standing just behind James.

"Everyone, this is Silvia," Charlotte said. She introduced Silvia to each person in the room, pointing to each of us and rattling off our names. Then Charlotte told everyone that Silvia was her protégée.

Silvia stood at the door with a large leather bag hanging across her shoulder. She was wearing a black business suit meant to signal "professional career woman who was going places," but it reeked of a Macy's one-day sale. She stood with her back as straight as if she were in an inspection line. She waited for a moment, scrutinizing the room and its occupants with a quick sweep of her eyes, and then she unceremoniously dropped her bag on the side of the door, an act that would have normally caused a severe reprimand from Charlotte. But Charlotte seemed not to notice this faux pas.

Silvia's hair was cut very short, a boyish cut, my mother would say, and in that light it was a rich burgundy. She wore a pair of oval glasses with claret frames and a pair of onyx and diamond stud ear-rings that sparkled under the light.

"I'm so sorry to be late, but I had to finish up some work," she said to no one in particular.

"You're exactly on time," Charlotte said, dismissing her apology with a wave of her hand.

Silvia's arrival changed the dynamic of the room almost like a sigh of relief. People started to shuffle about, finding new seating arrange-ments. They were relieved that it had not gone worse. I suppose any-thing less than an all-out shouting match would have been seen as a good sign by them.

This was silly. We were all friends. How hard could it be? Not that hard, right? I was still eyeing Vera, and she was trying to ignore me. It was like I was a teenager again, scared of talking to a girl and jealous of the boy who received her attention.

Nadir walked over and grabbed Vera's hand to be inviting. I could see he wanted to find a way to make everyone happy. He looked at me with imploring eyes and took a small step toward me. *Not smart*, I thought, and I looked away as he walked back to his seat.

Herman came over and asked, "Something to drink, James?" He grabbed James's arm and pulled him out of the room behind him.

Vera followed them without looking at me. Rajiv served another round of drinks, and once again little conversations started.

"It'll be okay," Charlotte assured me as I sat next to her.

"Of course." I barely heard Charlotte's words as I focused on Vera, James, and Herman. James sat in the very same spot I had been in earlier. Vera sat on the arm next to James. Her hand rested on James's shoulder. She treated him like a cat, too, but more like a treasured family pet. Squeezing him and petting him and cooing in his ear. The three of them, thick as thieves, all started laughing. Herman's boisterous voice cut across the room. Apparently James was something of a cut-up, or at least that was how they all wanted him to appear.

"Donte!" Charlotte shouted in my ear.

"What?" I looked her in the face. She rolled her eyes, stood, and an-nounced dinner. And, like good guests, they started to move toward the dining room.

Vera and James started, too, but I felt if I didn't say something at that moment, whatever hope I had would be lost forever.

I called out, "Vera, could I speak with you for a moment?"

"Why?" she said coldly.

"Just for a minute, please."

She looked hesitant. She even continued to walk toward the dining room but then turned back and nodded her consent. James idled for a moment deciding whether to stay or go. His eyes darted from Vera and then to me.

"Do you want me to stay?" James asked.

"No. You go on in. I'll be there in a second." She shooed him like her pet cat again.

James turned around at the door and once again looked at Vera with quizzical eyes, which Vera, to my joy, ignored. Herman clapped him on the shoulder, and they were swept out of the room with the other dinner guests.

"Please join us presently," Charlotte ordered but didn't wait for acknowledgement and walked out of the room, leaving the two of us alone. That was the point of their plan, after all.

CHAPTER FIVE:
TEN YEARS IS A LIFETIME

Vera and I were in the same room for the first time in many months. Yet it seemed we had nothing to say. Where do you start when there are so many unresolved questions? How do you fix everything in a two-minute conversation? Especially when she had decided it was finished.

I stared at her, daring her to speak first. I had practiced all the things I wanted to say, had run them through my mind month after month, but I was so angry then that I could not voice them. There were things that I never wanted to say to Vera, and I knew that if I spoke then, one of them would likely come out.

"Stop it," she barked, her arms folded across her chest like she was protecting herself.

"Stop what?" I said.

"Staring at me like that. You make me feel exposed when you look at me like that. It's exhausting," she said.

But I felt empowered because she moved closer to me, and she lost her boxer stance. Her arms dropped down to her sides, and I thought she looked like she regretted what she had just said. For an instant there was hope. She had the face of a younger Vera, from when we had first met, with the way she bit her bottom lip while considering a tough decision. Me or James.

However, she jabbed me in my chest with her fingers and said, enunciating every single syllable, "Why can't you—just for once—be happy for me? What is wrong with you, Donte?"

That was the one-two punch that one expects but is never ready for. She took a small step back, giving us more space.

"Wrong with me?" I fought back pathetically, a weak punch in the air. "I'm not the one who disappeared for months and then shows up with this, this…" I stammered, choking in my own anger, "*James in tow*." I managed to expel his name like a cowboy spitting tobacco. The words splattered all over her. "We've only been separated, what? Three months, four months?" It had been longer than four months, much longer, but I was making a point and couldn't be bothered with facts. "But you work pretty fast, don't you?"

Vera's face flared red with blood. "You know what, Donte? I didn't even want to come to Charlotte's fucking party. Why would I? She didn't even invite me directly, not that she ever would."

"Then why are you here?"

She looked at me for a moment. "I'm not sure. Maybe because they are my friends, too, and maybe because Nadir and Tess insisted."

She was right, of course. She had as much right to be there as I had. And I was angry with Charlotte for not trying to be a friend to Vera after knowing her for more than ten years.

I loved my friends and was happy to be part of their group, but they belonged to a different world than the kind I grew up in. None of them had to work while going to college (or, for that matter, high school). Money was a different set of problems for them. None of them worried about it like I did or like Vera did. I think that's why Vera and I got along so well in the first place. We were the same, or at least we were once the same. Vera used to complain to me about keeping up with Herman or Charlotte, but I'd shrug it off. It was understandable; I wanted to be with them, but a simple summer vacation with Herman and Tess cost us months of salary. It wasn't their fault. They were used to a certain lifestyle and couldn't fully understand our limitations—though at times they did find excuses to help pay for our trips with mysterious extra tickets or complimentary hotel rooms.

"I am sorry," I said, but I wasn't sure what I was being sorry about.

"You know what Nadir told me?"

I shook my head.

"Nadir said, when I initially refused his invitation, 'Ten years is a long time to throw away, Vera.' And then, as if I needed reminding, he added, 'It's a lifetime.'"

"He's right," I offered.

She gave a mirthless laugh. "Is he, now?"

"Yes, and that's my point. I agree that our relationship reached its natural end, but we can't just throw away more than ten years of life together."

"You're delusional, Donte. There was nothing natural about the end of our relationship. Death should be the natural end, not malaise or wishful dreams."

We became silent again, and I could tell she had imagined a different scenario as well. She had probably expected me to be contrite and apologetic. She imagined herself walking in the room, and I'd notice her and walk over to her. We'd greet each other tentatively but cordially, and then I'd go through a long speech apologizing for my horrid behavior, and she would, after listening carefully to my long list of errors and misjudgments, forgive me. After all, she had won so many of our arguments over the years. Then she'd introduce me to James, who would have enough sense to show up later, and he and I would bond together over dinner and exchange little fun stories about Vera. She imagined us parting the night as good friends.

In a utopian world I would have been that person, but in the real world I could only see a boxing match where my only choice was to throw a low, dirty punch to finish her.

I was taken aback by her "wishful dreams" remark, so I went at it again. "Don't you have any sense, Vera?"

"What?" she replied. She looked confused.

So, I delivered. "You don't have to say yes to the first person who happens to cross your path, you know."

"Fuck you," Vera replied in a low voice, and then bolder, "Fuck you." She started pacing in front of me with her finger jabbing the air. "You abandoned me, lost in your little dreams. You knew very well where I was. You had my address, you had my number. You could've called, you could've written. At least I wrote you. Should I have just become a hermit like you, Donte?" she yelled. "How dare you make me feel guilty for wanting someone who loves me? You don't even know James." She stopped, exhausted and out of breath.

She looked up at me, and I knew I'd pushed too hard, but that had never stopped me. "James," I said, mocking her. "I know his kind."

Now she was taken aback by my harshness but did not retaliate. Her eyes searched the room rapidly. She was fighting back tears. She braced herself again and took a long deep breath. She tried a different tact.

"Just for once—" She paused for a moment and closed her eyes as though searching for the right words and tone that would add to her dignified stand. "Just for once," she said again and bit her lip, needing the pain to control her rage. Then she declared, "Just for once, I would like you to be kind."

I thought it would be the final moment. She had spoken with such tenderness and confidence that I knew, in her mind, it would be the conclusion of our relationship. She apparently didn't need all the questions answered like I did.

She continued, "I know you love me…So why can't you love me enough to be happy for me? You know I need it." She smiled faintly, a sad, pleading smile of a woman who has been injured but cannot bring herself to blame.

Vera took a step closer and reached out and touched my face. Her short blond hair smelled of lavender and honey. I froze. She still had power over me.

But then she added, "I just want you out of my life."

I took a step back and said in a cool, paternal tone, "I want you to be happy, but why him? You can do so much better."

I really wounded her, and it took me by surprise. She started to cry again. Her tears used to make me angry, but now they made me feel desperate. I tried to think of what I could say to make her stop, but I couldn't even deduce why that had been the thing that was the final straw.

"Like who, Donte?" she said. "Someone more like you? Please tell me how I can make you happy because, in the end, it's all about you, isn't it?"

"I don't know…Like…"

Her voice was calm even as she cried. "I told Tess this was a fucking mistake. I wish you a good life, Donte, I really do, but I pity the next person who falls in love with you. I'm going to get James and leave."

She started to walk out of the room, but I grabbed her arm and turned her around. I hadn't planned it and couldn't believe I was stopping her. I thought my grip on her wrist was maybe too tight. She tried to twist away from me, but I held fast. I pulled her closer to me.

"Don't leave," I pleaded. If she walked out of the room now, it would be the end of us. No matter what, I couldn't have that. "If anybody has to leave, it should be me," I offered, but neither of us moved. I really didn't want to leave now, and I didn't want Vera to leave, but at the same time, I didn't want them to stay. I needed more time to think, but I needed her to be close. But I wasn't ready for someone like James. Not yet. Maybe in a few months I could handle it, but not now.

Vera didn't seem to want to leave either. It seemed she wanted closure as well. "Okay, let's call a truce, then," she offered.

She grabbed my hand to lead me to the dining room, but I didn't respond quickly enough. I still wasn't convinced, and she saw it on my face as plainly as I was feeling it.

She shook her head in disappointment and said, "You don't get it, do you? Jesus!"

I stared at her, not wanting to understand her accusation.

"I don't think you ever got it," she continued.

She was right, of course. I didn't get it, and my feeble attempt to regain some advantage now was just a vapor in the air.

"Honestly, Donte..." Her face had now changed into something like the young Vera who I'd known, and also the Vera who I'd married, and the Vera who'd left me, and some Vera I'd never known. She looked simultaneously angry and sad and frightened. "Fuck off," she said.

She pulled her arm away and stormed off to the dining room. She still had tears in her eyes, but her head-held-high, resolute look of confidence was classic Vera.

I hesitated for a long time, grappling with my instinct to flee and never talk to any of them ever again. Feeling defeated, I walked to the dining room, though I didn't enter. I paused at the door, waiting for Vera and James to dash to the front door in a huff, like a bad storm. But they never appeared. Instead, the dining room had filled with the buzz of conversation, low and whispered. Vera wasn't leaving.

Somewhere between our argument and the dining room chair, she must have decided it was her right to be at the dinner party, despite it being thrown, however perversely, in both our honors.

I thought about what Herman had said earlier about being blind while surrounded by love. I'm not sure what he meant or whether he was referring to me. It was typical of him to be profound and shallow at the same time. It was unsettling enough to marginally recognize one's own narcissism, which showed an abundance of selflessness—but learning, even obliquely, that that's how your friends thought of you, too, was too much.

Vera wanted me to be someone else, not the Donte she had fallen in love and spent close to ten years with. She wanted me to be more like James. I wanted to run in shame, but James would stay. He would fight for his friends and his life.

I stepped into the dining room, and I instantly realized my mistake. If I wasn't going to turn and run like I wanted, then I should have never let Vera enter the room first. In this battle of friends, which I discovered just then that I had little stomach for, Vera had landed the first victory. Still in tears, she had walked in and established the narrative; she was the victim and I was the villain.

Our table of friends turned to me, frozen like a scene on a Grecian urn. It only lasted a moment, but their stares made me sick to my stomach. Tess quickly looked away, angry herself. Charlotte looked at me with pity, nodding toward the empty seat, begging me to sit so that we could all move on. Herman just shook his head, as if his profound but shallow statement should have been heeded better. James had his arm around Vera's shoulders and gently stroked her skin while she, in what I considered to be a low blow, dabbed under her eyes with a tissue. I am sure she was hoping that I would leave and not ruin the night for everyone. Knowing Vera, I was sure she felt guilty for wanting that, but I was also sure that my antagonism had pushed her to the limit.

I had to prove her wrong. I had to prove all of them wrong. I knew the more I hesitated, the more selfish I would look. I took a deep breath and followed the path Vera had just taken, without even the smallest intimation of her resolve.

CHAPTER SIX:
DINNER

Charlotte's dining room was grand. She had placed her grandparents' ornate oak dining table in the center, and, even though the original chairs were no longer available, she was able to find a set very similar to the original that only an expert could distinguish. She had put two large candlesticks on each side of the table, and the candlelight flickered as we sat around the table.

As soon as I sat down, Charlotte instructed Vera to sit next to Herman, and Vera reluctantly moved away from James. Charlotte was a stickler about seating arrangements. Vera wasn't going to fight this battle.

Nadir was sitting at one end of the table with Anat on his left followed by Herman, Vera, and then Akron. Charlotte was sitting at the other end followed by me on her left and then Silvia, James, and Tess, who ended up sitting to Nadir's right.

Small conversations started, and I was happy that I was no longer the center of their attention.

"We have wonderful hors d'oeuvres," Charlotte announced while ringing a small bell, and the two maids showed up with two large carts with trays of food.

They were like synchronized dancers in a Hollywood musical, waltzing into the room in an orchestrated fashion with their trays and then splitting into two mirror images of each other, one approaching

Charlotte and the other, Nadir. We were all transfixed by these serving ballerinas.

Charlotte inspected each tray with a nod of approval but only selected a small mound of caviar. One lady moved to Akron as the other started to serve Tess. Akron too surveyed every tray intently but settled for some stuffed mushrooms. Vera passed, and Herman took a large portion of every item.

Rajiv walked in the room and started serving wine and champagne. He also moved in a precise manner, stopping at each guest and offering the choices without a word and nodding with approval no matter what was selected. The dance lasted only a few minutes. Then the ladies disappeared, and Rajiv took his post by the door. He sat by a small desk and started working on some papers, his work never-ending.

I felt out of place. It was high school all over again. I looked up at Herman for support, but he was too busy speaking with Vera.

Nadir stood up and tapped his wine glass with his pinky ring. Everybody looked up, and he raised his glass and waited for a moment to give his pending toast a dramatic gesture.

"Here's to good friends—"

We all raised our glasses and echoed his toast. Vera reached across the table and touched her glass with James's.

At the same time Nadir, who wasn't finished with his toast, continued, "... and to the great real estate market—"

Herman took the opportunity and chimed in, "And to our rich friends, Nadir and Charlotte, who provide the best drinks—"

"And, of course, to our new baby," Charlotte finished.

With this, everyone turned towards Charlotte with a raised glass.

"This is really exciting, Charlotte. Do you know whether it's a girl or boy?" I asked.

"It *is* exciting. Nadir and I have planned this wonderful regimen of body and brain food, special exercises, healthy music, and the ocean air is going to be great for the baby."

"I think you can drink a bit of wine now and then," offered Herman.

"Oh, no. No wine, no tea or coffee, nothing that is going to harm my child."

"Pretty brave of you," Anat shouted from the other end of the table. "I think I could give up all of it except the occasional, you know—"

"I admit, I'll miss my morning coffee." Charlotte sighed. "But it's important to keep your body as wholesome as possible." She pointed in the general direction of Vera.

"Why are you pointing at me?"

Vera normally wouldn't let Charlotte's regular life lessons bother her, but at that moment she was like a volcano ready to erupt.

"I wasn't. I was making the point that one should keep a wholesome body," replied Charlotte in her matter-of-fact way, completely misreading Vera's anger.

"Meaning?" Vera stared down at Charlotte like a venomous snake ready to strike at any moment.

Charlotte, as usual, was not aware of anything beyond her little bubble of reality and was already bored with the conversation. She was about to move on to the next subject, but I couldn't let it go. I was evil that night.

"I think Charlotte is referring to your habitual drug use and years of unprotected and rather wild sexual habits," I offered with a broad smile, as though I was teasing.

In normal times it would have been just fine, as Vera would have had a similar come back. That was our usual lighthearted banter, our own version of terms of endearment. But that was back when we were good together. That was our routine, going after each other with our hyperbolic innuendos of sex and drugs. But that was then, and, like Charlotte, it seemed I was trapped in my own bubble of the past.

"What the fuck?" Vera erupted in a voice that chilled my back. "Don't listen to this fucking idiot, James," she added.

She picked up a steak knife and pointed it directly at my face. Everyone froze for a moment, and it was clear that I had crossed the line (again). I could at that moment have said something kind, which I knew would have soothed Vera, but I couldn't relent, choosing to dig this hole of self-indulgence deeper.

"Are we having steak, Nadir?" Akron asked, staring quizzically at the knife in Vera's hand—staring so closely, in fact, that I thought it might pierce one of his eyes at any minute.

Nadir laughed at the absurdity of the suggestion and others joined in, desperate for any distraction. They all needed the release and were grateful for Akron's timely and deadpan question. Everyone was ready for anything that would bring down the tension in the room. Even Vera herself couldn't help but smile even while holding the knife.

Nadir, however, took the question seriously and mistook the nervous laughter as a confirmation of Akron's apparent ignorance.

He waved his hand as though dismissing the foolish notion of serving steak. "No, no." He chuckled. "These are special knives for artichoke. They might look like steak knives, but—" He picked up his own knife and inspected it very closely like a trained professional evaluating an antique piece of cutlery. "That is, to an untrained eye, of course," he continued, inspecting the room to make sure everyone was following.

"Of course," Herman confirmed while keeping a wary eye on the knife in Vera's hand. "I think Donte's father had a set."

"Really? I'd be surprised, Herman." Nadir shook his head in disbelief. "These are actually from the Xavier collection that just came out. They're a new design."

Vera was trying hard to stay angry, to defend her virtues, to show me that I had gone too far, but others were eagerly inspecting their own artichoke knives, pretending that nothing had happened.

I closed my eyes as if meditating. I finally recognized that I had gone too far. "I'm sorry. I am truly sorry. I meant it as a joke. It was in poor taste, and I do apologize."

"I don't even drink," Vera pleaded, looking around the table and then to James. "You know I don't."

"I think your *dear friend* is having fun at our expense," James said grandly and then leaned over to hold Vera's hands.

This act put Vera in an awkward position because she either had to relinquish the knife that she was still holding or ignore James's reach. She chose him.

"Well, that was fun," Anat chimed in from the other side of the table. "It's nice to get all that out, and now we can have a great dinner."

Again, like magic, the servants appeared. They served small bowls of lobster bisque that I declined at first as I hated it with a passion, but I had to accept it when I saw the disappointment in Charlotte's face. The horrid soup was followed by a plate of mixed young vegetable salad with a strange white dressing that everyone raved about, but I thought it just tasted like ranch dressing. And then, of course, artichokes with a lemon-butter sauce.

I looked up at Vera, who was displaying the same distaste for the dressing as she casually tried to push the white, gooey substance to the side of her plate.

Now everyone was eating and talking nonstop with two or three different conversations going on at once, but I couldn't get involved in a single one. I felt tired. I played with my soup and salad, taking baby bites and swallowing them down with large swigs of wine.

Meanwhile Charlotte kept pushing me to have a conversation with Silvia. It was becoming annoying, but she was my only friend in the room full of enemies.

I had met Silvia a few months earlier when I was at Charlotte's office to meet up with Nadir (just a convenient place to meet). She was nice then, but now she completely annoyed me. I wasn't sure why but from the first moment Silvia walked in the room, her black bag annoyed me; her silly haircut with the seventies bangs annoyed me; her overly stylish eyeglasses annoyed me; and her nonstop talk about her work annoyed me. I think after a certain age you just want to hang out with your old friends, and you don't want anyone new in the group. I hated thinking that way as it made me sound like my father, but you can't deny the point. Silvia didn't seem too keen on me either because she started a conversation with James, and they seemed to get on handsomely.

I was fine with that.

By the time the main dish of salmon and shark was served, Silvia and James were deep in conversation. The shark tasted great, though. The pieces were tender but firm, lightly charred, with a thick aromatic glaze that I couldn't identify. Everyone was talking, but their voices were just background music to my ears. I was too focused on cutting, chewing, and drinking to be bothered by everyone's problems.

Nadir was holding court on the other side of the table with constant interjections by Tess, who would never allow a comment to go unchallenged.

We finished eating, and as soon as the dinner plates were collected, Vera asked Tess to switch places with her and focused James's attention back in the right direction. Herman winked at her, and she smiled back sweetly.

Silvia had no one to talk to anymore and looked impatient and bored. Charlotte bluntly told me to keep Silvia entertained.

"Silvia," I called, but her head was turned and she didn't hear me. "SILVIA."

She turned her head slowly and looked at me with curious eyes, like a doctor examining a mental patient.

"Sorry," I said, "I didn't mean to shout. I was just wondering if you're having a good time tonight." She didn't answer for a moment, but her look told me that she really thought that I was mental. "I meant—"

Silvia shook her head slightly, and I stopped talking.

"Tell me about how you guys met. I'm rather curious." She spoke rather loudly, and no one would have missed traces of condescension if they were listening.

"Good question," I replied, raising my artichoke knife and pointing it like a gun at her. Bits of sauce dripped onto the tablecloth. "Good question, Silvia." I said her name by almost spelling each letter. "It's an exciting and long story—"

"Not really that exciting, and I can tell it in a minute," Herman interrupted, perhaps fearing my rendition of our lives, in particular the part that would involve Vera and me given my earlier accusation. "Charlotte, Nadir, Donte, and I went to the same high school—"

"Well, more than that," Nadir chimed in.

But Herman wasn't ceding to anyone. "As I was saying, the four of us went to the same school, and then Charlotte went to some little university in France where she met Tess, and later they became roommates."

"He means *Sorbonne*," offered Charlotte.

"Yeah, that's what I meant. Anat and Akron were neighbors of Nadir before he moved to this little cabin. And, of course, Nadir, Vera, Donte, and I went to the state university on Holloway. And that's it."

"That's not it," I called out indignantly, and Herman stared back at me blankly.

"Oh, yes," said Herman. "Charlotte married Nadir."

"Interesting," Silvia said, clearly not satisfied.

"That was the stupidest history of our friendship that I've ever heard," I said.

"Let me tell a better version," said Nadir, standing up but then sitting down immediately when Charlotte shot him a stern look.

"It's fine," said Silvia. "I just wasn't sure who knew whom first. James and I were talking earlier, and he wasn't sure either. But obviously you guys have known each other for a long time. You can tell with all the *love* in the room."

I was about to respond, but the arrival of a dessert tray, an opulent array of puffed pastries and coffee, distracted everyone, and the mood for storytelling vanished from everyone's mind.

Akron wanted to speak with Nadir, so he switched seats with Herman. Then Tess wanted to be closer to Charlotte, so she walked over to the other end of the table with her cup of coffee. Rajiv quickly brought a new chair before anyone had a chance to ask and put it between Charlotte and Herman.

"So, this was fun," Herman said.

"I had fun," I offered.

"I'm sure you did, mister, but I don't get you sometimes," Tess rejoined.

"I'm not sure what you mean," I said, trying very hard to sound innocent.

"Come off it. Why do you torture Vera? What's happened to you?"

"You're being rather harsh, Tess, don't you think?" Charlotte chimed in.

I leaned closer and whispered, "I just can't see this working, if *you know* what I mean?" I looked from one face to another meaningfully, as though parting with the weightiest of state secrets, and Charlotte nodded in agreement.

"I like James. He's a fine boy, though a bit too young," Tess said.

"It's not going to work, and it has nothing to do with his age," I claimed.

"How do you know?" Tess wasn't convinced. "Vera looks happy, and I mean really happy, the happiest I've seen her in months. If *you know* what I mean, Donte?"

"Yes, yes, she's happy, I get it. But for how long?"

"How long? It doesn't matter. And, by the way, this is more than we can say about you. You can't be content. You never were, and you never will be. We all know that. That's how you are, but why can't you let her have her life?"

Tess's comment about my inability to find fulfillment was like a heavy blanket over a campfire. In my heart I knew Tess and her no-nonsense approach were right, but I felt strangled by her words and naturally grabbed blindly to defend my position. And when I couldn't come up with anything reasonable, I cried out, "You don't understand, Tess. None of you do."

"I don't understand what?" Tess asked in her calm fashion.

I offered rather feebly, "Look, I want her to be happy."

Herman looked me with pursed lips for a moment and then said, "You do, Donte? I'm sorry, but I'm confused about how you can say that."

I don't necessarily subscribe to men supporting men no matter what, but at times I wished Herman was more supportive. "Yes, I do, Herman. I want her to be happy, but I can't see her with him."

I was angry and perhaps drunk as words came out of my mouth in a slurred, listless gush, like a drowning man expunging the water from his lungs. It was absurd to get angry, and my fury made me sound dishonest and self-serving even to myself. Even Charlotte looked dismayed.

"I'm sorry," I added without much conviction.

Tess wasn't accepting any interpretation of it anyway. "What are you sorry for? Why are you apologizing to us?" She paused for a moment and then added, "We're not the ones you should apologize to, Donte. You should look across the table."

Charlotte must have felt they were ganging up on me and told them to back off a bit. She followed her own advice by reaching over and grabbing my hands in a gesture of comfort. "Go and sit with her, Donte. Just be the sweet boy I know you are." And when she saw hesitation in my eyes, she added, "For me. Please."

To my own surprise, I nodded to Charlotte and then stood up. I could be the sweet person that Charlotte hoped I was.

CHAPTER SEVEN:
THE GAME

I walked over and joined the rest of the group at Nadir's end of the table. They neither welcomed me nor ignored me. I apologized again for my bad behavior earlier. They all nodded but continued with their conversation. I chimed in a few times, and Vera even replied, albeit in a dry, if not too cold, voice.

Silvia, who had been left out of all the conversations for the past thirty minutes, put her coffee cup down unceremoniously and called out to Charlotte that she needed to get back.

"I have a wonderful game," Charlotte announced enthusiastically, ignoring Silvia's plea for relief.

No one responded, but Charlotte loved party games and was unperturbed by the unenthusiastic response from the table. "It's a wonderful game that Elizabeth taught me. You know Elizabeth," she said in response to our puzzlement, as though it was the most obvious thing. Then she shrugged her shoulders in dismay. "Elizabeth is my body therapist at Angelina's."

"Oh yes, Angelina's. My favorite place," I shouted, perhaps too loudly.

"I go there all the time," Herman said and, after a moment of thought, added, "but Elizabeth and I don't get along that well."

"Have you tried Rosalina?" Akron chimed in, nodding knowingly.

"I have, but she's so nosey, always asking me about my personal life. She makes me so, you know, so…" Herman waved his hand.

Both Akron and I nodded in understanding.

"Oh, but Rosalina. She does wonders, I tell you." Akron closed his eyes as though reminiscing about his time at Angelina's.

Charlotte was shocked. We all could see the horror on her face. "I...I...I didn't know you guys went to Angelina's."

Charlotte sounded rather perturbed. We all knew what she was thinking: that Angelina's wasn't what it used to be if they let the likes of us in. It was typical of Charlotte's crowd to expect the rest of us to know the names of their decorator, their therapist, their tennis pro, and the dozen other minions who supported their daily life. But the idea of people like us—well, really Akron and me—going to their people without their so-called introduction was mortifying.

"I think they were thinking of Angela's on Van Ness, but that's even more troubling," Tess said as she wagged her finger at Herman.

"Never heard of it," Akron and I said in unison.

"Isn't the place on Van Ness a massage place?" Nadir asked innocently.

"I wouldn't know, Nadir," I replied earnestly, "but I'm sure Charlotte wants to know why you would give patronage to such a place as Angela's Hot Tubs and Massage?"

"Me? Me? I'd never...I've never been to those places in all my life," Nadir said.

"Are you sure?" asked Herman.

"Of course I'm sure. Think how dirty those places are. Can you imagine me in such a place?"

No one could.

"How come *you* know so much about it, my darling?" Tess asked Herman, looking serious.

"Me? I know nothing about it, and in the divorce court, I'll deny ever seeing Rosalina. Akron will swear to that as he was with me at the time."

"I was not," Akron said.

"Then I guess it was Elizabeth, after all," Herman offered.

"I'll confirm that in court," I added.

"Of course. Anyway," Charlotte said, tired of our antics and satisfied with the integrity of Angelina's class barrier, "Elizabeth's shrink used this game to let people come to actualize their own feelings. It has done wonders for Elizabeth. I've been dying to try it, so, if you're up to it, we can give it a go."

"I'm in," Herman said rather quickly.

"Count me in, dear," said Nadir, sending a kiss across the room.

"I'm sorry, Charlotte, but James and I need to go soon. In fact, it's already late."

"Oh, come on, Vera. Stay," Anat urged, crossing over to Vera for more emphasis and reassurance.

"I'm sure James would want to see Charlotte's game," I said, trying to be the sweet boy Charlotte had asked me to be.

"I need to go too," said Silvia in a pleading voice.

"What do you say, James?" I asked, not looking at him but staring straight at Charlotte.

Finally trying to help, Herman offered, "Yeah, I think we all should stay and play Charlotte's shrink's game."

"Not my shrink, my body therapist," Charlotte said.

"Sorry, I meant to say Charlotte's body therapist who works at Angelina's but certainly not at Angela's...Let's play," Herman said.

"We really must go," Vera said.

"Let's take a vote," Tess chimed in, sensible as always.

Charlotte, disappointed with the outcome, saw an opportunity to salvage her game. "I think Tess is right. Let's take a vote and let the majority rule."

"Let's drink to the tyranny of majority," Herman cried out. He stood up, raised his glass. Anat, Nadir, and I followed suit.

"What about you, Akron?" Herman asked.

"I think I want to go home."

"I'm sorry, Charlotte. I'd love to stay and play this game, but it's been too intense," offered Tess.

"Okay, that makes four nays. It's all up to James," Herman said, looking at James.

With that, everyone stared at him intently.

"Come on, buddy, it's all up to you," Nadir said warmly.

I was sure Vera was not happy, but her face betrayed nothing. She said nothing.

Herman and I were echoing Nadir by repeating, "Come on, buddy."

"I think I'd like to try this new game of Charlotte's, whatever it is," he said rather resolutely.

"Brilliant," Charlotte said. "Let's move to the next room where it's more comfortable."

We all got up and started to move toward the reading room, where, to our surprise, ten large brown mats had been arranged in an oval, all facing one another. The fireplace glowed a daring red. The lights were dimmed. A faint scent of sandalwood lingered in the air.

"So, the voting was rigged," Akron observed in a near whisper.

"It's too late to figure out Charlotte. You know that," Nadir whispered.

The room felt solemn, more like a place for worship than the setup for a party game, so we all kept quiet, whispering to each other if we spoke at all. We had no idea what Charlotte had planned, but she had yet to disappoint us in the past. Charlotte believed in mind-body experiences, and, although she would deny it, I knew she designed her games to stoke sexual tension.

The fire made the room warm, and Herman took off his large sweater, showing off his Dead T-shirt. I always envied his muscular body, though not enough to follow his strict exercise regimen.

Rajiv showed up with a bottle of cognac and offered a glass to each person except for Charlotte, who was pregnant, and Vera, who had gone dry. We held the snifters but waited as if the drink was part of the game. We worried any choice we made from that point on would be a violation of Charlotte's rules.

Charlotte asked us to sit.

We moved toward the cushions, but she told us to sit on the couch. We followed obediently like good boys and girls.

Rajiv stood by the door. He had a little smile on his face. He must have relished seeing Charlotte order someone else around for a change.

"This is a simple game," Charlotte announced.

"Can we drink?" Herman said.

"Yes, Herman. Of course you can drink. In fact, you need to finish it before we can start the game."

I took a small sip and savored the bittersweet taste in my mouth.

Vera eyed everyone, watching our faces as we drank. She must have wanted some too. She loved cognac.

"The game requires a bit of coordination since the room isn't very large," Charlotte continued. Being allowed to drink had broken her spell for a moment, causing a little distraction of chatting and sipping.

I smirked at her opinion about the reading room. It was half the size of my old house. I looked up and could tell Vera was thinking the same thing. I stopped myself from thinking "our house" because Vera lived there without me. It was her house now.

Charlotte moved to the center of the room and continued with her instructions. "Boys move to my right and women, to the other side."

We complied and stood awkwardly on either side, men in one line and women in the other. Herman made a move to sit on a mat, but he froze when Charlotte shouted at him.

"Don't sit," she said. Then, more softly, "The idea is to hide your location from the others. You may sit on the couch for now if you want."

Before anyone could ask any question, Rajiv produced ten blindfolds from a large, ornate box that was next to the wall. He walked over slowly and handed one to each person.

"When I tell you, I'd like each of you to blindfold the person next to you," Charlotte said.

Each group had started in loose clumps, but as Rajiv handed us our blindfolds, we moved closer to the mats. We waited there, hesitant but excited.

"Kinky," Anat drawled.

"Nadir, you devil. I didn't know you had it in you," Herman chirped in.

"It'll be all right. No need to worry," Charlotte urged. "Rajiv will help us."

We shrugged and started to help each other with the blindfolds, and then one by one we stopped talking. In a short while the room returned to the hushed reverence from when we had first entered. Only the crackling of the logs in the fireplace dared disrupt the eerie silence.

I stood in total darkness. The loss of my vision made me feel calm, along with all the alcohol. I imagined everyone had started to feel hypnotized in their inebriation. The silence only lasted for a few moments, but it felt like hours before we heard Rajiv's voice. He had hardly spoken all night, so it sounded odd to suddenly hear his precise, crisp voice. But it was also paced and reasoned, and it seemed to combine with everything else—the blindfold and the incense and the warmth—to relax me even more.

"Gentlemen, I will move you around and have you sit at one of the mats," Rajiv said. "Please stay where you are, and I'll move you. At that time, you may sit down. But, as Ms. Charlotte has instructed, please refrain from speaking. Please do not identify your location. Ladies, I will do the same as soon as I have placed the men."

Rajiv guided us in silence. When it was my turn, he took my hand into his like the way my father used to do. Rajiv was not a big man, but his grip felt strong. He walked me for a few steps and then whispered to me that I should sit down.

After a few moments, he announced, "I'm done with the men, and I'll start with the ladies."

Charlotte said in hurried voice, "Oh, I forgot. I think it'd be good if you take off your earrings and glasses."

I heard the faint movement of people, the soft padding of feet, and Rajiv's whispered instructions. Then everything went quiet again.

"This is the last instruction," Rajiv said, "and I won't speak until it's time to switch places." Rajiv rang a little bell. "When you hear that chime, gentlemen, please stay where you are, and ladies, please move to the right. I'll step out of the room during the round but will be here to help you move, ladies."

There was a long pause as if he wanted to give us ample time to absorb his instructions. However, he hadn't provided us with any actual instructions for Charlotte's strange game. I started to get an idea of where it was all heading, though.

Rajiv said, "So this is how this game is played. First, no one should speak. I'll chime the bell twice to indicate that I'm leaving the room. Then, reach across and touch the face of the person opposite you. Not any other part of the body. Just the face."

He paused again. I heard the burning of the logs more clearly. The room seemed even warmer, and I felt drowsy.

Rajiv spoke again. "I've been instructed to advise Mr. Kennard that he should seriously refrain from reaching for any other parts."

Herman must have exercised an immense amount of self-control, swallowing all of his replies to Charlotte working through Rajiv to single him out.

Rajiv said, "Ladies and gentlemen, when I ring the bell, you may commence. And of course, you may stop at any time, but please do not move until I return and ring the bell again."

Again, there was no sound for a moment, and then, without warning, the chime of the bell echoed throughout the room. Then everything was quiet again—no movements, no sounds, just the slow crackling of fire.

I was sitting closest to the fireplace and could feel the heat on my face. Its glow penetrated the edges of the blindfold, and I saw traces of the red of the dancing fire. I felt my heart pounding against my chest, and my hands felt clammy from the anticipation. But it didn't last long as my body relaxed and my heart slowed down. I was amazed how this little act of sitting blindfolded on a soft, comfortable mat could bring so much tranquility. Vera and James, the dinner—all of my life was in the distant past. I was sitting and waiting without being impatient.

Suddenly I became aware of another person inches away from my face. I faintly felt her breath on my cheek.

I reached rather tentatively across the space between us, wondering whether I'd recognize the person instantly or if it'd take me a few minutes. My finger landed on her cheekbone. Her skin felt warm and soft. The moment of the touch was electric but not informative. The skin was soft like Vera's, which seemed to never age. But my touch had been welcomed, so it couldn't have been her. After our conversation, she wouldn't be hospitable to a stranger's touch—after all, it could be my hand on her face.

It wasn't Silvia, either, as she was new to the group. This person's reaction was inviting, though I had not felt her hand on my face yet. You would think her reciprocation would be instantaneous; after all, I'd known these people for ages. Our history together gave us a kind of ease in matters of physical affection, and the excitement of all of us being blindfolded made me assume that everyone would be ready to dive in.

I reached with my other hand and touched the side of her nose, feeling for any feature, any bump or scar that might convey more clues. But my second hand also failed in its mission, although, for the first time, I was keenly aware of every single nerve at the tips of my fingers. I moved my finger down her face and reached the sides of her mouth. I felt her warm breath on my fingers as I lingered on her lips, but I still could not recognize the person. The feeling was intense, to move a finger over her bottom lip, to caress just under her chin to her cheekbone, from nose to ear.

Then ten fingers started probing my own face, and I knew those fingers in an instant. They belonged to Tess. As quickly as the feeling of tranquility had worked its way into my body, just as quickly, it was replaced with anxiety. I wondered if she knew my identity. We probed each other's features for a few moments more. When I couldn't take it any longer and was ready to take off my blindfold, when I thought everyone else had already done so and was watching me making a fool myself, I heard Rajiv's bell ring in the far distance.

Tess's fingers instantly withdrew, but mine remained glued to her face. When she had pulled back sharply, the connection severed. No more electric touch. So I took my hands away and placed them in my lap.

Tess disappeared in the sudden movement of air as she shifted to the next mat. Someone new sat in front of me, but the game was different now. Tranquility refused to return. I wanted to pull off my blindfold, throw it to the floor, and leave the party. Disrupting the game would give me away, and I knew there was a chance that Tess had not discovered my identity.

So I remained on my mat and forced myself to keep playing. I reached and touched the face of the new person. This new player enjoyed the touch and eagerly searched my skin and lips and eyebrows. I only moved my fingers in a perfunctory way. There were no feelings in my fingers. There was no intensity. After a few moments, Rajiv rang his little bell again.

After the third session of gentle touching, I think Charlotte grew tired of her little game because she spoke up. She told us to stand up and slowly move to the center of the room where we all gently collided in a mass of people. I never knew whether Charlotte intended it to be some concluding group hug or one last collection of our energies, but almost as soon as we gathered, she called off the game. I quickly pulled off my blindfold and looked over at Tess. She leaned over and kissed Herman. She avoided making eye contact with me.

We all felt subdued, as if the game had somehow exposed us. The mood in the room had lost all of its giddiness and schoolyard charm. Instead, everyone milled around in various states of embarrassment, with sheepish looks at the floor and too quiet, murmured conversation. Even Herman had lost his normal boisterousness. He typically would have made a joke by then, filling the space with a hearty laugh. Perhaps we had gone too far with all the intimate touching.

Charlotte's announcement had resulted in some half-hearted grumblings, but as we watched Rajiv collect the blindfolds and stack the mats, a sense of welcome swept through us because the party had finally ended. Vera and James said their goodbyes to Charlotte and Nadir and left without talking to me. I saw them walk out, holding hands. Despite her inhospitable mood, she clearly didn't mind someone else touching her. While I knew I didn't have the right because time had passed between me and Vera, I felt rejected all over again.

Silvia followed them quickly as well.

I kissed Charlotte and offered to help with the cleaning, but she dismissed the offer as though I was crazy. I was glad to be leaving, anyway. I felt drained from the intensity of the dinner and the game. Akron and Anat argued about something in the corner of the room, so I skipped my goodbye with them and simply left.

The party next door was still pushing forward in full swing, but the golden-haired woman was not at the window. I walked over to my car and drove home as quickly as I could. I fell into a dreamless sleep without any ghosts from my past or present.

The cannolis were never served.

THE LATE SIXTIES

CHAPTER EIGHT:
ST. FRANCIS LOWELL HIGH SCHOOL

St. Francis Lowell High School is one of the oldest and most affluent high schools in California. It was situated at the edge of the city with several buildings forming a strange hub-and-spoke structure. In the midst of its one-story buildings was a large clock tower that stood out like a lonely giant, watching over the campus. The 1906 earthquake damaged the clock, leaving it a relic, an impotent overseer, and age damaged everything else. As rich as it was, the school could never collect enough donations to restore it; it seemed the administrators and parents always had other projects with higher priority. There was a group of citizens who prevented the school from tearing the tower down on more than one occasion, owing to its historical status in the Bay Area.

By the time I started at St. Francis Lowell, the tower's doors and windows were boarded up, and the building was cordoned off by a tall wooden and metal fence, imprisoning the tower for the remainder of its life.

St. Francis Lowell, like every other high school, was gerrymandered around different cliques, with each spoke of the campus housing a different social, economic, ethnic, or cerebral cluster. And, of course, there was Charlotte's group all by itself. She practically owned the campus. The majority of students had rather wealthy parents, so one would have thought wealth wouldn't carry much cachet, but life in high school can be more complicated than real life.

In those days I had my own so-called gang—students who came from particular neighborhoods. In retrospect I think we added a touch of spice to our bland school. Other students, however, through their adolescent imaginations, made us scarier and more colorful than we really were. Charlotte and her very close friendship with me were the bridge from my group to the rest of the student body. She gave me legitimacy, and in return I gave her opportunity to be bad without going too far.

At the end of our senior year at St. Francis, Charlotte and Herman decided to revive the old tradition of climbing the clock tower. It seemed there was no way they could get in that old building without getting caught; from afar, the barrier looked impenetrable.

Charlotte turned to me for help. It wasn't too difficult to find weak spots given the age of the barrier. We entered the school at night and cleared the way in the back of the building so that they could get in without being seen.

Charlotte insisted that I join them in the tower, but I refused. She was trying to set me up with her close friend Donna, and naturally she thought the tower was a great place for us to meet, ignoring the fact that Charlotte and I still had unresolved issues of our own.

I stood on the school side of the fence surrounded by my friends, trying to blend in with the other students, who had started to notice all the commotion on top of the clock tower.

Herman called me by name and shouted at me to come up. I nodded a few times but didn't move. Naturally, they were spotted by some of the teachers, and there was a huge row between the administrators. Most were ready to come down as it was becoming inevitable that they were going to get caught, but Herman wouldn't have it.

As expected, it didn't go well. But, ironically and perhaps not surprisingly, after the staircase gave in and they completed the destruction of the old building, the only person who was punished was me. They didn't catch any of the real culprits except for Charlotte, who was injured. However, from the school's point of view, Charlotte was not the right person to punish in order to set an example. Her father had contributed too much money to have his daughter disciplined. I, on the other hand, had the right pedigree to satisfy the angry parents, and I was spotted crossing the fence. Those who had actually been in the tower were all spotted crossing the fence, too, but Mr. Loverly, the principal, only mentioned my name during a large parents' meeting.

There was talk of expelling me from the school, but I had already met all the requirements to graduate. Charlotte tried to help and forced a meeting with Mr. Loverly. He invited me to show that he was fair and understanding, but after listening to Charlotte's plea for a few minutes, he stopped her. He then looked at me while speaking to Charlotte and offered his wisdom: "An Ethiopian can't change his skin."

We were confused and waited for him to say more, but he just stared at me a bit longer and then told us the meeting was over.

Neither Charlotte nor I understood what he meant, but that was his verdict until Charlotte's father had a private conversation with Mr. Loverly. In the end, I was *permitted* to receive my diploma, as if I had not earned it.

Overall, it wasn't a good end of the year for me, and to top it off, Charlotte announced that she would go to Paris for school, despite our earlier agreement that all of us would go to the same university.

The rest of the summer was crap as well. I spent weeks trying to convince Charlotte to change her mind, and she refused my pleas. A few days before her departure, I tried again.

We were sitting in her room listening to music when I asked, for the hundredth time, "Why can't you stay and go to SF State like the rest of us?" I never said it directly but also didn't try to hide the undertone of 'you owe me' in my voice.

"I told you already. I need to get away from Nadir, but even more, I need to get away from my crazy parents."

Charlotte's father and stepmother were going through their annual major fight—as opposed to their monthly regular fights—and the house had become unbearable mostly because they used Charlotte as a pawn in their battles to humiliate each other.

Junior year had been even worse for Charlotte in that regard, and she thought she would teach her parents a lesson by dating as many strange boys as possible. Self-destructive mode had never helped her before, but facts had never stopped her either. She repeated the foolish path over and over again to get the attention and love she desperately needed from her father.

They didn't even notice.

At first I tried to be supportive, but when there was no reaction from her parents, my protective brother mode took over. I started grabbing her from her dates' cars or calling the house to make sure she was back early, and when nothing else worked, I started acting like a jealous boyfriend. And when that didn't work, I started the cycle again.

"We've never been apart this long," I complained, back in my boyfriend mode even though she was dating Nadir at the time.

Charlotte looked at me funny. "We have to grow up some time. I'll write you often, but I need to get away."

"It won't be the same without you."

She laughed at my childish remark. "Of course not, but you and Nadir have become friends, haven't you? I think it'll be good for you."

"Are you dumping him?"

A few months earlier, when I was in brother mode, I convinced her to think about dating a nice, decent boy like Nadir. His parents roamed in the same circles as Charlotte's, and I thought they would certainly approve or at least notice.

It worked, and by the summer of our senior year, she and Nadir had been dating for several months. I liked Nadir, but there was always that jealous part of me that needed curbing.

"To be honest, I don't know. I like him. He's a nice boy, but he may have other ideas," Charlotte said.

"What do you mean?"

"Don't freak out. I don't mean that he's pushing me to have sex with him or anything. To be honest, I think I'll end up forcing him." Charlotte looked up and smiled. When I didn't say anything, she added, "Lighten up. You're so serious."

"I thought you liked serious people," I replied.

"Nadir thinks we'll get married and have children one day, and I'm not ready to even think about that. And definitely not with him."

"Then why can't you stay?"

"You know better. I need to get away, and the offer is too good to pass up, anyway."

I nodded, and then, without thinking, I blurted, "I love you. You know that, don't you?"

She said, "Of course I do, silly. I love you too. Why do you think I spend so much time with you?"

I wasn't sure what to say next.

*   *   *

The summer before Charlotte started dating Nadir, she had a horrible fight with her stepmom and consequently showed up at my doorstep. She cried, and I was comforting as I'd been numerous times before.

But that time was different. We were more affectionate to each other, and then one thing led to another, and we started making out. It was the first time ever, but nothing serious. It felt good, and in a way, I'd been wondering for some time if there was more between us. I had never made a pass at her, not once, and Charlotte at times had hinted at my lack of interest. We had grown up together, and she had always acted like my sister.

But when we kissed, it felt nice and comfortable. I wondered why we hadn't done this years earlier.

It went on for a while, but then, for some reason, it started to feel all weird and incestuous. It was Charlotte who complained first.

We were kissing on her bed. She pulled back and said, "I'm sorry, but—"

She waited for me to say something, to protest, but I withdrew and nodded, neither confirming nor denying her unspoken dissent. Perhaps she was expecting something different, but it seemed my neutrality made her change her mind. She leaned forward and kissed me again. I responded more eagerly, and then, as if both of us decided without any words, we barricaded ourselves against the unpleasantness we both surely felt.

We made love with such tenderness that, in my mind, I saw nothing wrong with our action. At least I felt that way in the moment. For a brief month that summer, we were lovers, and it was one of the greatest times of my life. By and by, however, the earlier, eerie feeling that I had kept in check reared its ugly head. But again, it was Charlotte who was brave.

"We can't, Donte. We can't go on like this," she said as she lay next to me on the bed.

We had just come back from a swim and were both wearing our swimsuits. I was holding her hand after we had kissed. I certainly had not planned to stop even though the kisses felt wrong, as they always had. But it seemed Charlotte's brain, if not mine, had finally caught up with the situation.

I was still holding her hand but hadn't said anything, nor had I attempted to kiss her again. Like most teenage boys, I was conflicted and confused. So I did what I thought was right.

I rolled over and faced the ceiling. "I love you. You know that, don't you?"

"And I love you. But this will ruin us. I'm sure of it. I cannot help but think of you as a brother, and as wonderful as this is, it still feels incestuous."

"It doesn't to me," I replied. I had to say it out loud to believe the lie.

"It's hard on me. I really tried to dismiss this nagging feeling that has been festering in me, but I can't. I can't help but believe what we're doing is wrong. I told myself that it'd diminish in time, but it hasn't. In fact, it has grown stronger."

"Don't you want me?" I insisted.

"Look at me. Look at my body trembling next to you. It's aching to have you, but my mind tells me differently. I kiss you, and it feels wrong. You touch me, and it feels painful. Don't you feel the same way?"

"It'll get better," I replied, trying to sound resolute.

"You're wrong. I'm sorry, but I know us better, and this will destroy us."

I let go of her hand, hearing the finality of her words. I could see tears rolling down her cheeks. She turned around to hide from me, and I felt as though I'd been hit by a ton of bricks.

We ended it, though. There were no arguments. No fighting. No begging. It was clear that we both felt the same way.

And a few months later, I encouraged her to date Nadir. I thought he was a safe bet—a nice guy with no expectations. She agreed, I think, to confirm the end of our romantic relationship.

*   *   *

Charlotte and I never spoke of our summer together, and several months after that, we were both our regular selves, or so it seemed. But then she decided to leave for Paris, and it felt as if I was driving her away.

Then, to add to my pain, she offered, "You know, if you find your-self a girlfriend, you won't feel so left out. You should try to hook up with Donna again. You seemed to get along with her at the Tower."

My response: "Fuck you, Charlotte."

"Why so angry? I wasn't trying…I was just thinking that you'd be happier, and Donna is really a nice girl—and she would love to go out with you."

"How do you know?"

"Donna is my friend, and you've met her so many times too. I don't even remember the last time you had a date. You seem so discontented."

"I don't have to run around with a girlfriend to be content. I don't have to date everyone in school to prove myself. I'm content with things as they are, and you're fucking it up."

"I have a life too. Do you expect me to stay here forever? I thought you understood. I thought you agreed that we cannot be together," Charlotte said.

"We tried that once, but it didn't work for you, did it?"

"Did it for you? Be honest." Charlotte was angry now.

I didn't answer.

So she persisted, "Come on, be honest."

"I don't know, Charlotte. I guess not, but I still don't want you to leave."

"I'm leaving for Paris," she said.

I opened my mouth to respond, but it was clear that there was nothing else to say. I knew her well enough to recognize defeat.

"Will you ask Donna out?" she asked.

"If you want me to."

"Yes, please do. It'll be good for you."

I never did, and I didn't show up to the airport when Charlotte left. For a long time I didn't answer any of her letters. But many months of separation changes you. When she came back for the holidays, she was with a new friend, Tess. Charlotte had changed, but I had as well; by then I was with a new girl, Vera Pacient.

CHAPTER NINE:
A FAILED CAMPAIGN

I met Vera in my first semester of college, during the first week, in fact. I was taking an introductory philosophy class, a required course for all freshmen, and the room was packed. I walked in halfway through the first day of class with a slip to try to add the course. I tried to look tough and defiant with my motorcyle jacket and my big hairdo. In 1968, the campus was a mix of students who wore suits, white shirts, and ties, and others who stood out with long hair and colorful clothes.

The professor stopped the lecture as soon as I walked in, and instead of yelling at me for interrupting her class, she pulled a chair from behind her desk and offered it to me. Later I learned that everyone was dumbfounded since the first thing that professor did was kick all the unregistered students out of her class. Yet she accommodated me, as if I deserved the extra attention.

I grabbed the chair and parked it next to a blond, slender girl with a long ponytail. She was all dressed up as if she was going out to dinner.

I nodded and said, "Donte."

She smiled back and said, "Vera. Vera Pacient."

The professor loved Plato, and given that this was a basic intro class, she focused on the *Apology of Socrates*, the simplified version, for the whole semester. She required everyone to speak out and debate.

In the end it was a good class, and by and by all of us changed and learned to have at least a semblance of thoughtful public discourse. Vera and I sat next to each other throughout the semester and became de facto partners in debates. For the first month or so we only saw each other in the class, but after a while our arguments over the nature of political thought spilled over to the campus's only café.

One day while we were debating and drinking coffee, Vera pointed to someone across the room and asked, "Who is that? I've seen her with you on campus."

"What? You're spying on me?"

She turned red and quickly offered, "No...No, I was just wondering."

"Just kidding, Vera. She is a good friend," I replied and then waved at my friend to come over.

She saw me and waved back and then started to walk toward us.

"She's very pretty," said Vera.

"Yes."

And she was. She was tall with dark skin and large brown eyes. She was wearing dark pants and a cut-up shirt, showing her muscular upper arms. She had loads of pamphlets in her hands, some of which she dropped unceremoniously on our table when she arrived.

We kissed each other on the cheeks, and then she sat next to me.

"Hello," Vera exclaimed and then added hurriedly, "I'm in Donte's philosophy class." She sounded apologetic. "My name is Vera, Vera Pacient."

"Oh, yes. I've heard of you," she replied pleasantly. "I'm Tilly Losch, and I bet Donte hasn't even mentioned me." Tilly leaned over and kissed Vera on the cheek, then got up and sat next to her.

"I was about to leave," Vera explained unnecessarily, standing up.

Tilly pulled her down and said, "No reason to go, girl."

"I like your name," Vera offered as she sat back down.

"Yeah, it's cool. My name is the same as Ottilie Ethel Leopoldine 'Tilly' Losch, Countess of Carnarvon," she said in one breath and in a matter-of-fact tone. Then she added, "I don't think we're related, but of course you never know which of my ancestors were raped by some of these dudes." She looked at me, smiled, and then concluded thoughtfully, "I think she was a famous dancer or ballerina or something from Austria, fifty years ago or so."

"Wow," Vera said.

"Or it could be random," Tilly offered dismissively.

With that introduction, we sat back and talked about school and our work and the upcoming election. Vera fell in place with us in no time, as if she'd known us for years.

Vera had grown up without a mother, who had passed away when she was young, and more or less without a father, who was a merchant marine and away from home more often than not. During those long absences, her grandmother would stay with her, though not every day, so Vera had to grow up quickly in order to survive the empty house.

When Vera started college, her father was back living at home with her. He had been forced to resign his commission due to an injury but kept busy with odd jobs. But there was still no money. Vera had to pay her way through college, as did I.

She ended up taking a job as a bartender at the Cliff House. She wasn't even eighteen yet, but when the manager saw how much she knew about drinks (thanks to her father), he hired her without asking too much about the age thing.

At the time, there was already a great movement across the states for lowering the drinking age to eighteen, and a majority of them did by the mid-seventies. The argument that young boys were dying in Vietnam but could neither drink nor vote was too potent to ignore. California never changed its law, though, and all the states that had lowered the drinking age in the seventies had to raise it again to comply with the 1984 Drinking Age Act.

As it was, Vera was allowed to work, and she and others like her served as many young people as they could—it was our generation's little protest.

Vera had kept her job secret for months, but somehow Tilly found out and told me. I insisted on going to see her, and, seeing that we had a connection, I wanted to bring some of my friends.

We all showed up one Saturday afternoon in November. I remember the day because it was a few days before the election and many of my friends couldn't vote. There was, however, a movement to amend the constitution in order to lower the voting age to eighteen. It was an exciting time. And we were all very hopeful that Humphrey would beat Nixon. There was a lot of anticipation; after a year of assassinations and sadness, 1968 was ending on a positive note.

Vera told me she had the "shit-shift" that night—a shift that started around noon and ended by the time customers actually came in, around 7:30. We showed up around seven o'clock and took a table by the window as Vera had instructed. She was behind the bar and nodded as we sat down. She spoke to one of the waitresses, who then came to our table.

The waitress smiled. "Okay, Vera's friends. My name is Gloria, and I'm your server tonight. If you behave, you can have whatever you want."

We ordered our drinks, and I followed behind her as she walked away.

"Something wrong?" Vera asked when I reached the bar.

"No, I just wanted to say hello and apologize for bringing so many people," I offered and then added quickly, "But they're nice kids, and they'll behave, I promise."

"No problem. I'll join you as soon as my shift's over."

I nodded and walked back to the table. A few minutes later, Gloria came back with our drinks.

"Okay, three whiskey sours and two Schlitz," she said, putting all the drinks in the middle of the table.

We grabbed for our drinks like thirsty animals, and Gloria smiled and walked away without a word.

At 7:30, Vera came over with another round of drinks.

"Vera. Hi," I said as I stood up.

The two other men with me stood up as well. People were more courteous then. I introduced each person in turn as Vera sat down.

Herman and Nadir were both wearing gray suits with white shirts and thin dark ties. Vera shook hands with the men and then leaned over to kiss Tilly.

The last person was Herman's girlfriend, so I let Herman do the honors.

"This is my girlfriend, Edna," Herman said.

Vera reached over to shake hands. Edna recoiled as though she was going to bite her but then begrudgingly touched her hand. "Edna" was an old-fashioned name for an old-fashioned girl. Edna means "pleasure" in Hebrew, but there was nothing pleasurable about this person who held the name.

"Thanks for the drinks, Vera," Tilly offered, smiling broadly as she took a big gulp of her whiskey sour.

"Happy to do it." Then she turned to Edna. "Would you like another beer?"

Edna shook her head.

No one spoke for a moment, an odd silence, but then Tilly looked up at Vera and said, "Hey, Vera, do you want to help out with Humphrey's campaign?"

"Me? Are you serious?"

"Sure, girl. Why wouldn't I be?"

"I thought you had to be twenty-one," Vera said.

"Not at all," I chimed in. "We need more help, and it'll be great to have you work with us. We need to do a massive get out the vote campaign."

"Oh, I'd love to. What can I do, though? I don't have anything to offer."

"You'll have plenty to offer, girl," Tilly commended. "Fuck! Don't ever undersell yourself."

"Wow, this is so cool," Vera said.

"It'll be exciting. We'll go door-to-door, and we'll offer rides to voters." Tilly was animated now.

"How about you guys?" Vera asked, looking at the rest of the group.

"Sorry, Vera, I'm not with Humphrey," Nadir confessed rather shyly.

"What? Shit. You're crazy, man," Tilly roared.

"I don't support Nixon, but my dad will kill me if he hears I'm helping you guys," Nadir said.

Herman and I nodded with a clear understanding.

"What about you, Herman?" Vera asked.

"I might, but I'd have to do it very carefully. My dad is worse than Nadir's."

"Have you heard from Charlotte?" asked Nadir, using the lull in the conversation.

There was a momentary discomfort in everyone's face, but then I replied in a low, even voice, "I got a postcard from her last week."

I could see the hurt wash across Nadir's face, but he smiled weakly and murmured, "That's good. I was wondering if she'd completely forgotten us."

"Don't take these things seriously, man. You know Charlotte. It was just a postcard saying she has a new roommate named Tess something. Nothing more. A basic Charlotte," I said.

"I know, and I try not to, but it's—" Nadir looked rather distraught.

I thought he might burst into tears. By this time, I had become Nadir's friend and was genuinely troubled by his state. But I wasn't sure what to do for him. I knew how Nadir felt. I'd gone through a similar pain months earlier.

I hadn't told Vera about Charlotte and worried about what might come out that night, so I quickly offered, "Charlotte is Nadir's girlfriend, and she has gone to Paris to study."

"Oh, I see," Vera said.

"Charlotte loves him," I said as a confirmation and then, to Nadir, "She loves you, man. We all know she does, but we also know she has an eccentric way of showing it."

Herman nodded, but Edna just snorted.

"What's wrong?" Herman asked.

"'What's wrong?' Nobody thinks it's strange that Charlotte *loves* Nadir but only writes to Donte? I find it more than peculiar, don't you, Vera?" Edna said.

"Be nice, Edna," Herman admonished her softly, but there was no conviction in his voice, which surely wasn't missed by anyone.

"I *am* being nice, but I'm being honest, too, since no one else is. It seems Donte loves to keep all the girls for himself." She waved her hand, pointing to Tilly and Vera.

"What a fucked-up thing to say," I rejoined. I then added, mainly for Vera's benefit but perhaps for everyone's, "Charlotte and I grew up together, so we're very close. We're like siblings."

Edna snorted again and said in a singsong voice, "I bet you are."

"What are you trying to say, Edna? I didn't even know you knew Charlotte," Nadir said, looking more distraught.

"Of course I know her. Who do you think introduced me to Herman?" She then faced me and continued, "Of course, I'm not as close to her as you, but, then again, no one is."

I was furious, but I kept my cool. Nadir seemed shocked, and the rest of them were too embarrassed to look at each other.

"What's going on?" Nadir asked in a desperate tone.

Vera looked up at me and our eyes met. I was embarrassed to be caught in this situation in front of her. I had to do something.

I smiled and tried to look nonchalant. Then I looked at Nadir for a moment and, when I had his full attention, asked, "Do you *trust* me?" I wanted to add that if he didn't, he shouldn't be my friend, but I hoped he saw that message in my eyes.

To my relief, Nadir replied, "Of course, Donte. Why would you ask that?"

"And you know how much I like Charlotte, right? You know this because you've known us for a long time, and we've been through a lot."

I was expecting Nadir to dispute my latter assertion, but he simply nodded.

"And I introduced you to Charlotte, didn't I? I pushed you to go after her when you were shy and hesitant, right?" I said.

"Yes. But I still don't understand," Nadir said.

"Would I have done all that if she wasn't like my own sister? Do you seriously think Charlotte would want someone and not go after him?"

Nadir nodded again.

"You're a wonderful person, Nadir. You can either believe this and be happy or let others ruin it for you. It's your choice, not mine, not Herman's, and certainly not Edna's."

"I'm sorry," moaned Nadir.

"Don't be sorry. Just trust yourself."

"How about another round?" Vera asked. Then, without waiting for an answer, she signaled Gloria, who was hovering at the bar.

"Let's meet tomorrow, Vera," Tilly said. "I can show you what you can do and work out the details. You may have to miss a few classes, though."

"I'm in. I think it'll be great."

"I need to pee. Where's the bathroom?" Edna asked.

Vera pointed to the back of the room, and then, as if not trusting her to make it there, she followed behind Edna.

Gloria brought our new order, and we drank in silence.

When the girls didn't come back, I said, "I'll go and check on Vera."

"Yeah, make sure she's still alive," Herman offered.

I knocked on the door, but no one answered, so I pushed it slightly, hoping no one would catch me. I didn't go in and was about to call Vera when I heard my name.

"And it's not just him," Edna was saying.

"Why do you say that? They seem like nice people," Vera replied.

"Herman is the only nice one; the rest are all assholes. Wait until you meet Charlotte. Then you'll see. They have their own little club, and they don't let anyone in, so don't get your hopes up," Edna said.

"I'm sure she is a nice person. Donte—"

Edna snorted loudly. "Donte!" she cried out. "Donte is the biggest fucker of them all. He's banging that crazy woman Tilly while he's in love with Charlotte, who's really his sister, and stupid Nadir is worried about his dad. He should be worried about losing his girlfriend to that asshole."

"His sister? Are you sure?"

"Listen, honey, get away from these guys as soon as possible. Now go away and let me pee."

I closed the door quickly and went back to the table. A few seconds later, Vera showed up followed by Edna. She asked Herman to take her home. He refused, but took her outside to hail her a cab. Vera gave me a funny look but didn't say anything. Nadir also found an excuse to leave soon after, without ever finishing his first beer.

Gloria came by as soon as Nadir left. "Chub ain't a big drinker."

"But we are, Gloria. How about another round?" Vera looked at us. We all nodded.

Gloria brought a new round, and we started talking about the election. Tilly was very knowledgeable about every single candidate on the ballot. We finished our drinks, and then, as if we had run out of ideas, too, we all fell silent.

"Could we sit outside?" asked Tilly, after a few minutes.

There were no seats outside, but people sat on the cliff's edge to watch the sunset. The sky was already dark. No drinks were allowed outside, but Vera said, "Sure. If you keep it quiet."

She went to the backroom and grabbed a small bottle of whiskey and a large checkered blanket, and then we went through the side door that had a large red sign warning against exactly what we were doing.

We sat on the edge of the cliff where we could hear the heavy rush of the waves below us. It was a clear evening with an easterly breeze, and the four of us sat close to each other, sharing the blanket. The stars were out, but it was a new moon, so the area was darker than ever. Our only source of light was from the windows of the bar. We sipped from the bottle and passed it back and forth and stared at the deep, dark horizon. Tilly carefully rolled a joint and, with some difficulty, used a match to light it. It felt like the most natural thing for us to do that night—smoking a joint and drinking a quart of whiskey.

I felt mellow and comfortable and a bit sleepy from the rhythmic crashes of the waves against the rocks a dozen feet below us. I think we all felt that way as we sat staring into the dark sea.

Vera broke the silence by asking, "How long you guys been together?"

Tilly gave a sweet laugh and replied, "We're not together, girl. We're just friends. Just very close friends."

"Oh, I thought—"

"That's okay. It's natural to think so. People look at us and just assume," Tilly said.

"I'm sorry, I didn't mean to imply—"

"There is nothing to be sorry about, girl. I won't push him out of my bed, but I don't want him as my boyfriend. He is too wild." Tilly winked.

"I second that," Herman chimed in. He was holding the roach in the corner of his mouth, trying very hard not to burn his lips. He spat it out when it got too hot and took a large swig from the bottle, which made him cough hard.

I said, "What kind of talk is that, Tilly? You're going to scare Vera."

"I'm sure she can handle it. Can't you, Vera?" Herman offered kindly.

"She doesn't look like a woman who would scare too easily," said Tilly, and then she added, "If anything, it's the Charlotte-Donte-Nadir triangle that might scare her more."

"Please don't start with that. I think I've had enough of it for one night," I rejoined.

Vera looked at Tilly and then me and then back to Tilly and said softly, "Oh, I see...Yeah, of course. I didn't get it...I'm fine."

Tilly laughed out loud, and Herman and I joined her. Vera tilted her head and smiled meekly. Tilly pulled Vera close and kissed her on the mouth. Vera looked surprised, but before she could do anything or say anything, Tilly kissed her again.

Then abruptly she stood up and said, "Gotta go. Herman, could you drive me?"

"Sure," he replied and stood up too.

"Let's work out the details tomorrow, Vera. Donte, you can drive her over?"

I nodded. "See you tomorrow."

Tilly bent over and kissed me hard and walked away with Herman.

"I'm sorry about Tilly. She likes to play games," I offered.

"I'm okay, I think," Vera said.

"I'm also sorry for Edna. She's a nice girl, but she doesn't like me, and she doesn't understand my relationship with Charlotte."

Vera didn't respond, so I asked, "Do you want another sip?"

She nodded and grabbed the bottle.

"Charlotte is like my sister, really," I said. "And Tilly and I are just friends, nothing more. You believe me, right?"

"It's not any of my business."

"It's just that I like you, Vera. I really like you, and I don't want tonight's misguided conversation to taint our friendship."

"I'm still here, aren't I?"

"Yes, and I'm happy that we didn't upset you too much," I said, grabbing the bottle from her.

I don't know why—perhaps because of Tilly or perhaps because of the alcohol or maybe because of the beautiful night—but Vera leaned over and kissed me. And I kissed her back.

It was strange to be kissed by someone who within the span of a few minutes had been kissed by another, but it was also delicious. I could taste them both at the same time. I pulled back, and Vera smiled knowingly.

We sat there for a long time sipping from the bottle, and once we were completely smashed, we walked back to the street and grabbed separate cabs back to our apartments. I slept soundly that night, visited by occasional images of Tilly and Vera.

CHAPTER TEN:
REVELATION

It was early December 1969 when Charlotte and her new friend Tess
touched down in San Francisco. They had been away for more than
a year. The plan, which Charlotte had described in her postcard, was
for Tess to spend a week with Charlotte and then spend Christmas
with her own family in Montgomery, Alabama.

They walked into the reception room where Herman, Nadir, and I
had been waiting for hours, tons of luggage in tow. Their plane was
several hours late, but in those days, it was an event and pleasure to
spend time at the airport. Herman was wearing his formal gray suit
and thin tie; Nadir was wearing a checkered green suit that was a tad
large for him, as though he was planning to grow into it later. I was
the odd man out with my T-shirt, fringed leather vest, and jeans. I
was also sporting a massive hairdo and wearing a rolled-up red scarf
around my head. The other boys had their regular crew cuts.

We all smiled broadly when we saw them, and Nadir took a tentative
step toward Charlotte. She hugged him affectionately and then Herman and then me. She introduced Tess to us, and we all shook hands.

"God, I missed you guys," said Charlotte. She then looked at me and
asked, "How come you never wrote me back? I wrote you tons. It's
been six months since your last letter. What happened?"

"I wrote back, but I've been so busy with school this year," I offered
feebly.

"It doesn't take much. Nadir has been writing nonstop."

Nadir made an indeterminate sound and then said, "I just love writing."

She ignored him. "What about summer? Busy then too?"

"We were expecting you back for summer," I rejoined.

Charlotte opened her mouth to respond but then shut it for a moment before asking, "Is my father here?"

"Ms. Charlotte!"

The voice startled us, and we all turned around and were face-to-face with Mr. Johnston, Charlotte's family driver.

He nodded and continued, "Ms. Charlotte, your father sends his regrets but"—he paused—"I am sorry, he had to go to Belize." He stopped, not sure what else to say.

Charlotte looked crestfallen for a moment but recovered quickly. "Did he go alone, Mr. Johnston?"

"No, Ms. Charlotte."

"That's good. At least we don't have to deal with her in the house."

"May I take your bags?" he asked.

"Yes, please." She turned toward us. "You guys want to come over?"

"If you're not tired, I was thinking we should go out," I offered.

"That would be great," Charlotte replied cheerfully. "Can you manage, Tess?"

Tess looked exhausted but replied, "I'd love to."

"Let's go to Sea Cliff," I offered.

Charlotte pursed her lips and said, "That's a place for old people."

"It'll be fine," I said.

To my surprise Charlotte didn't argue back. She instructed Mr. Johnston to take her and Tess's luggage home and then come and pick them up in a couple of hours since Nadir had his car and we all could go with him.

Nadir insisted that Charlotte sit in the front, so Tess sat between Herman and me. After a while she fell asleep, and Charlotte continued with her complaints about my lack of letter-writing.

We went back and forth for a while, but then we were all jolted into silence. Nadir slammed on the brakes before parking at the side of the restaurant. Tess sat up straight, looking bewildered.

"Do you want to go home?" Charlotte asked her.

"No, I'm fine. It'd be good to stay up."

We all walked into the place like the ragtag group that we were; for a second I feared that they might not let us in. I took a left turn and took them to the other side of the restaurant where they did not serve "proper" food. This was the casual side, with younger clientele.

We grabbed a table, but I didn't sit down. I walked over to the bar and asked Vera to join us. I had to wait for her to serve a few people, but then we both walked back to our table.

"This is my friend Vera Pacient," I said and then, pointing to Charlotte, added, "Vera, this is Charlotte and her friend from France, Tess."

Vera was wearing a long green dress with huge yellow flowers. She shook hands with each of them and then turned to Tess and asked, "*Comment allez-vous?*" But before Tess could respond, she added, "That's the extent of my French." She then kissed Herman on the cheek and shook hands with Nadir.

"What can I get for you guys?" she asked.

Charlotte wanted a glass of Pernod. I knew she was doing it to test Vera, but Vera was good-natured about it and said that they didn't carry Pernod but could offer ouzo, which was very similar.

"No, I'll just have a glass of red wine, maybe a Burgundy."

"I'll have a beer, please, Vera," Herman said. Nadir and I asked for the same.

"And what would you like to have?" Vera asked Tess. The way she carefully enunciated each word gave the impression that she thought Tess was French.

"I'm from Alabama, Vera," Tess cried out with a big smile.

Vera gave out an affectionate laugh and said, "I'm so stupid. I'm so sorry, Tess, but the way Donte introduced you, I thought you were French."

"I'll take that as a compliment. I've never had ouzo. Is it good?"

"Not my drink, but if you like Pernod, you'll probably like it," Vera said.

"Then let's go for it."

"I'll try it too," Herman said quickly.

"Okay, three beers, a glass of Burgundy, and two ouzos coming up."

"I want to try it too," I said. And with that, Nadir said he wanted one too.

As soon as she walked away, Charlotte said, "I can see why you were too busy to write."

Herman replied for me. "Come off it, Charlotte. The man was busy. We're all busy dealing with all the craziness that is going on here."

Charlotte opened her mouth to respond but closed it sharply and sat back. I knew she was excited to see us all and was disappointed that her father had ditched her yet again.

Vera brought back our drinks but didn't stay. We drank slowly, and Tess talked about the flight and her plans for Christmas. As soon as we were done with our drinks, Vera came back with another round, but this time she sat down with a glass of her own.

Charlotte eyed her warily, but Vera continued to smile back at her. She wasn't going to let Charlotte intimidate her.

"Did you hear the UK ended capital punishment today?" Vera asked.

I had heard about it and was glad that they'd had the courage to do it.

But before I could say anything to that effect, Charlotte leaned forward a bit and replied, "That's stupid. How are they going to deal with their murderers?"

I wasn't sure where that came from as it was not like her, but Vera didn't back down.

"You know how many people we put to death in this country? Hundreds, thousands."

"Not to mention all the people we're killing on the other side of the world," Herman chimed in.

"My God, I leave the country for a year and you all have become communists."

"Is this you talking or your dad?" I asked, staring at her intently.

Charlotte was about to respond, but Tess preempted her and said, "Oh, I heard about the draft lottery. It was just a few days ago, right?"

I looked at Tess and offered, "You know how fucking lucky we were, the three of us, just because we were born on certain dates?"

"What does that mean?" Tess asked.

"What does it mean?" Herman responded. "It means we're not going to be drafted yet. It means the war may be over before we are even called."

"That's wonderful. To tell you the truth, most of the people I know in Alabama would probably volunteer as soon as they could. Though,

I tell you, it was odd to live in a foreign country and hear about the U.S. making decisions about the futures of young boys by picking plastic balls."

Nadir spoke up for the first time. "It's part of the craziness of this country, but we were lucky. I was born November 3rd, and my number was 348. Donte was born on September 24th, and his number was 194, and Herman was born on July 25th, and his number was 67. If he had been born a day earlier, just one day earlier, his lottery number would've been 23. Can you imagine that?"

"But somebody was 23, right?" Tess asked earnestly. "Who's going to be first?"

"September 14th, those unlucky bastards." Nadir voiced everyone's thought.

"I was born on September 14th," said Vera solemnly.

I felt scared for her even though she would never get drafted.

"Somebody has to fight the war, Tess," Charlotte said. I was surprised again as she was the one who always spoke against the war.

"This is a sad conversation," Nadir said. "Let's not talk about this now. We're students, anyway, and they wouldn't send students to war." And then, with a less resolute voice, he asked, "Would they?"

"You're too rich to worry about that, Nadir," I offered, punching him hard on his shoulder.

"I heard Jim Morrison got arrested last month for harassing a stewardess. That's all the Parisians talked about for a whole week," Tess offered in turn.

"Fuck Jim Morrison," I said harshly.

Tess was taken aback a bit.

"Jesus, Donte. Don't be rude to my friend," scolded Charlotte.

"I wasn't being rude. I just don't like The Doors. People are dying, and he's spanking little stewardesses," I said.

"How about another round?" Vera offered.

We had our third, and I was feeling light headed and queasy. Charlotte stood up and said she was going to the bathroom. She looked wobbly walking through the restaurant.

Vera noticed me watching Charlotte and whispered, "Do you want me to go with her?"

I nodded, thinking, Déjà vu. Vera stood up and casually walked behind Charlotte but kept a pace or two behind her. We continued talking, and eventually it felt like hours had passed since they left.

I didn't want to go after them, so I leaned over and asked Tess, "Do you mind checking on Charlotte?"

Tess stood up rather unsteadily and made her way to the bathroom.

After a few minutes, they all returned.

Charlotte said, "I wanna go home."

"I'll take you," Nadir offered.

"No. Mr. Johnston should be outside by now," Charlotte said.

They said their goodbyes.

Tess offered to pay, but Vera dismissed it and said, "Welcome home!"

They started to walk out, but Charlotte stopped, turned around, and said, "Donte, could you come with us?"

There was an awkward pause, and then Charlotte added, "Just to the house, and then Mr. Johnston will drive you right back."

I stood up and looked at Vera, but she didn't say anything, nor did she make any gesture.

"Sure, Charlotte," I replied. I turned to the others. "I'll be back in a few."

Charlotte was right. Mr. Johnston was outside standing next to a black limousine. He stood up sharply and opened the back door for us.

"Thank you, Mr. Johnston," said Charlotte. "Will you take us home?"

Charlotte went in, and Tess followed and sat facing her. I went in and sat next to Charlotte, allowing her to put her head on my shoulder as she closed her eyes. Charlotte's efforts had exhausted her, and she looked rather ghostly.

She opened her eyes and looked at Tess for a moment and said, as though confirming something, "You know I love Donte; he's my brother." She then closed her eyes.

We drove in silence for a while through the dark streets as rain started to fall, making the roads slick. Charlotte stirred a bit, and her head fell off my shoulder.

Tess reached over and adjusted her so she would be more comfortable. She then looked at me and said, "Vera is lovely."

I nodded with a small smile and replied, "Yes."

"She was helping Charlotte in the bathroom, you know?"

"It doesn't surprise me, and I'm sure Charlotte wasn't very grateful."

"No. In fact she was a major bitch about it."

"She doesn't mean it, not really. She just can't help but to have this aristocratic air about her."

"Vera was gracious, though," Tess said.

"She is."

"You two look good together."

"We do, don't we?" I replied.

"I'm sure Charlotte and Vera will become good friends soon," Tess said in earnest.

"I guess you don't know Charlotte as well as I thought."

Tess didn't respond, and we drove the rest of the way in silence.

Ten minutes later, the car stopped. Mr. Johnston opened the door for us.

"Do you need help with Ms. Charlotte, Donte?" Mr. Johnston said.

"No, I think we can manage."

"Do you need a ride back?"

"No, thanks."

Mr. Johnston didn't insist; he never did.

We managed to wake Charlotte up, and she walked to the house under her own power. Mr. Johnston walked ahead and opened the door. As soon as we entered the house, he said goodnight and left.

"Everybody's gone to bed, I guess," said Charlotte, slurring every word, sounding rather disappointed.

"Should I wake up Mrs. Norris?" I asked.

"No, let the old bag sleep. I'm sure she left us some food in the kitchen," Charlotte said.

"Don't you want to go to bed?" I asked.

"No, let's eat something. I haven't seen you for months. I want to talk with you. How come you didn't respond to my letters?"

"Let's eat," I ordered.

We walked to the kitchen, and, as Charlotte had predicted, there were plates of food and a note for Charlotte. She picked up the note and read it. "She says, 'Don't make a mess, Donte,' and, of course, she loves us."

"She always says that, and she's always wrong."

"You're the messiest boy I know, but I love you anyway. Even though you can't write one lousy letter."

We grabbed some food and then took our plates to the living room. Charlotte put her plate on the table and lay on the sofa. She was asleep within minutes.

My eyes were glazed over, and my eyelids weighed a ton.

I put my plate down and was ready to tell Tess that I was leaving when Tess said, in a soft voice, "I need to ask you something."

"Sure," I replied.

"It's about the necklace—"

"How do you know about that?" I asked, but it was obvious how. In fact, Charlotte had told me about it in one of her letters. But I added, "I don't know why or what Charlotte told you, but I don't want to talk about it."

"I'm sorry, but her story has been sitting on the back of my mind for months, and Charlotte told me that I need to speak with you about it. In fact, she insisted."

I was surprised but also glad to be able to talk about the incident with someone. Yet I wasn't sure how to respond, so I replied lamely, "It was just a silly childhood prank."

"You think so?"

"Why? You don't?"

"It may have been for you, but not for her," Tess replied.

"If it was so important, she would have talked to me about it. She hasn't said a word about the incident for years. I don't think she has ever talked about it with anyone," I said, not trying to hide the anger in my voice.

Tess gave a small smile and said, "Except me."

And the silliness of my statement was clear. "No, you're right, except you. That makes you special."

I meant it as a casual comment but then again, maybe it wasn't.

Tess said rather stiffly, "I don't think I'm so special. I think I was in the right place at the right time. She needed to unburden something, and I was there for her as I'm sure any good friend would be."

"I'm sure," I replied. Then we both fell silent again.

After a while I said, "I'm glad Charlotte told you because it also caused her to write me about it. I didn't know she felt so responsible for everything, and I didn't know how to tell her the truth."

"There is more?" Tess asked.

"Of course, and that's why I didn't write her back. I wasn't sure what to do. Either way I was damned. If I agreed with her version, then I was agreeing that she was at fault, and yet, if I told her the truth, then I would be hurting her in some other way."

"What way?" Tess said, sitting straight up in her eagerness.

"I don't know if I can tell you."

"You're kidding me? You can't do that. Why would you bring it up in the first place?"

"I didn't. You did."

"Still, why indulge me at all?"

"I don't know. Maybe because I knew you knew, and if Charlotte trusted you, then I should too."

Charlotte opened her eyes for a second and said, "Did you call me?"

"No. Go back to sleep," I said. I got up and indicated for Tess to follow me.

We walked back to the kitchen and sat on the tall stools.

"She trusted you, and I need to ask somebody what I should do," I said.

"Then tell me," Tess pleaded.

I wasn't convinced. I didn't know if I could trust her. And if I did, it would mean revealing so much more. We were behaving like adults and not like college kids. I was tired and still drunk. I stared at her for a moment but didn't respond.

Tess looked tired, too, but it seemed her curiosity had perked her up a bit. I didn't know it about her then, but it was her sense of empathy that was driving her and not an eagerness for more gossip.

She made an offer: "I'll tell you my secret if you tell me yours." She smiled and her eyes twinkled.

So I did.

CHAPTER ELEVEN: SECRETS

It is true that my father knew Charlotte's father, and it's true they met in a far-off land where differences were lessened by the kinship of nationality. And it is true that when they came back home, they stayed friends despite all the barriers that existed in those days, and there were so many. They stayed friends but couldn't be too close, not in public, anyway—not even in San Francisco.

My father ended up working for Charlotte's father, but their friendship was a cause of distress for Charlotte's mother and stayed so for a long time. Charlotte always felt abandoned by her father, and when she was younger, the feeling was more intense. As little children, Charlotte and I liked each other, but, at the same time, she also saw me, and my father, as barriers to her own father's love.

Charlotte didn't mean any harm, but she was young and wanted to punish us for, as she felt then, stealing her father. It was meant as a simple, childish prank to gain if not her father's love, then at least his attention. She wanted to show him that there were others who loved her. She stole her mother's pearl necklace and then pretended it was a gift from me. She was only ten years old, so she didn't see the ridiculousness of her plan. She wore the necklace as she paraded around her father's office. Her father noticed it immediately and told her to return it to her mother's room.

Charlotte insisted that I had given it to her, and her father laughed at the notion that I could, at the age of ten, give her such a gift. She hadn't thought it through, and so, facing her father's ridicule, she made a decision, a change of plan. She felt trapped, so she blurted that it was my father who had bought the gift and given it to me to give to her. Her father had laughed harder, amused by his daughter's theatrics, and even asked why my father would give her such an expensive gift.

He would have dismissed the notion and moved on, but then Charlotte, in her authoritative voice, said something that in retrospect sounds benign but felt ominous at the time. She told her father that it was because my father loved her, and she apparently insisted that my father loved her very much.

Charlotte wanted to hear her father say that it was not true, that he loved her more. But he didn't say that; in fact, he was silent for a moment. Perhaps he was hurt by Charlotte, or perhaps he was thinking of something else. Charlotte couldn't really tell, so she only saw anger. He demanded that Charlotte give the necklace to him, and, fearing the worst, Charlotte gave it back without a protest.

This could have been a simple lie without any major consequences, but, three days later, my father was arrested. Charlotte knew it had something to do with the necklace, and although my father didn't spend more than a day in jail, Charlotte blamed herself for everything that happened after that. My family and I had to move away. Charlotte and I didn't see each other until her mother died of a brain aneurysm about a year later.

They were all disconnected events, but in Charlotte's mind they were all consequences of her lie. She not only didn't gain her father's love but also lost her best friend and then her mother. We eventually came back, and her father remarried. Charlotte was fearful that we would blame her as she did herself. But as I recall, our first reencounter was warm and loving. I think the events made Charlotte more protective of me.

She had been carrying this secret with her for years and never revealed it to anyone until she met Tess. And I'm sure she didn't think she would become Tess's lifelong friend.

That was Charlotte's view of the events since she did not know about her mother's role in this sad affair. Charlotte's mother was also upset with my family, seeing us as overreaching interlopers who were crossing the line that people like us should never cross. When

Charlotte's father relayed Charlotte's childish story to her, it gave her the idea of using the necklace to frame my father. It was her mother who got my father in jail. You didn't need much evidence to entangle people like my family.

For the longest time I only heard Charlotte's version of the story, her little prank. I didn't know about the jail or about the ultimate twist—my father's short affair with Charlotte's mother and her hypocrisy that came with it.

When I was in college, my father told me the rest of this long, twisted tale. At the time I was utterly confused and hurt and couldn't understand why my father would tell me about all this, but after a while I appreciated the burden of guilt and betrayal that my father had endured all those years. My mother had left us when I was a little boy, and I understood my father's loneliness and the allure of Charlotte's mother. I understood the complexity of their lives. I felt closer to my father despite his betrayal. My father didn't know anything about Charlotte's little lie, so, when I read Charlotte's letter confessing to having betrayed my father, I was dumbfounded as the two narratives collided.

"So now you know," I told Tess as I finished my story.

She nodded but didn't say anything. I wasn't sure if there was anything for her to say, and I regretted my decision to share at once. There was no real answer, anyway. If I told Charlotte, it would kill any nice memories of her mother, but if I didn't, then I'd leave her with the guilt.

"Don't tell her the truth," Tess said. "Tell her that your father's time in jail had nothing to do with her and you guys left because of work. Tell her that children make silly mistakes, and we can't carry the burden all our lives." She stopped and closed her eyes. She took a deep breath and said again, "Don't tell her the truth, at least not your truth. Make her believe that none of these events are connected. I think you should talk to your father and tell him about Charlotte's role and then ask him to speak with her and free her from this guilt. Do all this so you can free her."

"Are you sure? If she ever finds out, she'll never forgive me."

"I'll swear to you, I'll never utter a word about this to anyone. Your secrets are safe with me."

"If you're really sure." I needed the extra reassurance, but I was already feeling confident about her. She was one of us, as my father would say.

"It wouldn't be a lie," she offered kindly.

I nodded and then walked back to the living room. I picked up Charlotte and carried her to her room, and Tess followed behind us quietly. She stood on the threshold and spied on us as I put Charlotte on the bed and carefully and slowly took off her shoes and socks. I took a quilt from the closet and put it on her. I held her hand for a moment and kissed her on the forehead, meticulous and tender, like her father might have done if he were a better person.

I walked out of the room and asked Tess if she wanted to go to bed. She nodded, so I directed her to a room next to Charlotte's.

"This is yours," I offered. It was nominally my room, and I assumed Charlotte would offer it to her.

Tess thanked me and walked me to the door. I shook her hand formally and thanked her for the advice. I said goodbye and then walked out of the house without calling a cab. Tess stood in the doorway. I could feel her watching me as I crossed the driveway and walked through the front yard and then disappeared into the darkness.

We didn't know it then, but on that cold night in December 1969, Herman met his future wife. I don't think they even exchanged more than a few words that night, and what was said was mostly about the politics of the day, Vietnam and the draft. And yet, without any of us knowing, they were destined to be together. Herman asked Tess out a couple of days later, and she said yes. That simple.

Tess never told me her secret, though, and I never asked. I thought I didn't need to know.

SPRING 1981

CHAPTER TWELVE:
A POOL PARTY

Charlotte had her baby, and she, Nadir, and the baby moved into their new house, Charlotte's dream house, one with a beautiful backyard and heated pool. All of our lives seemed to fit back into a comfortable and regular routine. It helped that I never saw Vera. Tess informed me that after Charlotte's dinner party, Vera told everyone to stop inviting her to such events. I wondered if it would ultimately be for the best, this avoidance, and while I remained uncertain, I knew it would at least breed peace, even if a false one.

With Vera and I out of the spotlight, a boredom set into the group, or at least that was Herman's take on it, and soon Anat and Akron's relationship became the new gossip. I would catch Herman, Nadir, Tess, and the others in a corner at a party, making bets on Anat's behavior or Akron's aloofness. I suddenly saw what it must have been like when Vera and I separated—our friends dissecting the intrigue of each minute event like we were characters on their favorite primetime soap. Nadir surprised me the most of all as he, a reasoned interpersonal diplomat, never seemed to be someone particularly interested in gossip. This was doubly strange because Nadir and Akron were close friends, but then again, we were all friends. But something new had taken hold of him since the baby had come along, as if Nadir needed some new excitement.

One thing was certain, though: our middle-aged life was injected with intrigue and strange sexual tension that we experienced vicariously through each other. Anat and Akron's possible extra-marital activities peeled a layer from the façade of our wholesome relationships. And couples started to talk and whisper in gatherings with hushed and conspiratorial voices that eagerly demanded more detailed information, more graphic illustration.

Rumors abounded about them, and each person had a different version of the events that actually spoke to their own domestic life more than to the facts. Not being that close to Anat or Akron, I stayed away from the fray, though I did call her, not him, to offer her my support, knowing full well that she wasn't going to ask for any help from me. It was a shameful and transparent faux offer.

More unusual was Tess's attitude toward them. I'd have expected her to jump in and try to help, but it seemed she was afraid to even talk about them.

"I don't want to hear about failed relationships," I warned Herman when he tried to talk to me about Anat and Akron.

"They're just going through rough times," he replied, refusing to believe there was anything serious going on. "Some couples thrive on lively bickering."

But I wasn't in the mood to hear about other people's problems.

And there was Anat. She would arrive at a bash without her husband, claiming that he was away on business or not feeling well. Other times they would appear together, very friendly and warm, but then one of them would disappear in the middle of the party without a word.

Initially I saw this as part of their relationship, and I think the others thought the same way. Then, their disappearing act became routine, and that's when Herman and Nadir started to make little childish side bets about who would leave first at the next dinner party. It was terrible how we found solace in a simple action of pretending to be better than others—more stable, more forthright, more realistic.

Friends making bets on another friend's misery. We thought we were clever for being so lighthearted about it. Nevertheless, the simple suggestion of "I bet you…" took on a life of its own, and, though memories become hazy, I have the lingering belief that our actions might have hastened the demise of their marriage.

I was at a large party at Charlotte's new house. It was uncharacteristically warm that spring day, and the party had spilled into the backyard. Charlotte had placed several gas heaters around the patio, which made it more than comfortable even for San Francisco. Anat and Akron showed up late but were very perky and happy, which had become a rarity by that time, but everyone welcomed the mood. Charlotte was proud of herself, certain that she'd had a hand in saving their marriage.

Perhaps it was this momentary warmth in their relationship that permitted Herman to push his game a bit further. Anat and Akron, who had been at each other's side at first, had slowly drifted apart. Nadir quickly came over and made the usual signal for a bet on who would leave first. These bets had become an obsession of sorts, and they couldn't help playing for higher and higher stakes. Still, even while it was mildly interesting in the beginning, it was tiresome by then. It was becoming like a bad soap opera that would never end and needed closure.

Nadir and Herman were still debating and setting up the rules of the game, a repeat. I could see Anat sitting and drinking with a few people, and I had seen Akron disappearing into some other room with some of his smoking friends.

"You're on," Herman said, sounding rather serious. "Why don't we make a proper wager this time?"

"Whatever you want, mister," Nadir replied, confident in his abilities.

"I'll bet you a case of Scotch that Akron will leave the party as soon as he's done getting high," Herman countered.

But Nadir wasn't about to give in, so he said rather casually, "No problem, but it better be a nice single malt and not the cheap stuff you normally buy. In fact, what about two cases?"

"Two cases of fine single malt Scotch, then."

They reached an agreement and shook on it solemnly. And with that they quickly separated, hoping to avoid Tess, who was walking toward them. But she caught them and ordered them to set up something or other. Nadir quickly obeyed and walked outside.

"What's going on?" asked Tess, staring at me intently.

"Just chatting," I replied.

"Are they betting again?" She wasn't happy and stared at me, trying to extract the information.

"Tess, please don't ask me. I'm not involved," I replied.

Tess turned around to ask Herman, but he shook his head solemnly. To my surprise she didn't pursue the subject. Then Charlotte walked over, so Tess lost any chance of interrogating him any further.

Charlotte came in, stood by us, and grabbed my hand. Tess noticed and reached out and took Herman's hand into her own. She was good about such things.

Charlotte's voice broke my concentration. "I'm so glad you came, Donte. You seem happier."

"I think I am," I said. "I feel good at least."

"I'm glad."

"Look at you," Tess said, looking at Charlotte. "You look so great and you just gave birth."

"Me?"

"You look fabulous, Charlotte," Herman offered.

And she did look good. She looked as though she had never been pregnant. Her stomach was as flat as ever, her thighs were long and athletic, and her arms were solidly toned. The only thing she had carried over from her pregnancy was her perpetual glow. Tess looked at Herman meaningfully, and he looked back at her with the same intensity. The unspoken question hung between them for a moment.

"We're not ready yet." Tess spoke for both of them.

He nodded, though he didn't look as certain as she.

"I'm going to talk to Anat," Herman told us.

Tess kissed him as a reply.

It was always amazing how Tess knew the right gesture—a hug at the right time, a kiss on the cheek versus on the mouth, holding hands, or any kind terms of endearment. She simply had a gift for it.

"I'll go with you," I offered. We walked over by the pool where Anat and Nadir were speaking.

"Hello, darlings," said Anat as soon as we reached them.

"What are you drinking?" Herman asked.

She shoved her glass toward us, and I took a small sip. It was a strong gin and tonic.

"Is it heated?" Anat pointed to the pool.

"Of course," Nadir answered.

Anat dipped her finger in the water and nodded approvingly.

"We should give it a try," Herman said.

I knew he was trying to create drama.

"You're crazy," Nadir replied incredulously.

"I'll bet Anat would jump in," Herman insisted.

"I'll go in if Tess does," she said.

"Well, if you're game, I'm game too. I haven't even used the pool since we moved to this house," Nadir said longingly. He thought for a bit and then said, "But I don't think I've got enough bathing suits for all the guests."

"Don't worry about the details. I don't need a bathing suit; I have my boxers," offered Herman.

"Don't be silly. This is not the way," I warned.

He ignored me and started to take off his clothes. Nadir followed with some trepidation. I looked over at Charlotte and Tess. They were standing behind a large glass wall that separated the patio into an inner and outer section. They were staring at us intently, and I knew they had figured out what Herman and Nadir were about to do. I could see Charlotte was getting agitated and speaking rapidly to Tess. I was expecting Charlotte to walk over and put a stop to it, but she just stood there, seething.

This spontaneous change in the character of the party left many of the guests puzzled at best. Most had passed the age of dropping their pants on a moment's notice. Others could aptly be described as nonparticipants. Nevertheless, there were some serious activities happening by the pool. Charlotte stood in silence watching two grown men racing to get into the water. The other spectators' faces were passive, neither encouraging nor discouraging; they stood around watching and sipping their drinks. And in the middle of the sea of poise was Anat, who hooted and cheered them on.

I walked over and stood with Charlotte and Tess. We continued to stare as more guests entered the pool, abandoning their jackets and dresses for boxer shorts and silky slips. Charlotte bit her lip harder with every single guest who surrendered to the pool. She looked miserable but still controlled her anger with a Herculean effort that must have taken a great toll on her. She looked defeated.

I reached over and held her hand.

She asked, "Can't you stop this?"

"No," I replied in earnest.

She then turned to Tess and asked, "Why does your husband always...always try to ruin my parties?"

Tess was taken aback but wisely said nothing. So we stood there, all
three of us, simply staring. I'm sure Tess had not realized the mag-
nitude of the situation until Charlotte's comment. Otherwise, she'd
have fished Herman out of the pool before anyone else had a chance
to join in.

I don't think Herman expected to have such "success" either, but
it seemed that the situation had taken on a life of its own; Anat
came closer to the edge of the pool and stood there while someone
whispered something to her. She laughed slyly but didn't do what we
knew he had asked of her. I was heartened by Anat's refusal and by
the steadfast resistance of the large number of people who had not
compromised their self-restraint. They continued to sit nobly around
the beautifully decorated tables and chairs, sipping from cut crystal.

All this time there was no sign of Akron or any of his friends.
But as soon as I thought about him, he appeared as though I had
willed him. He walked over to the nearest table and sat with an
elderly couple. There was a bottle of champagne in the ice bucket
next to the table, and he poured himself a large glass and then, as an
afterthought, offered some to the couple. They refused with polite
smiles.

Anat was still engaged with the few men around her and had not
noticed Akron's approach. This time Nadir shouted for a few others
to join, and a couple more people, after some more urging, started to
disrobe. One of the guests moved closer to Anat and said something,
perhaps echoing the earlier pleas. Anat looked back and noticed her
husband. Another guest urged her to get in, and this time Anat relented. With a swift movement she stepped away from the circle and
grabbed the bowtie that was binding her long dress. Then, with a
snap like a magician's assistant, she stood outside of it.

Akron stood up sharply, like a soldier called to attention, but then
slumped back down without a word, looking disheartened. Anat
jumped in and then held onto the edge of the shallow part of the pool,
fully exposed through her wet slip, laughing with several admirers
watching on the sideline. Nadir stood behind her, chatting with another couple, each holding a tall glass.

I walked over and sat next to Akron. I needed to speak with him and try to be his friend. Akron handed me the bottle of champagne, and I poured some in a flute and gingerly took a sip. The tables next to us were crowded with men and women who not only would never consider wetting any part of their bodies but didn't even deign to pay any attention to the crowd in the pool.

After a few minutes of silence, Akron said, "I need to go." He stood up, and I followed him.

"I'm sorry, Akron," I said.

"Why?"

"I don't know. I feel we've ruined Charlotte's party," I said, though I'm sure he understood my true meaning.

"I wouldn't worry about it."

"Herman was just trying to get Nadir in the water. He hates Charlotte's stuffiness." I don't know why I felt the need to defend Herman. He deserved Akron's anger.

Akron chuckled. "You guys think too highly of yourselves. He didn't force anybody."

"I know, but Herman upset you."

"No, he didn't. If anything, I'd say it was Nadir's fault. Nadir didn't do anything that he didn't want to do. He tries too hard to be cool."

"Are you mad at Anat?" I asked, even though I had no right.

"We're past all that. You all know that. I'll see you soon."

We shook hands. He walked away without saying another word. I watched him as he collected his coat and left. I was still staring at the closed door when I heard Tess behind me.

"I just don't get this silliness," Tess said.

"Herman was just trying to add a bit of excitement to the party."

"I'm surprised Charlotte continues to invite us," she said.

"It's rather simple, Tess. Nadir wants to be playful or, as they say, tries to be cool. Herman has the charisma. He doesn't have to do much to be the life of the party. Nadir needs Herman to shield him from his other friends' snobbery, and Herman needs Nadir to provide the snobbish audience. And Charlotte and you are alike. So it's easy to see why you and Herman are always invited. Nadir wants Herman, and Charlotte wants you."

"But why punish Akron?" she said.

"Nobody is punishing him," I protested. "He doesn't blame anyone."

"How do you know?" Tess asked in her serious, clinical tone.

"He just told me," I replied feebly.

"So what? Just because he doesn't blame anyone directly doesn't mean we're not responsible."

Tess was getting angry, so I said, "You read too much into things, Tess."

In the end Nadir lost a couple of cases of Scotch, a small price to pay for one of the best parties he had ever hosted. But, as Herman told me later, the winning wasn't worth it given the hell he got from Tess later that night.

CHAPTER THIRTEEN:
ORGANIZED PARTIES DON'T WORK

Three weeks after Charlotte's pool party, Anat called to tell me about a get-together, a sort of "I-have-been-sad-and-depressed-for-some-time-and-I-need-to-get-out-and-show-people-that-I-am-still-standing" celebration. She complained that she had wanted to have a small gathering, but it was growing too big. Size is, of course, relative, and what Anat thought of as large was what most would consider simply friends dropping by for a drink. I thoroughly hated structured celebrations, and Anat's sounded like one: come at five, leave at nine. So I mentioned that I might not even be able to attend. That got her started on how she really wanted to see me and how it had been such a long time. Long time! I thought that was strange given that I'd just seen her a few weeks earlier—more of her than I thought I'd ever see.

"Okay, okay," I said. "Maybe I'll come for a drink or two."

"That'll be fine. Just come and say hello. I really want to see you."

A wise man would have thought there was something funny about this overly accommodating Anat and her selective invitation. She started telling me some other stuff, but I tuned her out.

As she talked, her phone clicked, announcing another incoming call. "Can I put you on hold for a second?" she asked.

"No, Anat, just give me a call later and tell me what to bring." I hoped she wouldn't try to put me on hold anyway.

"Just bring a bottle of wine and come around five," she said hurriedly as she hung up.

I was going to yet another structured party where I only would know a couple of people, but I had a plan: go in, have a drink, say hello, listen to a couple of strangers tell the synopses of their lives and then tell them mine so that we could quickly pigeonhole each other, satisfying our human need for categorization, and then, finally, sit in a corner and, when Anat was distracted, get out.

I arrived too early and managed to be the first guest. Akron answered the door, which was quite a shock. The way Anat had spoken, I thought she needed the party because of her relationship. It had sounded like it was about marking a step in a new direction. So I was surprised but rather happy to see Akron.

Before I even walked in the door, Anat flew across the hallway and gave me what would be called a bear hug if she were a hundred pounds heavier.

"I hope I'm not the first person," I said.

"But you are, and we are so glad of it," she purred. "Go in the back, and pour yourself a drink and pour me one too."

I turned around to ask Akron if he wanted one, but he was gone without making the tiniest noise. It had started to become rather eerie with Anat's purring and Akron's disappearance. The bar was set in the backyard but poorly stocked. I surveyed the bottles and heard Vera's voice in my head making fun of the limited selection.

I grabbed a wine bottle and fumbled with the corkscrew, but the cork refused to dislodge. It became a battle of wills as I pulled and pushed the cork with all my might. I only managed to push it farther in, and one more hard push would have dropped it inside. Akron appeared like a ghost, as soundless as ever, and from nowhere, which freaked me out a bit, so I almost dropped the bottle. He grabbed it from my hands and, with an efficient pull, managed to take the cork out. He gave the bottle back to me. His eyes shone black, and he had a queer, mirthless smile that seemed frozen on his lips.

"You want a glass?" I offered in a metallic voice, a gurgled noise like a patient trying to respond to the dentist's idle chatter during a cleaning.

He refused, drifting across the yard to rearrange some patio furniture. Although Akron and I were not that close, we were always friendly enough, laughing at each other's jokes, chatting during parties, but that day he seemed like a different person. He seemed to be floating from one corner to another in an aimless pattern. When Anat joined us, she was eager to grab the large wine glass and slurp it down smoothly.

"So, what's going on?" I whispered to Anat, pointing to her husband, who was greeting a new set of friends with the same frozen smile.

"I don't know," she said. "I just thought that I needed him to be here."

I guess that said it all, and I knew that if I pushed to understand what she meant, I would only get drawn in further. I didn't even want to be at the party.

Other guests flowed in like floodwater, as though the road that had been closed for a long time had just opened, allowing them to come through the barriers all at once.

They came with bottles of wine and baskets of food. A woman with golden hair—and a light green ponytail—walked in carrying a round glass jar. She walked toward me like she was on a mission, and I feared she might collide with me if I didn't step aside. She came to a sudden halt next to the bar and unceremoniously placed the jar on the table next to me. It shook violently as it hit the table, and some yellowish liquid splattered from the open top. The solid particles in the jar were bobbing up and down like broken debris from a shipwreck.

She wiped her hands on her skirt, surveyed the room like a pro for a second, and then turned her gaze on me. She had a round, chubby face that fit well with her body. She smiled broadly. Her eyes twinkled as if a bright light was reflecting from them.

"Wanna try?" she said with a loud, deep voice. She pointed at the jar and then, without waiting for an answer, started to pour the yellow liquid into a large red plastic cup. "Give it a try, man. It's great." She shoved the plastic cup in my face.

I grabbed it with my left hand while holding my wine glass with the other.

"Let me hold that for you," she offered. She grabbed my wine glass and smacked it on the table, spilling half of its contents.

I lowered my head toward the red cup and tentatively smelled the liquid. I jerked my head back as the strong, pungent smell of pepper penetrated my nostrils. I sneezed hard.

The woman laughed and stared at me expectedly, so I took a quick sip. It was like drinking acid. My throat burned as the liquid drilled its way to my stomach.

"It's great, huh?" Her smile grew. My eyes started to water, and she almost started to jump up and down. "I've been perfecting it for months. My name is Maryjay, by the way."

"It's great, Mary Jane," I managed to croak.

"No," she replied, shaking her head slowly.

"No, what?"

"Not Mary Jane. That's a dumb ass name. It's Maryjay, just one word."

"Donte," I offered.

"Sure thing, man. Guess what's in it?" She waited for a moment, and when I didn't speak, she continued as though I had said something. "No. No." She shook her head as if admonishing a dimwitted student. "There's gin, pear liquor, and some herbs and spices that I can't divulge."

She batted her eyes like a small girl embarrassed about being unable to share a secret. "But I can tell you," she whispered conspiratorially, leaning very close to my ear, "there is"—she paused for better effect—"some rocoto peppers in it." Maryjay's face lit up with both her smile and eyes going wide at imparting her secret.

Maryjay urged me to take another sip, but I was liberated as soon as Charlotte and Nadir showed up. I shook hands with Nadir and kissed Charlotte, but before I could say anything else, Maryjay and her ponytail turned to Charlotte with a cup of her liquid death, which Charlotte refused in no uncertain terms.

I started to develop a horrible headache and walked over to get some food. Nadir used the opportunity to get away from Maryjay as well. We both walked over to the table and grabbed a plate. However, the food was horrid. I was glad Vera was spared from seeing it.

Akron appeared again, this time looking calmer. "Pretty awful, ay?"

"You said it," I said.

I dumped my plate into a garbage can near the table and heard the splatter of food hitting the rest of the trash.

"Let's walk over to the garage," Akron said.

The three of us walked into his converted garage in silence. We sat on the couch, shoulder to shoulder, not talking but sharing a blunt. Nadir took a puff but declined the rest of it. Our behavior was so mechanical and so contrived that I felt like a teenager having sex for the first time. It was just an act, and all in silence.

We finished the smoke, and I left the two of them feeling not high but very low. I walked to the bar and forced a large sip of the yellow, putrid liquid down my throat, and within seconds I felt scrubbed clean. My head felt as big as a balloon. My mouth, throat, and lips were numb. I swayed over to the living room and let my body fall on a large couch. I sat there looking like a lost child who had given up hope of ever finding his parents. My mind drifted away from me, and I lost track of where I was and how long I had been there until I suddenly, somehow, found myself in the middle of a conversation.

Maryjay was telling her life story, of which the highlight was her pursuit of making new alcoholic beverages. I wanted to participate now, so I offered my own secret drink that Vera had taught me. That got Maryjay excited. Then she said something that I don't exactly recall, but it was something benign, like a name or a place, and then, as though the floodgate of my well-guarded emotions had opened, I started to pour out my feelings for all to see.

I was sitting between Maryjay and this other woman named Jane, crying about how miserable I was and how much I used to love Vera and how I could never have that life again.

"You're better off, Donte. You're a single man now, so enjoy your life. There are so many opportunities," offered Charlotte from across the room. Then she started to rattle off a list of things I could do as a single man. Maryjay was agreeing with Charlotte and pushing closer and closer to me as I stared blankly at the wall.

Then, out of nowhere, as if I'd had an epiphany, I cried out, "But I love them."

"Them?" Charlotte asked.

"Who do you love?" Maryjay asked as she leaned even closer.

"I love…" I paused and looked at everyone around me. "I love," I said again and paused for a long time. "I love too many people," I finally exclaimed.

Maryjay grabbed my face and turned me around so I would face her. "Hey, that's why I make my drinks. Because I love people too."

"No. No. I don't love people. I love them."

"You're a deep man, Donte," a man from the other side of the room said. The sarcasm wasn't lost on me, but Charlotte shook her head in disappointment at the man, clearly thinking he was a moron.

Jane, who had been sitting silently on the other side of me, pulled me back from Maryjay's grasp and offered, "I know what you mean. There're some people who have too much love in them, and they're bursting from the inside." She looked at Charlotte and then added, "I'm that way."

"That's it. That's it. I have too much love," I cried out.

Maryjay wasn't going to let Jane have all the attention, so she grabbed my face again and shouted, "That's what I'm saying—"

I looked at her blankly.

Jane looked at Maryjay and said, "You don't understand."

"What do you mean, I don't understand?"

"You confuse the tender feelings of love and affection with inebriation, Maryjay," offered Jane without a smile.

"I'm not stupid, Jane. I think my friend Donte understands. Don't you, Donte?"

"I think it's time for you to go home, Donte," Charlotte commanded.

I looked up at Charlotte rather blankly and offered, "I love you too."

"We all love each other. This is just a big love fest," Charlotte cried out, waving her hands around.

Charlotte pulled me off the couch, ignoring Maryjay's protest, and shoved me in the bathroom so that I could wash and sober up a bit. I took a long time in there, but when I came out and walked into the kitchen, I felt a bit saner.

Anat stood in front of the opened refrigerator, staring at its contents while talking loudly with Charlotte. I tapped Anat on the shoulder to say goodbye. She turned around with a swift movement and pulled me toward her hard. She hugged me and kissed me on the lips.

"Hey, we should go out for a movie or something sometime?" Anat asked as I managed to extricate myself from her grasp.

The request sounded innocent enough.

"That'll be great. Just give me a call, and we could do something fun," I agreed. And then, without thinking, I added, "Especially now that you're a free woman."

It was the sort of thing you might think but should never say, some primal half-thought born out of false masculine, territorial prowess.

Like a cartoon bubble, the words floated in the air, displayed in large capital letters, and I could tell, based on Charlotte and Anat's expressions, that they could see them as well. I knew instantly that I had said the wrong thing at the wrong time. I didn't mean anything by it, but I had already said it, so there was no taking it back. The kitchen fell into an uncomfortable hush, and I felt crushed under the weight of their collective eyes.

Charlotte looked horrified and stared down at her toes. She had noticed what I hadn't noticed at first. Akron stood just inside the kitchen doorway, back to us but within earshot. I'm sure he had heard my last words. But if he had, he didn't betray anything. Anat's eyes twinkled like two spurious beacons, and it occurred to me that she may have set me up—but she wouldn't have, would she?

Akron walked into the kitchen and grabbed a beer from the fridge.

"I got to go, man," I said in my most virile voice that I hoped would convey brotherhood and solidarity.

Akron turned around and shook my hand but remained silent, not trying to talk me into staying. He escorted me to the door, and I stepped outside, thinking he would walk me to my car. I thought I should say something to apologize for my poor taste, but then I heard the door slam behind me hard.

I felt exhausted, ready to be home and alone and asleep. I wished I could have apologized to Akron before he slammed the door. I had stupidly overstepped my bounds.

But part of me felt used as well. I remembered watching Anat run across Charlotte's backyard, having left her dress on the ground near the bar. Herman and Nadir in the pool yelling for her to hurry to them, her slip flapping as she ran. Her laughing and screaming as she jumped over the edge into the water. And Akron sitting on the sidelines, forced to watch his soon-to-be ex splash-fighting with Herman. Maybe that had been the point all along, why Anat just had to have Akron at the party; so that someone like me would behave like a horse's ass in front of him.

Anat hadn't needed to show people she was still standing. She needed to show Akron she could stand without him.

CHAPTER FOURTEEN: SILVIA AND HER DOG

I pressed the crosswalk button and waited patiently for the light to change even though several pedestrians rushed across the intermittent traffic. I did not want to rush. I wasn't ready yet.

I could see Silvia across the street, standing erect with her large black bag hanging loosely on her shoulder. She looked gloomy, and it seemed she was staring at nothing. She hadn't noticed me. I stood back a bit, letting the light change several times. She took a few steps forward and then back again, her black bag following each step like an obedient dog. Her hair was pulled back, and she was wearing a new pair of glasses, more oval than the ones she had before. I could see that she was looking for me in the waves of people as they rushed toward their homes. I waited.

It'd been almost a week since Anat's party and my disastrous pronouncement—though I still couldn't remember all the details of how I got home that night. I recalled waking up in the morning with a massive headache but no guilt. I'd said what I said, and there was nothing I could do. This is what I'd told myself all week long.

But when I left the office on Friday to meet Silvia, I didn't wait by the entrance as we had arranged but instead walked across the street and sat at the bus stop. I wasn't feeling guilty about what I'd said to Anat but rather for Akron's emasculation, whether my role in that was intentional on my part or not. I still felt the dark blanket

of sadness around my heart. He had stormed out of so many parties before Charlotte's pool party, when he had just sat there and
taken it.

I wasn't honest with myself then because if I were to be, I would
have to admit that I was bitterly sad. And I couldn't empathize with
Akron because I would also have to admit that I saw myself in him,
his experience in Vera and me. I'd also have to be angry with Herman
and Nadir for making the foolish choice to dive into the pool and
spurring Anat to do the same.

I wondered if my relationship with my friends, even those I had
known since high school, was conditional. If Anat left Akron, would
either of them continue to be my friend? How long before Vera and I
would partition our friends into hers and mine? I kept getting trapped
in my own mind, worrying that all relationships were conditional.

Dark clouds rolled quickly across the sky, promising a rainy night
ahead. The air turned cold, and a swift wind made me shiver. I
thought the weather would be a perfectly reasoned excuse to avoid
this meeting. But it seemed that was exactly what I'd been saying before every event, looking for the slightest provocation to cut off any
real contact. Yet I somehow ended up attending them every single
time, like a man who has been tamed after many years of marriage.
Just one more person in a group of coworkers who seemed to have no
family, no life, and no other interests besides the occasional gathering with a throng of other people like himself.

Though lately it seemed there were fewer and fewer people showing
up, and only I would attend time after time. Why I, who generally
hated people, felt compelled to be there every time was a mystery to
me.

I was standing across the street, letting the light change repeatedly,
and neither going over to meet Silvia nor turning around and going
home. Silvia had organized this thing so a few of us could meet with
a few of the out-of-town colleagues, but it seemed they all had a better idea—go wherever Silvia wasn't going. Throughout the day, one
after another, they canceled. I also called to do the same, but when
she picked up the receiver, I couldn't bring myself to go through with
it. She seemed very excited and assured me that a new colleague by
the name of Elliot would join us.

I didn't think Elliot was going to come, but I only said, "Great," and told her that I would meet her in front of the entrance. So it was going to be Silvia and me, all evening, once again.

Silvia had joined the company a short time after the December dinner party at Nadir's house. Charlotte had helped her get the job, and I only heard about it a week or so after when the new staff were introduced at a gathering. I saw her across the room. At first she seemed not to recognize me. She feigned surprise when I walked over to say hello.

"So nice to see you. I didn't know you worked here." She spoke impatiently, with her eyes searching the room.

She wore a dark tailored suit, with her long, auburn hair pulled back so tightly I was afraid that her follicles would tear from her scalp at any moment. We shook hands, and I pointedly reminded her that it was only a few months earlier when I told her about my company and our search for someone in marketing.

"You're so right. I completely forgot. And really, I owe you and Charlotte big." She said this with such a straight, honest face that I felt embarrassed about even thinking bad thoughts about her.

"Don't be silly. I don't know what Charlotte did for you, but I didn't do anything," I said. That certainly was the truth.

"Look, a few of us from marketing are going out for drinks after this, and if you feel like joining us, I'd like to buy you one," she offered sweetly, her eyes piercing mine.

"I'll try, but I have so much to do today," I replied unconvincingly.

She nodded while searching the room. She must have noticed someone. She quickly said, "I won't pressure you, but if you change your mind, we'll be at Charter at One Market." She grabbed my hand and squeezed it softly. "Hope to see you there, Donte, but if you don't mind, I'm going to network a bit."

She walked away and quickly zeroed in on the VP of marketing and started chatting as though they were old friends. I walked back to my office to finish the rest of my work.

I went to the Charter, of course, but made sure to show up around seven. The logic was that if they were a boring bunch, they would have gone home by then, and I wouldn't have missed much. To my surprise six or seven people were still sitting around a large table when I got there. I pretty much knew everyone, and they all, in their own way, acknowledged my approach. Silvia jumped up as soon as she saw me and rushed over to greet me as though we had known each other all our lives.

She made sure that I sat next to her by pushing one of her colleagues to another chair. She went around and meticulously introduced every single person. It was like a business meeting with an obnoxious twist. Silvia had released her hair from its oppressive prison, and now it flowed freely and wildly around her face as she pointed to each person.

It started with Joe.

"Here's Joe. He's been with the company how long, Joe? Right! For about seven years, and he's responsible for the Southern California sector, though his territory encroaches a bit into Nevada…"

She then tried to spice it up by adding a bit of personal zest. "Joe, as you can tell, is rather handsome, but, unfortunately for most of the single women in the company, he's married."

Joe, as though expecting this introduction, raised his large glass of beer. Silvia followed suit by grabbing her own glass and draining the soft-colored liquid with a smooth movement. She pointed to Linda, who at the moment was stuffing her face with fried chicken. Her fingers and lips glistened as she took large bites. She drained half a bottle of beer.

"Linda, the gorgeous lady at the end of the table, pretty much has everything except for the coastal states. She has been around for a long time, and she is our boss," Silvia shouted above the conversation. Linda looked up and gave a thin smile. Linda was a smart woman, but she couldn't hold her liquor.

Silvia's voice was laced with sarcasm. She winked at Joe, who promptly raised his glass and shouted, "To Linda."

Everyone followed suit. They laughed heartily at some inside joke. Silvia waved at Linda, who had resumed her concentration on the plate of fried chicken.

I nodded, unable to bring myself to stop Silvia. Although I worked in a different department, I knew most of the people in marketing, and they certainly knew me. Nevertheless, it seemed they were all enjoying Silvia's breakdown of people's characteristics. After the third introduction, I started to tune her out and ordered a beer from the passing waitress. Nobody seemed to notice my lack of attention and continued clinking bottles and glasses every time Silvia mentioned something interesting.

Overall, though, it turned into a fun night. I was more than surprised to see the usually mellow bunch be so gregarious. Silvia went on to invite me several more times, and I felt a bit privileged to be included in this marketing group's outings. The number of people attending such gatherings varied from as low as two to as high as twenty, the whole department. Silvia, with a couple of exceptions, was present each time I joined the group, and several times she and I were the only people remaining at the table when the others left to go their separate ways.

Both of us liked staying up late. Our conversations inevitably would turn to work and how good or bad—mostly bad—the company leaders were. Because she was new, she wanted to know more about who did what and the culture of the place. At first I enjoyed the older, more experienced role, but after a while it seemed like we only talked about work and only the part that pertained to her. She talked about her clients and her bosses and how she would really want to do one thing when she was forced to do something else.

When I would drag the conversation from work to something else, say, a book I had read or a movie I had seen, she would turn the conversation to what she called her first and only love, music—a secret that she tried in vain to keep from her coworkers. She played lead guitar in a female rock band, although the current drummer was a man, and she dreamed of fame if not fortune. Apparently the band practiced late nights and looked for gigs on weekends.

After we finished our bitching session about our jobs, the conversation always turned to her music. I'd inevitably say she should invite me to see her band. Every time, she would make an excuse about how nothing was happening at the time. For a few weeks there was no drummer, as he had walked out one night. Later I found out from none other than Linda, who knew about everything and everyone, that the drummer had been dating Silvia, and the walk-out was more of a lovers' spat than a musical conflict.

"Silvia thinks she's so clever with her glasses and never-ending schmoozing," Linda told me after a meeting when she and I were alone. "I know Silvia is your friend and all, but, well, you know what I mean…"

"I know, but I think she's harmless," I said. "She means well."

"I know she does," Linda replied. Though she took a moment to mull over her response. "But for example, she spends all night long with her stupid, ridiculous band that will never in a million years be successful. Then comes to work late pretending she was working at home all night long. Who is she trying to fool?"

I nodded in agreement, even though I didn't think Silvia was trying to fool anyone. She loved her music regardless of the odds of succeeding in the way that she dreamed. She was happy writing songs and singing them. She wasn't trying to fool anyone—she was just trying to balance too many things at once.

"Now she's screwing her drummer, and they are always fighting. And on top of it—" Linda took a deep breath, gathering strength to exhale everything she had. "And on top of it, she has recruited this other woman from my department to play bass guitar." Linda took a step toward me and said in a hushed voice, "Apparently her drummer boy was sneaking around with the previous bass guitarist, so Silvia got rid of her."

I didn't know what to say. Silvia did her job well; in fact, in her short time with the company, she had already received significant praise. So what if she wanted to try her luck with something else? I envied her tenacity and resilience. And frankly, I envied her direction. She had something in her life that meant so much to her that she sacrificed for it.

Perhaps it was because she had such a passion for what she was doing that I didn't want to spend that evening alone with her. The light changed several more times, and I still could see Silvia across the street. She had only to turn around to spot me.

I wasn't ready yet. Charlotte had been calling me every day to admonish me for being thoughtless at Anat's get-together. I didn't think I'd been thoughtless; I thought I was drunk and high and that what I had said to Anat had only been semi-serious. It certainly hadn't been for Akron to hear.

Charlotte told me it was fine if I stayed away from her friends.

Her friends! I had assumed there might be some divide with friends when Vera and I ended, but I never thought that line would come between Charlotte and me.

When I told her that I had wished I could have apologized to Akron, she became even more frustrated, like I had missed the point completely.

"Don't you remember that night?" she said.

"Did I miss something?"

"You're not seriously going on a date with Anat, are you?"

"Date? I'm not going on any date."

"Good. It would be foolish. Think about how Akron might feel. You're the one who freaked out a few months ago when Vera showed up with James, and you guys had been separated for months."

If she had meant that to be helpful, it wasn't. And I didn't want to talk about Vera and James either. I ended the call by telling her that I was going out with Silvia to get drunk and do some other foolish shit.

She had said, "Fine," and hung up.

CHAPTER FIFTEEN:
MISGUIDED EXPECTATIONS

I stood back on the sidewalk, looking over to see if this new guy Elliot would show up. I was hoping he would, as I wanted another person around besides Silvia that evening. I wanted to talk to someone new, someone who didn't know me; I was tired of friends and their insights. It had been a terrible week, what with Charlotte's nonstop phone calls.

Elliot was nowhere to be found, and I was already fifteen minutes late. I smiled inwardly as Silvia was notorious for being late or canceling at the last minute. She had taken over organizing these outings and had insisted that we all meet in front of the building and walk en masse rather than meeting at the bar or restaurant. She thought it was more dramatic that way, but her consistent lateness and changes of plan had reduced the number of attendees to near zero over time. I was not surprised that so many had canceled after Silvia couldn't seem to provide the address of the bar that she had promised to be the best in San Francisco. I suspected that several people had decided to just take the visiting colleagues to the Charter given its proximity to our office.

I pressed the crosswalk button again and malevolently thought of how I could walk over to her and cancel, just for the hell of it. She was still staring out into the distance when I approached her. The sidewalk was crowded with businessmen and -women in their tight dark suits, rushing toward the BART station on Market, avoiding the insistent panhandlers strewn across downtown San Francisco.

She didn't notice my approach even when only a few people were between us. She had her dark bag clutched tightly under her arm, as though shielding herself from the people around her. I took several more steps, stood very close behind her, and gently touched her shoulder. She jumped at my touch and raised her bag like a shield. She quickly lowered it when she saw me and gave an embarrassed smile.

"I'm sorry. I didn't see you coming," she stammered but then added quickly, "I was sort of worried that you might not show up."

I said nothing for a moment and then, perhaps a bit too late, uttered, "Oh, no. Why would you think that?" Then I compounded my lie. "I was looking forward to seeing you tonight."

"Really?" she asked, looking genuinely surprised. "Maybe we can go somewhere nice."

"Sure. What do you think about Boca Giovanni on Columbus?"

"I love that place," she said.

"I'll grab a cab." With that I walked to the curb to hail a passing cab.

She grabbed my arm and said, "Do you mind if we walk a bit?"

"No," I replied. However, I looked up to the sky to indicate the possibility of rain.

She started walking, ignoring my signal.

So I said, "It might rain, though."

"We can always grab a cab if it does," she said, already several steps ahead of me. She didn't hesitate or slow.

We walked swiftly through traffic, not waiting for any lights to change. We'd covered half of the way without uttering a single word, and I was wondering whether I should be happy that we were not talking or be fearful that it would all come out at once during dinner.

I liked Silvia. Most times she was fun to be with, but I could only handle so much drama, especially since I was trying to deal with my own. I was tired and hungry, so a peaceful dinner would have served me fine. I felt like an old married man who had heard every single story his wife had to offer. The wife was no longer appealing, just a companion in the night. I just wanted to eat a good meal, go home, read a chapter or two, and then go to sleep in a warm, comfortable bed.

The thunder in the distance snatched away the warm bed fantasy and brought me back to the long walk to the restaurant. People hurried to their homes as the evening promised to be wet and windy.

I picked up my pace. Silvia kept up without a word. We arrived at the restaurant quicker than I expected. As we walked down to the warm cellar, the rain started coming down hard.

"See? No problem," Silvia said, holding her hand out to catch a little rain.

The hostess seated us at a small table in the corner without any delay—clearly the weather had scared some of the potential customers away. Despite a few vacant tables, the restaurant still appeared to be busy, busboys and waiters rushing through the dining room, the noise of silverware and conversation.

The aroma of garlic, butter, and herbs was intoxicating. I congratulated myself on a great choice. I'd taken Vera to Boca Giovanni on our first real date. It had been a great place to impress a person who knew so much about food and wine.

Silvia and I sat solemnly as we listened to the waiter enumerate several specials of the night. I asked for a glass of house wine, and Silvia nodded her assent. The waiter quickly came back with two large glasses of dark liquid, and we each took a grateful sip. In less than ten minutes, we were working on a plate of young zucchini flowers stuffed with tuna.

We had only exchanged a few polite words during the wait. Now I was getting annoyed at Silvia for not talking, even though I had worried about it before, because it was really feeling more like we were an old couple out for a routine meal. Was this how it'd be after years of marriage? I hoped not. I certainly didn't want to believe that silent meals could be in my future.

"Do you think I'm a selfish person?" she asked in an abrupt and hushed tone.

Still deep in thought, living in my head with the faux resentment and frustration about the silent meal, I missed what she had said. I looked up, and she stared at me with her dewy eyes. I cursed at myself about how stupid I had been to want conversation. I wished we could just eat our meals and then go our separate ways.

"No, of course not," I replied. Even I could hear my own disingenuousness.

"Do you think I expect too much?" Silvia asked, looking straight at me.

I wasn't sure what all these questions meant. I sipped from my glass slowly to gather my thoughts. She did set some high bars for herself and others, and it seemed most of our conversations revolved around her life. But I didn't know Silvia well enough to delve into her true intentions. She was a nice person. She was pretty and, at times, very fun. Although she mostly talked about herself, in those rare times when she listened, she would give rather insightful advice. I felt good being with her and enjoyed hearing about her world. She was certainly clever and very strong-minded, but she could be rather high maintenance. Then again, on a few occasions she had gone out of her way to accommodate me. To me she seemed to be nothing more or less than a regular human being, full of good and bad, a walking contradiction.

"I don't think I expect too much." She paused after answering her own question, probably to confirm this belief for herself. It was a statement full of more pitfalls of doubt than I'd ever heard said aloud. She wanted to make sure she was convinced. "I just know what I want. It seems this is too much for him."

Who was she talking about? For some reason, I thought that I should know this "him," so I felt uncomfortable asking the obvious. Silvia had a bad tendency to talk in abstractions, but from her tone I could tell this was a definite person. Her vagueness signaled that she thought I should know to whom she was referring. However, until that moment we had never discussed anything intimate. Despite the volume with which Silvia loved to discuss herself, she had never offered anything beyond superficial complaints about work and her band.

Once she mentioned the drummer, suggesting their relationship, but in her abstracted sort of way. I already had the information from Linda, so I knew what she was talking about. I was under the impression that the drummer was out of the picture, but maybe not. It occurred to me that it was very strange that she and I had spent time together without any other colleagues but never talked about our personal lives. I knew all about her latest project at work and the song she was writing, but I didn't even know her age or whether she had siblings. Perhaps even more unnerving was that I never really cared to know, and apparently she felt the same way. Yet, here we were on this cold, rainy evening, and she was trying to open up to me.

I nodded, not knowing what else to do, the wine glass now empty, and I still struggled with the sudden knowledge that I hardly knew Silvia. I stared at her intently, realizing that in her own peculiar way, she was trying very hard to confide in me.

She adjusted her glasses on her face and pressed her forehead with her fingers, trying to massage out whatever demon was trapped behind her skull. She closed her eyes for a moment. "Do you know what I mean?"

She pushed her hands farther back and, in a swift move, pulled out the hair band. Her long hair flowed onto her face, obscuring it for a moment. When she pulled it away from her face, I could see that tears were welling in her eyes. The sight of tears on Silvia was so extraordinary and so surreal that I was taken aback, like being hit by a cannonball of bewilderment. Without thinking, I reached out and touched her hand; instinctively, she grabbed mine and squeezed it hard.

At that moment the waiter reappeared with our meals, but we didn't look up. Silvia pressed my hand harder, clinging to this small thread of connection. The waiter ascertained the situation and left without saying a word. And at that moment, without wanting to and hating myself for doing so, the only thing I was thinking was that Silvia was amazingly pretty. I tried to focus on thinking about what to do to console her, but my mind had its own agenda. Holding her hand was the most intimate contact I had ever had with her. There had never even been a situation where we were not colleagues on a business outing, except once. I didn't think anything of it then, but that night at the restaurant, it occurred to me that perhaps there had been a moment between us on that previous occasion.

A couple of months earlier we were out with several colleagues, and all night long Silvia was excited and happy. She told several funny stories and was even very kind to Linda. It was a great dinner, and everyone seemed to be enjoying the night out. Silvia treated everyone to a couple of rounds of drinks. Nobody bothered to ask why.

Everyone stayed later than usual, but when the dinner was over and when everyone had left, Silvia asked if I wanted to stay for another drink. I had no sooner agreed than she started to speak about her band. She had written a new song that she was rather proud of. She thought this song would be the one, and the band was going great; they had a couple of new members. It was then when I thought that was a hint that the drummer was out of the picture, although I didn't ask. Silvia rarely drank, and when she did, it was half a glass of wine, but that night she was celebrating. It was one of the best times I'd had with her, and it seemed we really clicked. We stayed until closing and then stumbled out into the street.

Our attempt to hail a cab was unsuccessful, so we walked toward her apartment, which happened to be only a few blocks away. By the time we reached her place, we felt warm from the brisk walk and the wine.

"Come up and let me call a cab for you," she said. She fumbled with her key.

I stood very close to her and felt the warmth of her body and smell of her hair. She was clearly inebriated, and no matter how much she concentrated she could not get the key steady. After she dropped it several times, I reached out to balance her hand. Our bodies touched in the slightest way. There was a pause, perhaps longer than it should have been, but then she turned the key and the door opened with a loud clank.

I straightened up and saw a cab driving by, which I hailed automatically. I was as intoxicated as her.

"I had a wonderful time. Good luck with your song," I said.

She looked at the cab and then looked at me and had a moment of contemplation. A decision. She leaned her body a bit closer, then another momentary pause, another decision. She leaned even closer and kissed me on the cheek and walked inside, closing the door behind her.

Perhaps that moment was a seedling of desire that was now being nurtured by Silvia's fragility at Boca Giovanni. She held my hand tighter, as if she was truly in need of some comfort.

"I'm so miserable, and I don't know what to do," she moaned softly.

I was never very comfortable with public displays of affection, but I felt compelled to go sit next to her and hold her in my arms, though

I still didn't know the full story. She sobbed quietly on my shoulder. I felt frustrated because I couldn't feel more empathy for her. I reached in my pocket and grabbed a few bills and threw them on the table.

Silvia, even in her despondent mood, tried to grab her purse to pay. "Don't be silly. Let's get out of here," I said.

I ushered her out of the chair, and we walked out of the restaurant.

"I'm so sorry," she said as soon as we were outside, looking embarrassed.

Thankfully, the rain had relented a bit. She straightened herself and wiped her face with a tissue from her purse. "I'm really sorry. I don't think you were planning for this tonight."

"Everything will be alright," I assured her.

She smiled faintly at my attempt. "He thinks I have unrealistic expectations of him. He's leaving tomorrow to see his mother for New Year's, and I asked if I could go with him. I thought, you know, it was time for me to meet his family, like normal people do. But no, this was too much. He isn't ready, and his mother is not ready."

And I thought, *That's it? It's just a silly "I want to meet your parents" fight?* So she was angry that he wanted to go on the trip alone. Why was I involved?

"Sometimes you have to be patient," I said.

"Patient?" she mocked me.

Fuck, I was just trying to be helpful.

She said, "I'm not asking him to marry me or anything. But after all this time, I think it's not too much to ask to see his family."

"Well..."

"He's leaving, and I'm not sure if he's coming back."

She stopped in the middle of the sidewalk and started to sob again. It was perhaps more serious, but still, the nagging question of "why me" was echoing in my head.

Despite it all, I moved closer and held her again. I felt like a fool, but then she sobbed more and buried her head in my arms. I felt her breasts heaving up and down against my chest and her soft hands around my body. I thought, *Not now.* Was I that insensitive and crude? I'd become what I had always despised about other men and yet there I was on the sidewalk, only able to concentrate on the contours of her body.

I took a half-step back to give a tiny separation between our bodies. *How rude of my body*, I thought, but it seemed it had its own will and its own objective. I tried to take control and willed myself to adhere to the solemnity of the situation as Silvia sobbed rhythmically. I stroked her hair and kept saying that it would be all right while trying to fight the urge to follow my baser instincts.

She pulled back abruptly and grabbed my hand and started to walk. We walked like young lovers for a short while, without speaking. This roller coaster of emotions was taking a toll on me as well, and I thought I should walk her home, go to my own apartment, take a cold shower, and just go to sleep. I felt the intense desire to be alone and away from everybody.

We walked and walked. Occasionally she needed to stop and be held for a moment before resuming. She kept talking about expecta-tions and needs but wouldn't elaborate more than what she had con-veyed already. Every stop made me feel guilty. Her distraught state had made her softer and a bit kinder and certainly more attractive. I wanted to grab her and kiss her, but even I knew it was wrong on so many levels. We walked so far that before I knew it, we were in front of her apartment. The rain had been falling softly, and our clothes were slightly damp.

"Can I make you a cup of coffee?" She had no more tears. She now looked tired and very stoic.

"I think I should go home now," I said.

"Come on. Please. This is the least I could do for you. I promise I won't start crying again." She smiled and grabbed my hand. Hers felt soft and tender in mine, and I couldn't resist the temptation, even as I kept telling myself that the whole thing was wrong.

Her apartment was on the second floor, a typical San Francisco one-bedroom with hardwood floors and a large, old-fashioned kitchen. It was the first time I had seen the inside of her place, and it looked how I had imagined it would, neat and organized. Her guitars, along with some other electronic instruments, were shoved against the wall in the corner of the living room. A few books were stacked on a makeshift bookshelf and a few more against the bare wall. She owned a large stereo system but no television.

I took off my jacket and sat on the large couch, uncomfortable and a bit agitated. The couch was overly soft, the kind that would suck a person in.

She took off her raincoat and then her sweater and tossed them on the sofa. She was wearing a white T-shirt underneath, with a gold medallion hanging from her neck. She disappeared into the kitchen and I just sat there, alone. She came back after what seemed like a long time with two steaming cups of coffee. She put them down on the small table and sat on the couch next to me. The couch wobbled a bit, but we managed to keep our balance.

"Thank you for being here," she said solemnly. "I didn't mean to dump everything on you tonight. I was going to cancel, but I thought it would be good to go out, and when it ended up being just the two of us, it all came out. I'm so sorry."

"Stop apologizing. I'm glad you're able to confide in me. I just wish I could do something to help you," I said.

"You have already." She reached out and took my hand again. "Honestly, you have."

My face was impassive, but she seemed to read more into it. "It has been an up-and-down affair, so it was inevitable that it would end like this." She sighed in resignation.

"You never know. Sometimes a break can do a relationship a lot of good," I said. I had no idea what I was talking about, but it seemed like the right thing to say. She smiled at my desperate attempt.

"Not this time," she claimed with certain finality and started to cry again.

I looked at the coffee cups, then at her guitars stacked against the wall, and then at her. She moved closer. I grabbed her and tried to pull her even closer, but I misjudged the distance and the force, and we both fell backward on the couch.

Her body was now partially on top of me. I thought she would sit up, but she didn't. She lay on my chest with her hair on my face. She was still wearing her glasses, which were pressing into my chest. My right arm was stuck between her body and the back of the couch. My left leg was hanging off the couch and my right leg was under her body. I waited for her to make the first move, but she seemed content to lie in that position, piercing my chest and crushing my arm.

I wiggled a bit to get more comfortable, and in the process she rolled onto her side with one leg hooked over me, her body between the couch back and me. I took her glasses off with my free hand and put them on the table next to the coffee cups. She snuggled closer to me. I worked my right arm free and managed to put it around her waist. I could now feel every part of her body, from her tear-soaked face to her warm chest to her hips covered by the rough denim of her jeans. Her hair pressed against my face, and I smelled faint traces of perfume and shampoo.

There I was in a situation I should never have been in. On the one hand, I was ready to take her with the smallest cue, and on the other hand, I knew that the whole thing was wrong. She didn't want me, and even if she thought she did at that moment, she would wake up with deep regrets.

She moved a bit and held me tighter, and in the process, I felt her soft breasts press against me. Electricity ran through me like a bull in San Fermín. If there was ever a sign, this was it. She wanted me, I thought, and I certainly wanted her, or at least was succumbing to lust.

I lowered my head to kiss her.

I froze.

I saw her face in the mirror across the room. She was staring into the distance. I saw that the weight of her distress had crushed the integrity of her defenses. She didn't need me to complicate her life; she needed a friend to listen to her and to know when to call it quits. She had trusted me.

I gently slid out from under her and stood up without a protest from Silvia. I bent over, kissed her on the cheek, grabbed a small blanket from the chair next to the guitars, and put it on her before grabbing my jacket and leaving the house.

I walked into the cool, fresh air of the night, filled with ozone from the rain. I could be that friend.

Silvia resigned from the firm a month later.

CHAPTER SIXTEEN:
MY DATE WITH ANAT

Anat called and wanted to arrange our date. Despite Charlotte's vehement and cryptic protests, I accepted. She had no good reasons that I shouldn't socialize with Anat. Even though my comment had made Akron angry, they were not a couple anymore. They hadn't even been a couple that night. And I kept reminding myself that what had transpired in the kitchen and with the slamming front door had actually been engineered by Anat.

Anyway, she was my friend, after all, and I didn't consider our outing a real date, even though I kept saying "date." But I only said it because Charlotte kept referring to it as such.

I also needed Anat's company after my episode with Silvia. I needed someone cuddly and warm to make me feel good about myself. I wanted to go out with Anat so that I could forget about Silvia's eyes in the mirror. I wanted to prove that I could have a regular life again.

I didn't want to pick her up at her place, so she said she would come to my place at about seven o'clock. She called around 6:30 to say she was running a bit late, which killed my whole plan for dinner and a movie. I asked her to meet me at Polk and California at about 7:30. I called Charlotte to tell her about my movie plans, hoping to prove that I was more interested in the movie than in Anat.

It only took me ten minutes to get to that side of town, so I waited for her at the Polk Café, a dingy place with bad, expensive coffee. Nevertheless, I was forced to order a cup that stayed untouched.

Anat finally showed up around 7:45, just fashionably late. She was dressed all in black—black pants; black lacy blouse that was partly unbuttoned, revealing a flowery-patterned black bra; black shawl to keep her warm; and black stilettos that made clicking sounds as she approached me. I sat with my back toward the window, turning around when I heard the approach of her shoes, like the sound of horseshoes on cobblestone.

She looked good despite the lack of color in her attire. Her frame fit nicely in her selection of clothing, which accentuated her body in the right places. The cold air had made two small bumps at the top of her shirt, and I forced myself to look a few inches higher. Her long brown hair was pulled back in a ponytail that revealed her neckline. She hadn't seen me and kept scanning the street outside, but then she spotted me staring at her.

She waved in one of those quick, jerky movements, walked over, and landed me a soft kiss. I tasted cinnamon on her lips. The night was going to be grand.

"I'm sorry," she said. "Have you been waiting long?"

"It's not a problem," I said evenly. I still couldn't get over how nice she looked. "You look very nice."

"Thank you," she said and sat next to me on a bar stool.

"Are you hungry?"

"I'm starved. It was an awful day, and I didn't get a chance to eat," she said, "but it's so nice to see you."

"We could grab a sandwich and then go see a movie. What do you think about seeing—"

She looked at me like I was crazy. I had missed some cue in her appearance. Obviously, she had dressed to be seen. It was clear that a movie and a sandwich on the run didn't go with her outfit.

I said, "Or we could go to this really nice Indian restaurant on Van Ness?"

"Whatever you want is fine with me." She played the game well. "I'm just so glad to be able to get out of the house."

We went to Gaylord on Van Ness. She wanted to drive, but I convinced her to walk the short distance. We clicked and clacked toward the place. At first the hostess tried to scare us away, promising a long wait due to our lack of reservation. But Anat worked her particular kind of charm, her subtle flirtatiousness and contagious warmth, which buttered up the hostess. Anat whispered something to her, and they shared a sorority giggle. Soon we were seated at a small table in the corner of the restaurant.

The restaurant was beautifully decorated with white and red linen cloths draped on the walls and mantels. The room smelled of burning incense that made us feel a bit sedated. The flickering candlelight gave an aura of richness that gently complemented the room. A fat man with a large mustache and a broad grin appeared at our table as soon as we were seated. He went through a list of specials in a hurried voice laced with a thick Punjabi accent. It was a long list. I missed the whole thing, and Anat didn't even pay attention as she applied fresh lipstick.

In many ways Anat appeared very modern, but in certain ways she lived in a bygone era. She seemed to hold onto specific date etiquette that never crossed my mind. For instance, I had already disappointed her by not picking her up and chauffeuring her to the restaurant. But I got back in her good graces by opening doors, taking off her shawl, and ordering her favorite drink from the mustachioed man.

"I'll have a lassi, and the lady will have a gin and tonic," I ordered, to Anat's nodding approval. I waited for the man to leave, giving us a little breathing room before starting our chitchat. "How's it going, Anat?" I asked.

"Fine. Just fine," she replied in a dreamy voice.

"No, really. What's going on with you and Akron? I heard that he has moved out?" Charlotte had, of course, filled me in on the latest from the Anat-Akron household, but she had meant it as a way of dissuading me from seeing Anat.

"We're divorcing," Anat said.

Her response was terse and matter-of-fact. I suppose in some sense it was expected, but I was shocked anyway. I had hoped that their rough time would only be temporary, just a minor hiccup in their love story. I'd thought that soon all their little side intrigues and passive-aggressive spats would smooth out and turn them back into the couple we'd known. It wasn't going to be a pleasant night.

"What? How could this be?" I asked, suddenly feeling guilty for sitting at that table with her. The word "date" echoed in my mind. I wondered if Akron knew about this or if my stupid moment of levity had exacerbated the situation.

"It's been a long time coming," said Anat in a drawling voice as she picked up the drink that the waiter had just put down. She took a long sip, then pointed the glass toward me. "I'm sure it's not a surprise to you."

I said nothing for a moment and sipped my tasteless lassi to buy some time. The waiter hovered around our table. He wanted our orders, and he didn't care about Anat's divorce. We both ignored him.

"It's a big surprise, Anat. I had no idea. I feel so—"

"Do you require more time, madam?" The waiter partially bowed to Anat.

"Nah, we're ready." She looked at me expectedly.

"Yes, I guess we are. What would you like?" I asked her.

She shrugged and said, "I'll have whatever you have."

"May I suggest a combination plate for two?" the man offered while moving his head from side to side. "It has all the great specialties of Gaylord, and I'll guarantee that you won't be disappointed."

I nodded in agreement just so we could get rid of him. The waiter nodded in response and started to leave, but Anat grabbed him and shook her empty glass.

"I'll have one too," I said. The lassi wasn't working.

Anat stared at me with a smile at the corner of her mouth. Her news hit me harder than it should have, but, despite my own history with Vera or perhaps because of it, I had faith in others' unions. Faith or blind hope. If it couldn't work for me, it should work for others. Herman and Tess, Charlotte and Nadir, Anat and Akron—even Tilly, for God's sake. I thought these people made the world a bit saner. So what if Akron was a bit aloof and Anat a bit footloose?

"What about the kids?" I said.

She mulled the question for a while as though she was just considering it for the first time. Her smile vanished, and I saw traces of worry lines across her face.

Anat wasn't classically beautiful with her angular nose and face, but she always looked fine. She was pretty in her own way and had a great body and a wonderful personality. She was getting older, as were the rest of us, but she never looked her age—at least not until that moment in the Indian restaurant when she was contemplating how to answer my question.

"We've talked to both of them, and we're not pretending that it's going to be easy. They seemed to be okay. On some level they seemed to have expected it." She smiled again to assure me.

It occurred to me that I did not know this couple as well as I thought I did. If the kids had seen this coming, then I was far more removed than I thought. I nodded in an understanding sort of way, though I had no understanding. Then I reached across the table and brushed my hand against her cheek. She leaned her head to the side and then put her hand on top of mine. She smiled lazily and patted my hand.

At that moment, the waiter appeared with our drinks and the first set of shuruat, or appetizers, consisting of small portions of chicken pakora, aloo chaat, miniature samosas, and papadum.

"To the future." She brought her glass up and drank most of it before putting it down.

I took a small sip and tasted only gin.

Anat was all business now. She surveyed the table and started serving me a little portion of each dish, like a mother would. She then put a small amount of aloo chaat on her plate and gingerly tasted it. She encouraged me to eat, and I took a bite of samosa. It was heavenly. The wrapping was tender and crispy, and the stuffing was not merely blended potatoes, like most ordinary samosas, but also onions and peas.

"I know it may be a bit of a surprise to you, but believe me, this has been long overdue." She again took a small bite from her plate and checked my plate to make sure it was full. She then took a sip of her drink, which left nothing in her glass.

"Sometimes you meet somebody and you think, this is it, this is how your life is going to be," she said. "And it's fine; at least it's fine at the time. But then you get married and you have children, and it turns out this isn't what you wanted in the first place. You tell yourself that you love him and he loves you. And there are, of course, the children to think about. So both of you get up every morning, make breakfast for the children, make sandwiches for their lunch, kiss each other goodbye, and go to work. For eight hours or so you're yourself, and you can pretend that there are no children, no husband, but then you have to go home, help with the homework, make dinner, and then go to bed to start the whole thing over and over and over again."

She ran out of steam and started pushing food around her plate.

"It sounds gloomy," I said to fill the silence. I meant to be sarcastic, to inject some lightness, the only part I could see myself playing in this conversation.

Anat smiled, shook her head, and replied, "You're wrong. Those were the good parts."

Oh no, I thought. How dark could this be?

"When I met Akron, he was exciting. He was different. He wanted to be different. He wanted to be an artist. He wanted to travel and work for the Peace Corps—he wanted to walk the earth. And his enthusiasm was infectious. I never thought about any of those things before I met him. I just wanted to go to school, get a job, buy a nice car and a home, and live. You know what I mean—just live. Just be like the next person in line." She paused and took another small bite from her food before nodding to the waiter for another drink.

I had emptied my plate, and she served me again without asking.

"I didn't know," I offered.

"No, you didn't know. How would you?"

I didn't reply, so she continued. "We traveled, and we had a grand time. He had inherited some money from his uncle or somebody, so we traveled like two jetsetters, staying in nice hotels, eating in fine restaurants, and seeing fine art in the great museums of Europe. All exciting! All fun! My family never had much money, and even if they had, they would have never spent it on travel. Travel to them was something you did when you had to, like going to a funeral."

I chuckled.

Anat's drink arrived, and she took the moment to pick up the glass. I thought she would down it like she had the first couple, but instead she just held it in her hands. "It's all exciting, and I'm in sort of a dream," she said. "I can see what's happening, and I can see myself participating in it, but I can't control it. It's just going on its own. I feel like a caboose that's being pulled by hundreds of train cars. But after a while it became clear, and I started to understand it and really desire it. I've always loved painting and drawing, but you can imagine how my parents would have reacted to the idea of pursuing a field that had no earning potential. It seems I wanted all the things that Akron had talked about and planned."

Anat stared beyond me as if connecting now to then. "So, when we came back from our trip, I dropped out of college and enrolled in an art school. My parents were livid. I didn't care. I had Akron, who created a type of comfort bubble that I could live and flourish in. I was happy."

She surveyed my plate like a mother and served me some of the main dishes that had just arrived. All standard Indian dishes, a variety of tandooris, masalas, and curries. There were also little bowls of mattar paneer and navratan korma, which I generally wouldn't order. There were plenty of naans.

Anat took my plate and carefully put each portion in a corner by itself as one would do for a child, but I appreciated that level of attention, which I hadn't had for a long time. She only served herself a tiny portion of mattar paneer.

"I didn't know you're a vegetarian." I pointed to her cheese and green peas.

She grabbed a piece of tandoori chicken without saying anything. We ate in silence for a while. I understood why Anat wanted to go out with me. I thought maybe she needed someone who wouldn't judge her, someone who would just sit there and listen. She didn't want assurance or sympathy. She also didn't want someone who would point out all the follies of her action, like Charlotte would. She just needed someone like me to give her some attention and hear her out.

"I wasn't happy," she continued as though no time had passed.

"I thought you said—"

"I meant to say I *thought* I was happy. It's easy to confuse contentment with happiness. I was lazy and felt safe living in Akron's little bubble." She smiled and looked into my eyes.

"I think I know what you're trying to say," I said, which seemed to reassure her.

"So life goes on the way you think it should, routine, but with occasional joy. However, you wake up one day and see that the man

who was supposed to do so many important things—be free, help
people—now drives a leased Mercedes he can't afford. But he must
have it because he wants to make partner one day in his law firm.
He works hard, but success, at least what he considers success to
be, is elusive. He's like a hummingbird fluttering from one flower to
the next, always eating but never satiated." She wiggled her fingers
around the table, imitating a little bird, which made us both laugh.
She sipped her drink.

"The funny thing is that by then I desired, really desired, the life
that he wanted when we met. I had grown to become an artist, but I
was no good."

She laughed nervously, and I saw tears gathering in the corner of
her eyes. She reached for her empty water glass, which I immediately
filled, but then she changed her mind and picked up my untouched
gin and tonic.

"You see," she said, "I wanted to travel the world, but I had no money
of my own. His obsession about his career and making money had
put us more in debt than ever. He had a new purpose in life, but I
didn't want to get on that ride. He worked hard, but he came home
tired and tense and needy. He wanted to tell me about his day at the
office and his clients, but I had no interest in that life. He would
talk and talk, and I'd nod and daydream about the life that I'd never
have."

She paused and took another sip from my glass, hoping to give
herself courage. "I still loved him, but I wasn't attracted to him. He
wanted intimacy, and as he worked harder, he wanted it even more.
It seemed lovemaking was his way of anchoring himself to his own
life's lost dream. But to me it was mechanical—I provided the vessel
but nothing else. I used to love sex, but now I saw it as a duty, like
making dinner. I needed a break from it, but instead of getting out, I
was pulled in even more. We needed the money, so I got a job teach-
ing painting and worked in an art gallery."

She stopped and started to play with her food, not looking up at
me. I saw she was debating something, so I sat back and waited, not
wanting to pressure her. She took a deep breath and held it for a long
time and then exhaled sharply, as if releasing what little trepidation
that was left in her.

"I met somebody, and he was everything that Akron wasn't, or at least I thought so at the time. He was interested in my needs. He was kind and gentle, and he knew about the arts. Boy, he really knew his stuff. It was just wonderful to sit next to him and absorb his passion, his love, and his knowledge of painting.

"And yes, it was foolish, and I shouldn't have done it, and in retrospect he was not so special, but then, at that moment in time, he was everything. I felt guilty two seconds after we said hello, even though I wasn't even thinking about infidelity, but you know Jews are worse than Catholics when it comes to guilt. But the guilt didn't stop me from meeting him at a downtown gallery. One thing led to another. And then we had a weekend together."

I guess it wasn't a surprise, but I didn't want to meet her eyes, not that she was looking up from her plate. I waited.

"I won't deny that it was wonderful and new and that I did feel free, as if the umbilical cord had been cut, and I was floating. I felt like I was me again, the real me for a change. Yet, I felt sick to my stomach, and every second I was with him, I thought about Akron and how I was betraying him. The sex was bad. It was hurried and dirty, and I broke up with the man after that weekend." She slowly looked up from her plate and took a deep breath.

"Do you hate me?" Anat asked.

I couldn't understand why she would ask such a question, especially of me, and it occurred to me that I had made a mistake by being there. I wasn't the right person for so much honesty. I couldn't decide what to say. What could I say anyway? Tell her that she shouldn't have if she really loved Akron? Or, I could tell her it was all right, that I could understand why she needed to find solace in another person's arms.

She waited. She wanted me to say something, and I wanted to give an answer that would please her, if only to take the immense pressure off the moment. I ran my fingers slowly down her forearm, and when I reached her hand, she grabbed mine and squeezed it hard.

"Why would I hate you, Anat? I fully empathize with you."

"Really...?"

"You're not eating much." I served her some food and pushed the plate closer to her.

Even though I had told her what I thought she wanted to hear, she still gripped my hand tight, in anticipation. And it dawned on me that what she was really after was some reciprocation, not just hollow words about empathy. She wanted to hear about Vera. She wanted me to break down every sordid detail. She wanted my apology to Vera, as if that could take the place of Akron's.

But I wasn't ready to share back, not with her, not with any one, not ever. But I fully understood what she meant by an absence of desire. That's how I felt with Vera, a sudden absence of passion. For a long time everything was fine, and then it wasn't. One day I was full of desire, and the next day there was nothing she could do to arouse me. We continued to be a couple, and we even would make love, if one could call it that, but it was just a routine.

I knew perfectly well what Anat was saying about living in someone else's bubble. I had been living in Vera's life.

For months I had pretended—no, made myself believe—that everything was fine, and I did such a good job that Vera never noticed a thing. I understood the comforts of habit. I could not put my finger on any action or any event that would mark my point of departure. I was miserable being with Vera without the courage needed to admit it to her or to myself.

I remembered that Vera was so puzzled by my sudden aloofness. She probably explained it away as stress at work and would reach out to comfort me. But my response, whether in words or actions, would only hurt her more. I felt ashamed of it later, and I knew that I was living a lie that would ultimately hurt her, but I couldn't will myself to change or make the move to stop it. I felt paralyzed—I could see the world around me collapsing but couldn't move to stop it. Yet Vera never relented, and she seemed, at least for a while, to have an unlimited capacity to endure without losing her faith in us.

So, I did what I knew would surely shatter her faith in an instant. I knew this, and yet I didn't stop myself; I couldn't stop myself. I wasn't being callous or hateful. Rather, like Anat, I thought the action would be my own salvation. And, like Anat, I found that I was wrong. I could see it again in Anat's story, but the world that I could have had was no longer available to me.

"Penny for your thoughts?" Anat whispered.

"I'm sorry, Anat. I was just thinking how hard it has been on you."

I expected Anat to push the point and try to get me to elaborate, but I was relieved when she said with her usual drawl, "I'm sorry to be such a miserable date." She let go of my hand.

"Is this why he's leaving?"

"Who?"

"Akron."

"Akron?" She laughed loud and then abruptly stopped. "No, no. This happened a long time ago, before the children. I broke up with the guy. The guilt was overbearing. And that man, bless him, gave me a piece of advice as a parting gift. You know what he said?"

She looked at me, and I shook my head.

"He said, 'If you want to save your marriage, don't tell your husband.' That's what he told me as I was leaving, feeling miserable. I was so eager to get out of the car and kept saying, 'I'm sorry, I'm sorry.' But he stopped me and forced me to look into his eyes. He said, 'Anat, dear, I know you're feeling horrible and think the right thing is to tell him, but trust me. You can get only temporary relief from this guilt, but you'll cause him a great deal of pain for a long time.' I just told him, 'Whatever,' and left the car, never wanting to see him or hear from him again."

"So you didn't tell Akron, then?" I asked.

"I was dying. I had to tell him. And you know what?"

I knew what was coming next.

"It was the biggest mistake of my life. It was never the same between us. Sure, we eventually made up and had a family, but the deep connection, the strong feelings that we had in the beginning were never recovered. I was going through the motions again, but after the initial intense feeling of love that my infidelity produced, I was back on a miserable, unyielding track. I was heading nowhere fast, and this time with two new lives in tow."

I was perplexed; perhaps I was too naïve to understand the complexities of married life, particularly when there were children involved.

"I'm confused, Anat. If this happened so long ago, why are you guys divorcing now?"

"Aren't you listening, Donte?" she said.

She grew angry, and I heard the bitterness in her tone. She grabbed my glass to drink, but she had already finished it, so she put it down heavily, looking miserable and lost. Tears started to roll down her cheeks as her eyes searched for the waiter. He was nowhere to be found. There was nothing else to do, so she looked at me straight and said, "This time both of us tried to derail our lives the only way we knew how."

Dinner ended quickly. Anat never got another drink, instead asking the waiter to box up the rest of the food, which she insisted I take home with me. She found a cab outside the restaurant.

I thought I should try to smooth things over with Anat before she left, but I suddenly became consumed with the realization that my apology would be misplaced. Even though our little date had ended on a bad note, it wasn't Anat I wanted to apologize to; it was Vera. That's who I wanted to talk to in that minute. Anat had tried to use me as an Akron proxy in the same way.

Anat kissed me on the cheek and hopped into the back of the cab. Before I could even tell her goodbye, she was gone.

I went home and mulled over picking up the phone and calling Vera right on the spot. But I knew that would be a terrible idea. I called Charlotte instead and heard her disapproval from the moment she picked up, something she tried to play off as frustration at sleeplessness because of the baby.

"I need to do something for Vera," I said.

"Leave it be, Donte. Why can't you leave it be? She's happier without you. Don't be stupid," Charlotte replied.

"I don't think you understand. You never liked her, and you're happy that she's out of our lives."

"Don't be childish. It's not about me." Charlotte almost sounded convincing. "You were miserable. We all could see that, and I told you so then and I tell you now. You're better off without her, and to be honest, she is better off without you too."

"But I owe her. I was horrible to her."

"That's exactly my point. You'll be horrible again. Think of what you did to Akron, trying to get a date with Anat right in front of him," Charlotte said.

I had explained to her so many times since that night, but still I persisted. "It was not a real date—"

"And now you are calling me right after that date, saying you want to make it right with Vera. You can be a very selfish person, Donte."

"Jesus, Charlotte. Can't you listen to me for a second? I wasn't trying to have a date with Anat. She's a friend. I can't go out with my friends anymore? Is that what you're saying?"

"Do you hear yourself? Anat is going through a bad time right now, and you think it's a good idea to ask her out at a big party right in front of her husband?"

"They're divorcing," I declared.

"Oh, that makes it alright, I suppose."

"I'm glad you think so. It was just a dinner, anyway. She needed someone to talk to—"

"What's wrong with you? I was being sarcastic, you ass," she yelled, and it was clear she was getting angry and frustrated.

"It wasn't a date, and you repeating that it was a hundred more times doesn't magically transform it into one. She felt miserable, and she needed someone to listen without judgment, or at least that's what I think she needed. I was just being a good friend, unlike you."

"Well, great. If I'm such a lousy friend, why are you calling me in the middle of the night?"

We sat on the phone in silence, neither one of us ready or willing to be the next person to talk. Charlotte had cut to the chase as she was known to do, but this time it seemed more hurtful than her usual remarks. She wouldn't apologize, but that, too, was her style. But her continued silence signaled to me that she knew she had gone too far.

Any other time I'd have slammed the receiver down and been done with her. Instead, I replied, as softly as I could, "I'm just calling because of what Anat said to me. How she talked about her mistakes and Akron's mistakes and how her life went off the rails. And it just made me realize that it's not too late."

"Donte..." Charlotte moaned.

"I don't mean too late for me and Vera to get back together. I know she's moved on, but it's not too late for me to make things right, as much as they can be made right. How else am I supposed to move on?" I said.

"I'm sorry, Donte, I wish I could help you. But I don't know what you expect. What can I do to help?"

"I don't know."

There was nothing else to say, so I apologized to Charlotte for calling her so late, what with the baby and all, told her goodnight, and hung up the phone. I put the leftover Indian food in the refrigerator and undressed and brushed my teeth. I lay in bed, holding a book to my chest that I wouldn't get to read that night, because all I could think about was how to mend my friendship with Vera.

SUMMER 1981

CHAPTER SEVENTEEN:
EXILED IN LONDON

In my company, if the big boss unexpectedly summons you, there can only be two outcomes, both unpleasant. The first would be an escorted visit to your desk so that you can retrieve your personal items, followed by an escorted trip to your car. The second would be a promise of a major promotion, *if*…But more often than not, this *if* was the pitfall that led you down the long, torturous route to an escorted visit to your desk.

Therefore, it was with great trepidation that I walked into Mr. Riasat's office after a terse phone call from his personal secretary, Mrs. Davis, the keeper of the gate.

"I was asked—" I started.

"Please have a seat. Mr. R. will be right with you." Mrs. Davis pointed to the low leather chairs populating the large, elegant outer office.

Mrs. Davis was the only one in the whole company who was permitted to call the boss by his initial. I sat, thinking about how I should update my resume. I was ready to leave, anyway, I told myself, and this would give me the proper excuse to take a month or two off. Anat's declaration, even after many weeks, still rang in my head. It seemed that life was deteriorating around me, and this impending layoff was just the final touch.

I waited for twenty minutes before Mrs. Davis called on me. "You may go in now."

I jumped up and walked straight in, fully resolved not to be intimidated by either of these creatures.

"I'm sending you to London," Mr. Riasat started without a preamble, and as soon as I heard London, the world that was disintegrating a moment before gelled together, as though a powerful adhesive was forming a new life right in front of my eyes. He was still talking, but the euphoria had taken hold of me, and his voice was just a background buzz.

"...fucked up. It's up to you to save the project." Mr. Riasat brought me back down to earth; there was the condition, and my future employment hinged on it. "I don't have to tell you that failure isn't an option. You'll need to leave today."

"Today?"

"Well? Fine, tomorrow. I want you to fire the old team and put together a new one." He paused to look at his calendar. "The presentation is in twenty-eight days. I want to get a progress report every three days." He thought about it for a moment. "No. Make it every two days."

He noted the change on a large pad on his desk and then looked up as though he was surprised that I was still in his office. He blinked once, expecting me to disappear, but I still stood there in the middle of the room, having not even had time to sit down.

"I don't have to say it, but I'm saying it so you won't forget. Your presentation must be amazing, gargantuan, novel, superior, strategically important, and yet tactically effective—but subtle and aesthetically pleasing." He thought for a moment and consulted his calendar again. "How's your wife, your girlfriend..." Again, a quick glance at his notepad. "Vera?"

"We separated over a year ago," I said automatically.

"Hmm...Well, it may be a good thing at this point. This way, you won't have any distractions," he said.

Bastard. Just tell him to fuck off and leave the room, I told myself. But, looking down, I realized that I had left my *cajones* back at my desk, or possibly even lost them years ago.

"Well, good luck and thanks for agreeing to this." He stood up and started walking toward me.

I wanted to go to London, to get away from my life, and I was eager to do a good job, so I mustered some courage.

"Mr. Riasat," I called out when he was a few feet away from me. The surprise of hearing anyone talking back to him stopped him in his tracks. I used this momentary advantage to continue, "I'm pleased that you have picked me, and I'm eager to do a good job, but firing the current crew is a bad idea."

He blinked once and took another step, then paused and looked over at his intercom. He had to make a decision.

"Fine. I trust you, Donte, but don't fuck it up." He started walking toward me again, and as he came closer, he raised his arm and, without touching me, guided me to the door and out of his office.

As soon as I stepped out, Mrs. Davis stood up and handed me a package.

"Here's some background information for your trip." She then took out a large envelope from her desk and put it on top of the package. "And here is your itinerary and hotel information. Your flight is out of SFO tomorrow at 7:30 a.m."

She sat back down, finished with me, and went back to work as if we had never spoken.

CHAPTER EIGHTEEN: TEMPTATION

After almost four weeks of long and potentially thankless hours during which we worked harder than ever and accomplished everything we had set out to do, the only task left was the final presentation, and this was all on my shoulders. I had checked the numbers, rehearsed, double-checked, and rehearsed some more. It wasn't enough that the facts and figures were perfect, since there was always a human element that could not be anticipated or practiced. I would either wow them, or I'd have to look for a new job. I wasn't really worried about my own job, but I was responsible for a large team, and many of them were dead set on keeping their jobs.

Although I could have gone alone, I thought it would be better to show up with someone on my arm, sort of an insurance for the human element part. It's better to come as a couple than a single. It looked more balanced, more centered. It's better for the corporate image. At least that's how it was during my time.

But then, I'm not being totally honest either. The fact of the matter is that I was terrified of public speaking—yes, I know. I do it all the time, but that doesn't diminish the fact that the idea brought me anguish to no end. Whenever I was asked to give a speech—and sadly, that happened way too often—I agonized over it for weeks. Every minute that I came closer to the appointed time, a growing fear that something could and would go wrong consumed me. I looked for excuses to avoid the task, and when they failed, I planned and re-planned how I could get away. I would try and dispel suspicion by showing disproportionate enthusiasm for the day and then call in sick or pretend that I'd had a major accident. And believe me, I had done this many times.

Unfortunately, I could only get away with that for minor functions as there were others who could do the job. Some events couldn't be avoided, and that's when I needed support. Before, Vera performed this task with utmost brilliance. I would have really liked to have her with me.

Nonetheless, I needed someone, and I didn't know anyone who would suit the position in London. I couldn't ask anyone from the London office to show up to this function, either, as no one was fit for the task. But, more importantly, these colleagues were explicitly banned by Mr. Riasat, who still thought they all should have been fired in the first place, though a few were allowed to come before the guests arrived to set up the prompts and double check everything.

Luckily, Tess had plans to go to Spain for a conference, and she happened to have time for a brief stop in London. I had called her a few days earlier to see if she was willing to extend her layover and be my date for the function, and to my surprise she immediately agreed. Tess was rather organized, and it wasn't very natural for her to change plans at the last minute, but I thought she was looking forward to getting away as well. I offered to pick her up from Heathrow, but she said that would be silly and that she would contact me later with the plan.

She loved planning. She called an hour later with detailed instructions of how she would get to my residential hotel and the time I should expect her. I said a lot of "yeahs" but really didn't listen. She asked whether I was writing it down, and I assured her as I flipped through the TV channels.

"Okay, call me in a day or two to finalize this," she said before hanging up.

Tess loved to finalize. As idiosyncrasies go, hers were harmless, though it could get under your skin after a while. But she was doing me a favor, so I wasn't about to complain. She called a day before her flight, forced me to write down her instructions, and then asked me to repeat the whole thing back to her.

On the day of the big presentation, I woke up late, after tossing and turning for most of the night, and took a long bath. I dressed and went downstairs and sat on the wide front porch. I ordered a pot of black tea, some toast, and *The Guardian*. The day was going to be fine, even though there was a low breeze blowing from the north, bringing a smattering of rain. I took a deep breath and inhaled the air fresh with the smell of rain from the warm sidewalk. I was as ready for this presentation as ever, and I wasn't going to waste another minute worrying about it. My tea and toast arrived, and the fragrance of the dark tea meshed with the smell of the morning. I gently sipped from the steaming cup and felt relaxed by both the taste and the smell.

The screech of tires brought me back, and the cries of its passenger announced the arrival of Tess, as punctual as ever. She jumped out of the cab and, with the efficiency of a pro, paid the driver, grabbed her rather large suitcase, and stood by my side before I could put down my teacup.

She wore ugly gray sweatpants and an oversized sweatshirt. She had let her hair grow and had it pulled back rather tightly and kept it in place with a colorful silk scarf. By her normal standards, she looked like a mess, but her smiling face made up for her disheveled appearance. We kissed and hugged, but she didn't linger and walked straight inside.

I dragged her suitcase as I walked behind her.

"Where's the elevator?" she said.

I pointed to the staircase by way of an answer and started dragging the suitcase up to my floor.

"You could have stored the suitcase at Paddington's," I rejoined, panting hard.

"I thought you wanted me to impress your bosses," she said without breaking her stride. She led me to my own room as though she had studied the layout of the place. I struggled with the key for a few moments before I finally let us both in.

I heaved the bag on the bed and asked if she wanted to rest or eat anything. She nodded but said she needed a bath first. She took off her sweatpants and shirt, meticulously folding each one and putting them on the corner of my bed. She turned around and walked toward the bathroom as she took off the rest of her clothes. I heard the water running as she hummed some silly song.

"Can you get me something to drink?" she yelled from the bathroom.

"There's only water," I yelled back from behind the ajar door, knowing that wouldn't do for Tess. "I'll go down to get you something."

"Can't you order room service?"

"It would take too long. There is a shop nearby."

I walked down to the corner of the street to a store that was owned by a Pakistani family. The owner greeted me warmly and was expecting a bit of a chat as I had been doing for the past few weeks, but I felt rushed. Tess always made me feel like I wasn't being efficient if I didn't do everything in double time.

"I need to make some gin and tonics," I told the Pakistani man rather tersely, and with a quick but fleeting tinge of guilt, knowing that he would be dismayed by my purchase of alcohol, "It's for a friend," I assured him. I wasn't sure why I felt compelled to explain myself or why he was so dismayed with his customers buying the alcohol that he stocked.

"Of course." He nodded knowingly and walked over to grab a bottle of gin and a couple small bottles of tonic water.

"I think you should get a couple of limes as well," he suggested and then added quickly, "At least that's how I think you make a gin and tonic." He put four small limes in the bag and gave me a couple of gold coins in exchange for my bills.

"Having a party, Mr. C.?" he asked.

"Well, there are a few friends over..."

"I see." He nodded with a tinge of a smile at the corner of his mouth. He said something to his wife, who crouched behind the counter, working hard on some sewing. She didn't look up but said something back in Urdu that made them both laugh heartily.

I stared at them, but he seemed unwilling to share the joke with me. His return stare made me nervous. I said I just had a friend from the States stopping in for a few days.

"Of course, of course," he said with a wink. I was about to explain further, but I stopped myself, still uneasy about feeling the urge to defend my actions to a shopkeeper who was more or less a stranger to me.

I dashed back to the room. I was happy to see that Tess was still occupied in the bathroom.

"Do you want your drink now?" I shouted.

"Is room service here?"

"Yes."

"That was fast. I hope you ordered a gin and tonic."

I cut the limes and made the drink the way she liked it, with very little gin. It wasn't even noon yet. I knocked on the door with a large glass in my hand.

"Come in," she ordered.

Tess lay in the bathtub filled with hot, steaming water and some remnants of bubbles. Her eyes were covered with a rolled-up towel. Her small breasts were halfway out of the water, swaying back and forth lightly. Her long body stretched to the fullest and looked very relaxed. Her complexion glowed soft pink from the heat of the water.

I remained at the door.

She pulled the towel off her face and waved me toward her. She grabbed the glass out of my hand and touched it to her cheek, ignoring my sophomoric look.

"I hope you're not going to stay there too long, or we will be late," I stammered and walked out of the room.

Tess had always been relaxed with nudity and had changed clothes in front of me many times over the years, but this was the first time I'd seen her whole body. We all read more into such things than may actually be there. That day of all days, I should have been focused on my impending presentation, but it's amazing how our minds can wander sometimes, like hapless sheep separated from the comfort of the flock.

I made myself a drink as well, though I really wanted a cold shower. I sat on the daybed, looking out at the wide roads outside with large, white Victorians towering over them. I opened the window, and the smell of fresh rain rushed in the room. Rain always made me feel melancholy. I loved the smell of the rain on the pavement, but it also forced me to be self-reflective, which always revealed my shortcomings and my failures.

I sat back down on the daybed, still nursing my now warm drink when Tess entered the room wrapped in a large, white towel, with another smaller towel covering her hair. She took the small towel off and shook her head several times to release the extra water before sitting down at the edge of the table, brushing her hair gently and meticulously.

"Why so gloomy?" she asked, smiling, showing her beautiful white teeth. Her lips were rosy red and looked even fuller from the bath. She had the kind of lips that most people would swear were created by an expert surgeon. Her dark green eyes investigated me thoroughly.

"We're going to be late," I said forcefully, in a futile attempt to focus my mind on something else. Tess prided herself on being punctual; this was my poor attempt to force her into action that would distract me from my feelings.

"No, we're not," she said, uncharacteristically calm for a person who seemed to be on edge all the time. She went on brushing her hair. "Plus, you want me to look beautiful for your boss." Her playful smile got on my nerves then.

"You always look gorgeous." I meant to sound playful like the way I always dealt with her, but it came out rather croaky, so I turned around to face the street again while she continued with her task.

She moved over to the daybed and sat next to me. I had my legs fully on the cushion, and she sat on my feet with her own legs stretched toward me. The daybed was too small for two people, and she leaned on the window, so I had to hold onto her feet to keep my own balance. Her feet were warm and soft and smelled of lavender.

I moved my hands up and down her feet in an absent-minded fashion, though, in reality, my mind focused on nothing but her lovely, soft legs. She leaned back and started to put on her lipstick, a soft, rosy shade. Tess had a small beauty mark below the right side of her mouth that I always thought made her look pretty, but she thought of it as unseemly. She started to cover it with some liquid foundation.

"Leave it alone, please," I said.

She looked up surprised and stared at me for a moment. "It looks horrid."

"Not to me."

She shrugged and put down the makeup kit; the little black island stood out delightfully in a sea of creamy skin.

"Thank you," I said.

"Up or down?"

"Up or down what?"

"You want my hair up or down?" she asked.

At that moment she looked intoxicating, and the only thing I could think of were her feet in my hands and my own feet lodged somewhere between her thighs. It occurred to me that this was the first time she and I had been alone—I mean, completely alone.

"I think down would be nice," I said.

"As you wish. It's your party." Her voice sounded deep and smoky.

I could feel a strong arousal within me and twisted to hide any evidence of it, but this only made me feel her body more and with that, any sense of morality or shame vanished.

She seemed oblivious to any changes in me and continued to chatter about her flight, though she didn't attempt to shift or move my feet. Was she flirting with me? Or was she not paying attention to any of the signals? I wanted to lean over and touch her face, but I sat back, frozen on the spot.

You read about these moments, but you have no idea what it means until you're right there at the crossroads, being pulled and pushed by powerful urges that you had only fathomed in your dreams. There was something unreal about it, and there was no clear guidance to help one decipher the signals. I was not into the idea of ancient gods, but I swore at that moment I could feel the Norse goddess Lofn hovering behind me, encouraged and resurrected by my thoughts.

Tess kept on talking, and I kept on nodding without really listening to her. My feet became numb, but I didn't dare to make even the smallest movement, fearing that any twitch would either alert her to my situation or, worse yet, terminate the delicious feeling that was running throughout my body. But after a while I had to adjust my foot, which was becoming horribly cramped. So I twisted a bit, trying my best to minimize changes to our relative positions. It seemed I was successful; I regained my circulation, and she continued to complain about the person in the seat next to her during her flight.

I thought at that instant—and without any expectations—that this was one of the best moments of my life. It seemed there was a solid bond between us that was beyond anything sexual. Silly, yes, but it proved that, once again, it's the little things in life that can, surprisingly, bring joy and solace.

I'd been so deep in thought, so oblivious to my surroundings, that it took me a moment to realize that Tess had stopped speaking. She too seemed to be focusing elsewhere. And then the connection broke suddenly when she jumped as if shocked by a powerful surge of electricity. She grabbed some clothes and walked to the bathroom, and this time she closed the door completely. We had barely looked at each other throughout the whole episode.

I sat there, dazed and embarrassed. A vision of Herman's big face hovered in front of me, just staring to the side, avoiding my own gaze. All I wanted was to smash his face and run after Tess, but I only admonished myself and then, like my mother used to do, bit my lip and tsk-tsked my own silliness.

I made myself another drink and sat back at the window, looking at the Londoners and their elegant and, at times, colorful clothes. I closed my eyes and rested my hand against the window, feeling the chill of the glass against my skin. I wanted Tess back next to me, but my logical mind reminded me of the pending presentation. *Snap out of it*, it yelled at me, and I opened my eyes to see that it was raining again.

CHAPTER NINETEEN: LUNCH

Tess came out of the bathroom wearing a pair of blue jeans and a white blouse, her hair hanging loosely around her shoulders. I was glad she had listened to me. I had opened the window to let the air in, and although it had stopped raining, I still could smell it in the breeze that flew through the window. The fresh air cleared my head and allowed me to focus on my task.

The earlier gray sky had given way to an occasional glimpse of the sun and the promise of a rare sunny afternoon. I felt happy.

I stood up and asked, "Do you want to eat?"

"I could eat, but do we have enough time?"

"We've got some time before we have to leave. We can have a light lunch. There's a place a couple of blocks away from here."

She nodded and grabbed her purse. She was ready.

We walked down the stairs, and I grabbed an umbrella from the lobby. We stepped onto the street and smiled at each other for no reason. There was still a drop or two of rain, but Tess stopped me as I tried to open the umbrella.

"Don't bother with that. It's not even raining."

We walked side by side for a moment.

"Are you nervous?" Tess asked.

"Not anymore," I replied, trying to sound certain. "I have a process for managing my anxiety."

"You do?"

"Yes, ma'am."

"You should teach me because I feel nervous."

"You don't trust me?" I asked.

Tess stopped and looked at me. "Of course I do. I'm nervous because I always want you to do well, and I know how much this means to you."

"Oh. It'll be fine, Tess. What's the worst case?" I asked but then answered my own question as cheerfully as possible. "The worst case is unemployment, and I can handle that."

"Good for you. Don't let them intimidate you."

After a couple more blocks, we reached the pub. It was a large place, but it was already getting full. The interior was painted black, giving it an eerie, Gothic look. But like most pubs in London, it was friendly and welcoming. We sat in a corner booth, the only one available. I'd been going to this pub almost every day since my arrival and had become a regular, if only temporarily.

The waitress showed up as soon as we sat down. "You're here early today."

"You've been telling me about your great lunches all these days, so we're here to try them before I go back to the States. By the way, this is my friend Tess, and Tess, this is Rosy."

"How do you do?" Tess offered.

"Doing fine, darling. What will it be?"

We ordered a pint of cider each and a ploughman's lunch, and then, with Rosy's insistence, Tess ordered the fish and chips, even though she hated fried food.

"I've never had cider before," Tess confessed after taking a sip.

"You like?" I asked.

"I like very much. I wonder if Mr. Stanton sells these."

"If not, I'm sure Vera can find us some," I replied and then felt embarrassed. I hadn't meant to bring up Vera.

"Speaking of Vera," Tess said, smiling broadly.

"Yes?"

"Well, Charlotte told me about your little maneuver to have her see Vera. That was brilliant, Donte. Did it work, though?"

"I don't know."

"I don't understand. Charlotte was excited about the whole thing, and you know Charlotte; she doesn't get excited that easily. She couldn't stop talking about Vera. You should've forced them to have lunch at Ernie's years ago. At minimum it has changed Charlotte's opinion of Vera dramatically. Strange what a little conversation can do."

"Yes, very strange," I said.

"So, how are you two doing, then?"

"I think better, Tess, but it's too early to tell. And to be honest, I'm still very confused."

"What is there to be confused about?" she asked.

"I don't know."

"You don't make any sense," Tess said, looking straight at me. "I don't mean to be brutal, but you must accept that Vera is with someone else and she's happy. She's the sweetest woman in the world, and I love her dearly. And I wished that you two could have stayed together, but it didn't work out. But that doesn't mean you can't be friends."

"I know," I said, not really wanting to continue with this conversation.

"You'll find someone."

"I know."

She stopped talking and took a sip of her cider.

The food arrived a few minutes later, so we concentrated on eating. But the silence didn't last long.

"Do you remember the first time we met?" Tess asked between the bites, without looking up.

"Of course."

"Charlotte asked you to escort her home after she threw up in the bathroom while Vera held her head."

"I only remember taking you and Charlotte home."

"That's my point. Vera is too sweet. Charlotte was a bitch to her all night long, but Vera was a gracious host and helped her in the bathroom and didn't even raise an eyebrow when you took us home."

"That's not fair, Tess. Vera understood…Charlotte is like a sister… Vera understood that I was needed—"

"I know. I didn't mean to accuse you. We are getting off the subject. It just occurred to me that this is the first time since our first night in Charlotte's house that we're together again without any of our friends."

"It is strange, but—"

She raised her hand to stop me. "That's not my point either. You and I shared something on that night. We shared a secret and because of that..." She paused and took a large sip of her drink, then she put the glass down and continued, "It was a very intimate moment."

"It was very intense. I was somewhat distraught, and you wanted to know why."

"Yes, yes. Because of all that, I felt a connection with you. I know it may sound weird, and I don't want you to feel uncomfortable. But that night meant something to me. I knew then..." She paused again and took another sip. "I knew then...I knew that night that I'd love you forever."

I looked up, confused, but before I could say anything, she quickly added, "That came out all wrong. I didn't mean it the way it sounded. I meant to say that I felt a bond between us, and it made me better understand how you and Charlotte feel about each other. I don't think the others do, and that has created a serious confusion amongst our friends."

"I don't understand, Tess. After all these years, you're mentioning it now?"

"I'm sorry; I know I'm rambling. This cider goes to your head."

"Do you want a glass of water?" I asked.

"No, I'm fine. I'm trying to say, did you ever tell Vera about Charlotte? Did you tell her about your secret?"

"No, of course not. Did you tell Herman?" I asked.

"Herman? No, why would I tell Herman? He's not a player here, but Vera is. She is—was your girlfriend, and as kind as she is, I'm certain she must be utterly confused by the extraordinary affection you show Charlotte. Nobody understands it, Donte. Nobody."

"Isn't it too late to talk about this now? You waited ten years to give this advice?" I asked.

Tess was taken aback by my harshness but stayed calm. "I know. Don't you think I know? I blame myself for keeping quiet all these years. I should have said something or at least pushed you to be forthright with Vera. In my defense, you two were so good together that I just assumed."

"I didn't deceive her," I objected.

"Don't be angry."

"I'm not angry. I just don't understand why you would bring this up now of all times."

"I'm sorry. I really am. It's because we're here together and away from everybody, and it reminded me of our first encounter and how strong it was. I won't say anything more but to say that I really think you should tell Vera everything."

"She won't understand. She'd think there was more—"

"But there wasn't, was there?" Tess asked.

I looked at her blankly for a moment.

"Oh, no! I'd never imagined. You and Charlotte are too good at hiding things. It's not normal."

"She isn't really my sister, Tess. And it was a long time ago, and it never went anywhere."

"I didn't mean it that way. I meant, it's not normal to keep so many secrets and keep them so well."

"It's best to keep some things hidden, Tess," I said.

"I don't want to agree with you. In fact, I hate to agree with you, but I think I must on this one. Nevertheless, you should tell Vera about the other things. I think she has the right to know."

"Maybe, Tess. I'll have to think about it. I have to think very carefully, but now is not the time."

"I know, and I'm sorry. I will not speak of this again. Who am I to advise you on these things anyway? I'm sorry," she said.

"Don't say you're sorry. I'm glad you can be honest with me, Tess. I need it. I need you to be my friend."

She nodded but didn't say anything. I still had my presentation to think about and no time to consider my past sins.

CHAPTER TWENTY:
A SEMINAR FROM HELL

A walk through the cold air suited us, and we managed to avoid any serious rain or conversation on the way back from the lunch. We returned to the hotel feeling full. Tess sat on the edge of the bed and rummaged through her suitcase, dragging out dress after dress, piling them up on the chairs. She took off her street clothes, grabbed an unwashed red silk dress that looked elegant just draped on the arm of the chair, and then walked to the bathroom. I followed her stride with my eyes, and once again I was presented with a shut door.

I waited.

She spent a long time there, but when she came back out she looked stunning. Her red dress fit her slender body perfectly. But she had put her hair up, despite my earlier request.

"Okay, I'm ready," Tess announced and grabbed a pair of shoes from her suitcase. "Is this your best suit?"

"Yes?" I said.

She pursed her lips and rolled her eyes. "I'm sure you have something better."

I opened the closet and presented her with what I had. She mused over the options for a few minutes and then pulled out a light gray suit and handed it to me. She then selected a tie and a new shirt from the rack. I had a whole new outfit.

"How about my underwear? Do you want to change that too?" I joked.

"I think I can trust you with that decision," she replied.

I changed quickly and grabbed the tie and, with a few expert moves, made a perfect knot.

"Impressive," Tess commented on her handiwork.

I grabbed my jacket, and we walked down the staircase. She almost tripped on the first stair, and I reached to steady her by grabbing her bare shoulder. A jolt of electricity ran through my fingertips like on the night of Charlotte's game, causing me to jerk back.

She didn't seem to notice, so I said, "Didn't you feel the static electricity?"

"What are you talking about?"

"Nothing."

"What's the matter with you? You're acting strangely," Tess said.

I ignored her and managed to make it to the curb without any further incident. I hailed a black-and-white cab that was parked on the other side of street. The driver made a quick U-turn and stopped right in front of us. I told him the address, and he stuck his right arm out of the window and opened the backdoor from the outside. Tess had to pull up her skirt a bit to be able to lift her legs to get in, but she managed to do so in her most ladylike manner. I climbed in after her and sat by her side.

"Big party?" the cabbie said.

"Just an office function. A bit of sucking up and kissing asses," Tess yelled out over the BBC Radio 4 program the cabbie was playing.

The driver nodded but didn't say anything.

"Humor is cultural," I whispered to Tess, though it was doubtful that the driver even heard her in the first place.

We sat in silence for a while, marveling at the beauty of the city and getting intoxicated by the deep smell of the gentle rain that had just started again.

She stared out through an open window. "I love the smell of rain."

"Me too," I said.

She reached out and held my hand in her own.

"You're going to be fine," she said suddenly, though she didn't sound very certain.

That more than anything else made me nervous. I felt a strong pang of failure in the bottom of my stomach. I wished it were over already. I continued to peer out the window as we crossed Hyde Park and drove north toward Portobello Road, which was packed with street vendors. The cabby efficiently maneuvered around the many vendors and made a left on Kensington.

"Will there be a lot of people?" Tess asked.

The driver slowed down and then maneuvered around a double-decker.

"I hope not." I knew this was simply wishful thinking. It was going to be hell.

She moved closer to me and laid her head on my shoulder for a moment. "You'll be fine."

"I shouldn't have had the cider at lunch," I said with somewhat of an accusatory tone.

"Hey, your own fault that you have no control. Plus, I think a few drinks will do you good. In fact, we should stop at a bar for another drink."

She was trying to be funny, but I wasn't in the mood.

Somehow all the euphoric feelings that were so real just a few minutes ago were gone, replaced with the fear of failure. I wished I hadn't called Tess. What was I thinking, bringing an unpredictable, rather loud, mostly obnoxious, and most definitely know-it-all girl to the most important event of my career? I must have been crazy. I noticed that she was still holding my hand in her own, so I jerked it away without a word and looked out the window. My mood seemed to have infected her as well, since she drew closer to the other side of the cab and peered outside.

And then a moment later, I felt ashamed for blaming her for my own insecurity. She was doing me a favor, and yet I was acting like a child. I should have apologized, but I sat in silence.

We reached Holland Park. I paid the driver as Tess walked ahead in her mangled way. I caught up with her, and she seemed to have regained her perkiness. There were already several cars queued, and many people in their elegant dresses were getting out.

"I hope they're not going to the same place," I said in a dismayed voice as I surveyed our rather simple attire.

Tess shrugged and, to my astonishment, took off her shoes.

"What are you doing?" I asked.

"There's no way I could climb that steep hill with these shoes," she said.

I looked up at the small pathway toward the top of the hill and then at the thin heels at the end of her shoes and couldn't find an argument against her. Except, of course, that there were a few other women in more restrictive dresses and shoes who were walking just fine.

"I'm not like them," she warned me before I even said anything.

"Whatever is the most comfortable for you, but let's do it as quickly as possible."

We dashed ahead toward the main event hand-in-hand, like a young couple on their first date. I tried to keep my face hidden just in case someone might recognize me, although it was a little arrogant to assume anyone would recognize me—my bosses, maybe, but definitely not me. Tess and I would appear like just another couple of overdressed Londoners out for a stroll.

We made it to the main area in no time. They had taken over a football field, which was nearly covered by a few large white tents. The perimeter was protected by a fancy combination of metal and wire, giving it the feel of a surreal corral. There were four people, two women and two men, standing at the entrance, politely but definitively asking for invitation cards and then checking the names on their pads. I handed them my invitation and announced our names. There were a few people milling around and sipping champagne while a rather good-sized orchestra played Vivaldi. We each grabbed a drink and strolled toward the largest tent, the only one that was fully enclosed by white walls, where I was sure the big boss would be.

We were not disappointed. Inside, the corporate leaders were holding audience with the peons of the company—that is, the mid-level managers like me; the real peons wouldn't even be invited to such a gathering. Three presentations from my company were scheduled, plus a handful from some companies from the continent—smaller than ours but not to be ignored.

It was odd to have business presentations mixed with a social event. It was odd to have it at Holland Park. It was odd to have all the competitors in the same place. The whole thing felt incredibly bizarre. But we all worked for so-called innovative and progressive companies, and they wanted to be different from traditional businesses. This was our way of telling those square people that we were better than them; a new era had begun, and we were trying to be pioneers. I still think it was odd, but I was just a minor player in a big game. I did what I needed to do to make my company successful.

It was rumored, and I was sure it was true, that the investors were only looking for two proposals. They wanted each one to be the opposite of the other in terms of style. Therefore, there was going to be at least one loser from my company. At least one team would be looking at the job ads in the morning paper.

We had been directed to work with other teams and were constantly told that it was the fate of the company that was most important. Like good inmates, we started with that comradely spirit. Naturally, this only lasted for a few days, and then we went out of our way to sabotage and misdirect the other teams' projects. Our savage behavior was fueled by a rumor that a poor performance would mean the dissolution of the branch and the wholesale firing of its staff; so much for the company's loyalty toward its staff.

Tess grabbed my hand. We strolled side by side and said our hellos and started several meaningless conversations with different people. In a short time we separated as Tess became engaged in an intense conversation with someone, and I roamed the tent doing what I was there to do. I overheard one of the guys refer to Tess as a beautiful "piece of ass," and at once I felt both pride and rage. I searched for Tess, and there she stood, talking to a young man. She laughed at something he said and tilted her head like a woman in one of those shampoo commercials. Again I felt a sense of jealousy that I knew I was not entitled to possess. I grabbed a glass of something from a passing waiter and downed it in one gulp.

Thirty minutes later several waiters and waitresses started moving around the tent with little bells in hand, calling everyone to the meal like old hotel bellboys. We all started looking for our pre-assigned tables. I located my table, where my name brightly shone on a creamy place card. I arrived first, so I stood by the table waiting for the others. One by one they showed up, and I introduced myself to each before I finally sat down. I looked at the name next to me: Angela Kilpatrick, one of the senior VPs of the company.

For some reason Tess had not been assigned to my table, and her absence made me feel more anxious. I'd noticed the mistake earlier, but there was nothing to be done. The usher assured me that it was merely an innocent error, though I saw it as a bad omen. I stood up glumly, staring at Tess being seated at another table.

"Have a seat, young man."

Angela had already sat and pointed at the chair next to her. She was a powerhouse in my company. In her mid-sixties, she looked better than many women in their forties. She had been with the company since she graduated from college, and she had done it all. She was a short, thin woman, but she could take over any boardroom like she was a giant. She had impeccable taste in clothing and, at that moment, wore a smart red Chanel suit with black trim. She wore a minimal amount of makeup, which made her look smart and power-ful. Her smiles were narrow and momentary, but this only added to her charisma.

She nodded again, and I apologized and sat down.

"Do you know everyone here?" she asked.

I shook my head.

She asked everyone to introduce themselves. This was more for her benefit than mine, but I appreciated it nevertheless. It was a distrac-tion that I needed. She introduced herself and then told them about me while I sat awkwardly with a frozen smile. With that out of the way, small conversations commenced around the table while I con-tinued to sit quietly.

Angela started to say something else, but I could not focus any-more. I saw her lips moving, and I even imagined seeing the words coming out of her mouth. Still, I couldn't understand them. I nodded and grinned so long that the back of my cheeks ached. I drank a glass of wine and played with the food that had been placed in front of me.

I was suspended in space with no sound. Then, as if someone had switched off the mute button, sounds began to filter through my ears again.

"It's definitely essential for everyone to do what's necessary…" An-gela said, holding a dessert fork like a pointer.

The man who had introduced himself as Kevin nodded and said, "Yes, Ms. Kilpatrick, but the data has shown…"

I had no idea what topic they were discussing. Tess energetically engaged with several people around her table. She talked in a loud, animated voice and drew laughter from everyone. How did she do it? How did she manage to blend in so easily while I struggled to even have a simple conversation in my own environment? Ironically, a few minutes later I would have to dazzle the people in this room. She moved so comfortably, was so relaxed. I knew the people around her, all stuffy and arrogant, but they melted like little groupies around a rock star.

I was still staring at Tess, lost inside my own head like usual, when I realized that everyone at my table was looking at me.

I panicked. Had I missed something? Did they call for me to give my presentation? Did I say something horrible without knowing it?

"I…I'm sorry. I zoned out for a second," I managed to utter.

"Nothing important," Angela said in her aristocratic voice, arching one eyebrow to indicate dismay. "We were just talking about your project." She paused to let her comment sink in and then continued by pointing her finger at the man next to her, though she was still looking at me. "And Kevin is confused."

Kevin started to explain himself but was stopped by a wave of Angela's hand.

"Never mind that." She dismissed him and then looked at me. "Please explain it to him so that he can understand."

Her tone left no doubt that Kevin was in trouble. Angela gave a quick smile to me and then returned to her dessert plate.

I thought, *Who the fuck is Kevin?* "Well, it's a construction of—"

A booming voice echoed across the field. I thought, *Thank God, I've been saved.*

Mr. Riasat stood at the podium with the confidence and the assurance of a man who knew he couldn't be beat. His white short hair was trimmed to an impeccable style, but I saw signs of male pattern baldness, though significantly less than men twenty years his junior. His tailored suit fit his round body perfectly, and he looked tall even though he was hardly medium height. He stood like a solid oak, strong and unwavering; there was clearly no doubt in his mind that he was the one who belonged up there.

He gave a brief introductory remark that I had heard a million times before, but he was a good speaker and made it convincing. After his speech he casually mentioned a change in the agenda: I, the person who thought he was ready to do it all, the person who had pulled Tess all the way from San Francisco to help, would be given the honor of being the first presenter.

No way.

I wasn't ready. It's a process, you see; I'm scared at first, but fear gives way to confidence, then I get really nervous, but I work through it, and then a few seconds before a presentation, I'm okay again. But now the agenda had changed. I needed time to adjust, but it wasn't going to be afforded to me. I was in between the confident and nervous cycles. I needed the order of the speakers to be the same as the published agenda. An agenda is like a contract. He shouldn't just walk up there and change it because he thought, in his distorted, manipulative mind, that he would gain some advantage without taking my system into account.

I saw him clapping and looking in my direction, telling me not to fuck up. Then everything was in slow motion. Angela had stopped eating, and she clapped very slowly while staring at me. The world slowed down. I looked down at the table and saw my hands on top of it. They appeared disconnected from my body. They looked abnormally large, and when I tried to lift them, they did not respond. They were these strange, long things sitting on top of the white linen. They were not even mine.

I heaved myself up with all my might, and the hands finally left the table, following my body upward. I stood next to the table with my arms next to my body, stretched beyond their natural limit by my heavy hands. I lifted one foot, but it refused my command too. I stared desperately at Tess, but she was still talking and laughing. I needed her help. I needed her to reassure me.

I was going to fail.

Then there was a rush of sound, a heavy and loud banging that jarred my body. I was now fully standing, and then everything was light and fast. The change in gravity almost made me knock my coffee cup off the table and into Angela's lap. But I managed to make it to the podium without stumbling or knocking anything over. One moment I sat by Angela, trying to coax my hands to behave, and the next moment, in less than a blink of an eye, I stood a hundred feet away at the podium.

Mr. Riasat shook my hand and then left me there, alone and unprotected. I felt like a child on the first day of school. I stared across the sea of faces. They stared back at me, mocking, waiting for me to fail. Even the waiters and waitresses, who only moments before were rushing back and forth, were standing still, staring at me expectantly. What did they want?

My hands felt wet but were no longer heavy. I wiped them on my pants, thankful that the podium had hidden this action from most of the audience. I was panting hard, and I heard the echo of my breathing from the large speakers scattered across the main tent. My heart ached, and I thought at any moment it would clench up, denying oxygen to my brain. I surveyed the field again, and, like a man stuck in quicksand, I tried to stay calm without much success. There was no floor beneath my feet. I gasped for breath but only tasted the rotten taste of failure in my mouth.

It must have been hours before I spoke.

"Good afternoon," I said hoarsely.

I couldn't remember my introductory remark. What was it? I wished I had brought my notes. I touched my jacket for a miracle, but the notes had been left in the other jacket, the one that was still sitting in my hotel room. I had planned to start with an anecdote, but I couldn't even remember how it began. I should've practiced more.

What was I thinking, inviting Tess? She sat out there in that sea of faces, laughing and talking to the men around her. I tried to pick her out of the crowd but failed. All the faces became the same face, indistinguishable in their judgment of me.

I opened my mouth. Some words rushed out in a ramble. I couldn't tell what I said, but it had extracted some scattered laughs. Not from Mr. Riasat, for sure. He detested gimmicky speeches. He had offered me some advice the first time I had to speak in front of him. It went something like: *Think of the podium as an anchor. Hold onto it, if you need to, so you don't hop around like a monkey. You're not a game show host.*

"Are you a lefty or righty?" Mr. Riasat had asked in all earnest. "Well?"

"I'm right-handed." I hated being made to feel like a schoolboy, and yet I sounded like an insolent child.

"No." He waved his hand dismissively. "No, I mean your eyes."

"My eyes?"

"Yes, depending on your eyes, you want to stay on the left of the podium or the right of it."

I never figured that one out, and I was wondering at that moment if I was standing on the wrong side. Maybe if I could inch myself more to the right—but then there was the anchor rule, and I could not possibly move and speak to such a large audience.

I grabbed a glass of water from the podium and drank the full thing in one breath. Then I started to talk about the project, the one that could make or break so many people's careers, mine included. Once I had rediscovered how to put one word in front of another, those chains called sentences, all linguistic prowess struck me at once. It was like I had always known how to do this.

After that point the presentation glided smoothly, the charts and graphs following my points in perfect harmony. I even located Tess's face, and she seemed to be caught in some sort of awe.

I returned to my seat to the sound of applause. I felt confident but exhausted. Angela kept patting my arm and my shoulder, and her excitement only grew as we watched the rest of the presentations. It seemed clear to everyone that we had outpaced the other companies.

As the official portion of the event came to a close, people broke ranks from their tables, and I found myself inundated with congratu-lations and well-wishers, so many hands to shake.

Tess appeared at my side and gave me a strong hug, whispering in my ear, "Well done." She drifted away from me as I entertained my hand-shakers, and I caught her and Angela sitting down at our table, talking.

I finally just wanted to get out of there and made my way toward Tess. Angela abruptly stood, shook Tess's hand, and walked off.

"Ready to go?" I said.

"Yes." Tess stood.

"What did Ms. Kilpatrick want?" I asked.

"Oh, nothing." Tess waved it off. "You know, small talk." She wrapped her arm around mine and guided me out of the tent.

CHAPTER TWENTY-ONE:
GETTING HIGH

We walked most of the way back as there were no taxis to be found. As soon as we stumbled into my room, Tess took off her shoes and stockings. We both fell on the bed, exhausted from the evening's event.

"My flight is at midnight, so I should leave soon," Tess said.

I didn't respond.

The walk, the tension of sitting next to Tess and wanting to touch her with all my might but knowing that the invisible wall between us was as solid as ever, had made me exhausted. I needed to lie down in one place for a long rest.

She surveyed the room and started to get up to pack her scattered clothes, but I held her back with a touch of my hand, and she laid back, giving a long sigh.

"I have a little thing for you to take away your fatigue," I said and rummaged through my bag in the corner of the large wardrobe, taking out a tightly rolled joint.

"How the hell?"

"Don't ask," I said.

"But I can't travel stoned. Are you crazy?"

"It's the only way to travel. This one is pretty light. It'll relax you before your flight to Spain." I opened the window and lit the roll, taking a long, slow puff before continuing. "This is the craziest flight schedule. You won't be in Barcelona until three or four in the morning."

"I know, but—"

"It's just crazy. I shouldn't have asked you to come to London," I whispered while leaning on the windowsill, the same way we started the day. This time, though, Tess remained seated on the bed. I took a few more drags and then realized that I had monopolized the now shrinking dooby. I turned around and tentatively offered it to Tess.

"I shouldn't, really," she said, though her body language gave the opposite signal.

The grass was more potent than I thought; when I stood up to take it to her, my head felt heavy, as though it might topple over. I stood by the open window and took a deep breath before attempting to walk the few feet that separated us. Tess sat rather still with her head propped up by a few pillows. I dropped onto the bed and stretched my hand toward Tess's mouth.

She took a deep drag and held the smoke in her lungs for a very long time, so long that I thought she might turn blue. But she seemed perfectly fine, sitting stoically with her legs stretched in front of her. She let out the smoke with a noisy exhale and pushed the remainder of the roll back to me, her arms stretching toward me but failing to reach me completely.

The burning paper floated between us for a moment before Tess quickly took it back to her mouth and took another long drag. I knew there was something that I had to tell Tess, but I couldn't remember, no matter how much I searched my mind. I still felt heavy, so I rested my head on her side. She looked down at me lazily with the joint still hanging from the corner of her mouth. She took it from her mouth and almost dropped it, as it was becoming a roach, but managed to hold onto it with her fingernails.

"Want more?" she said.

"I should warn you, Tess, this stuff is more potent than I thought," I said, finally remembering.

She blurted out laughing with a succession of deep breaths. She tried to stop herself but that made her laugh more.

"What's so funny?" I said.

She suddenly stopped laughing.

I waited for her to respond, but time seemed to have lost its continuity. For a moment my mind grabbed onto the word "funny" and drifted to this incident. But today wasn't funny, was it? I sat there thinking about "funny" for a long time, maybe hours.

Then Tess said, "Nothing, it's just—"

"Nothing what?" I asked.

"What do you mean, 'nothing what?' You just asked me what's funny, and I was thinking it's so funny that you said that now after I finished the whole thing and I need to be at Heathrow."

I said, "Wow. Heathrow is such a beautiful airport. I wish I were going to Heathrow on a train. Taking the train in the Black Forest with you sitting next to me while we sip red wine and eat loads of pasta."

"Can't we order room service?" she asked.

"I'd love to get some pasta and some black forest cake," I said.

"Let's go," she said but didn't move.

It appeared to me that I was walking in a dark corridor and suddenly a door opened, powered by a word that Tess had uttered, and I was compelled to move through the door. I felt so mellow and content walking through the doorway and exploring what was behind it. As I was getting comfortable in this journey, I heard Tess again saying something. It dragged me out of the dark corridor. I would say something incoherent, and she would reply with a non sequitur, and I would be back in the dark corridor with random doors.

I looked over at Tess, sitting so regally on the bed next to me with her tight-fitting, beautiful dress that made her small frame even more majestic than I would have thought possible. I looked at her bare legs and the glimpse of thigh that was made visible by the way her dress pulled up when she lay on the bed. She leaned closer, and the traces of her perfume lingered around my face. She said something, a whisper that I could not hear, so she tilted her head a bit to see me.

Her head tilted downward toward my face. I drew my face up to hers, only a wisp of hair between us. I did what I'd been dreaming of doing for eons and kissed her ever so softly on her warm lips. To my utter astonishment and heart-pounding surprise, she kissed me back. Emboldened, I kissed her again, this time deeply. She twisted her body so that she was now embracing me, and I felt every part of her body, from the top of her head to the tips of her toes. We kissed again and again, silently and ravenously. I put my fingers through her hair and pulled it away from her neck and shoulder. I pushed my lips against her neck, kissing it inch by inch.

She moaned, soft. She moved her hands under my shirt and caressed my torso and back, her hands warm and dry, her movements patient and concentrated. We kissed and embraced. She unbuttoned my shirt, and I fumbled with her dress like a teenager stumbling haplessly from zipper to hook. We sat up on the bed to accommodate each other. My shirt was half off, and her dress was crumpling under my persistent hands. We gazed into each other's eyes.

Then our hands became silent, and there was a moment of mutual hesitation that felt eternal to me.

She slowly pulled her dress up and leaned back on the bed.

"It's just—" she said.

"I know."

"It's just—" She tried again but failed to say what we both knew was the truth. "I'm going to be late for my flight."

"Yes." I put my arm around her shoulder.

She pulled closer and leaned her head on me. "I'm just going to sleep for a little bit."

"Okay," I said.

A moment later I felt her softly crying but didn't say anything, letting the softness of her body take me back to my drug-induced calm. Then she fell silent, and when I looked over, she had already drifted off. I wanted to sleep, too, but I also wanted to savor the moment, warm in bed with Tess.

But even that was a lie. I wasn't thinking about Tess. I was thinking about Vera.

Charlotte had surprised me right before I left for London. She called me and said she had gone around to Vera's place and taken her to lunch. I almost didn't believe her. How could the two of them ever stand to be alone, across the table from each other for a whole meal? But she said it had happened, no matter how tense, and that Vera was willing to hear from me, to accept an apology.

I thought that the moment the call ended, I would dial Vera's number, but to my surprise I chose not to. I waited. And before long, I found myself in London and busy with the coming presentation and the stress and anxiety of fucking it up and preparing for Tess's arrival.

But right at that moment, I couldn't stand it anymore.

I slipped away from Tess quietly, leaving her in the bed to nap before her flight. I walked to the front desk, requested to use their phone, informing them of the international charges, and pulled it around to the side for a little privacy.

It rang for what seemed like too long.

"Hello?" Vera answered.

I couldn't speak.

"Hello?" she said again, with anger in her voice.

"I'm so jealous of you going to Ernie's," I said, referring to the restaurant of Vera and Charlotte's meeting.

Vera sighed. "Hello, Donte."

"Was it as nice as it was before?" Ernie's had long been a dream restaurant for both Vera and me. As college students, we were always too poor to even think about going. I'd been able to get in a couple of times, all on Charlotte's dime or, rather, her father's. Vera and I had one incredible meal there together, but we never made our way back. Now I supposed we might not ever eat there in each other's company again.

"It was great, despite Charlotte's company," Vera said.

"Well, it's the price you have to pay if you want to eat there."

"For sure, but I think it was worth it."

I wanted to apologize right then. I heard an impatient tone on Vera's end, something like the tapping of her nails on a countertop. However, I wasn't sure how to phrase it. How do you go about apologizing to someone like Vera for something like this?

"Donte," she said.

"Yes?"

"I told Charlotte that I would forgive you, and I will, but I can't simply pick up and go as if nothing ever happened."

"I understand."

"Because you hurt me, and the wounds haven't healed."

"I know."

"Okay, then. Let's say goodbye, and perhaps we'll talk later, but much later."

"Vera, wait…" It wasn't enough, getting to where we were in this moment and then just deferring everything like a rain check on a dinner reservation.

"It's torture," Vera said. "Why do you enjoy torturing me, Donte?"

"I don't mean to hurt you."

"And yet you do," she said.

"I'm sorry."

"I don't think it's enough."

"I know. I know it'll never be, but I need to speak to you. I need to hear your voice," I replied in a halting voice.

"It's not always about you," she said.

"I didn't mean it that way. I'm trying to say I've changed, and I think for the better."

"Tell me why?"

"I don't know how to put it in words."

"Then I don't think we have much to say."

A clerk behind the desk started to click her tongue. I wasn't sure if it was because I had been on the phone as long as I had, at international rates. But why should they care? It was all going on my bill. Or maybe she had eavesdropped and had meant it as a commentary on the conversation itself.

"I want to tell you a story, Vera."

Vera sighed.

"It's about Anat," I said.

"Charlotte already told me." Vera sounded far off. Perhaps it was the transatlantic connection. Or, she had held the receiver away from her face in impatience.

"Charlotte is not a good storyteller, Vera. I need to tell you this." I didn't wait for her response, wanting to forge ahead before I lost my courage.

Even though she knew most of the story already, I told Vera about Anat and Akron's first meeting, their hopes and dreams, about the pool party and my dinner with Anat. All the while, I tucked my own feelings of guilt and shame into their story, expressing my sense of failure in terms of my own life, of destroying mine and Vera's future together, and how, over the last couple of months, I had maybe started to understand contentment.

Miraculously, Vera listened, not once attempting to stop me or interrupt me. But then she said, "I don't know what you want from me, Donte."

"I'm sorry about what happened at Charlotte's party. Between you and me. And James."

"That's fine, Donte." Her tone suggested otherwise.

"This isn't easy, and I haven't thought all this through, but I'm sure of two things. I'm sorry, and I don't want to lose you."

"Have you been drinking?" she said.

I still felt the joint pretty strongly. "I'm completely sober," I lied. "I wanted to wish you happiness and success in your new life, and I hope, as you said, one day we can simply be friends again." And that wasn't a lie.

I thought I had lost her. The other end of the call started to sound dead. "Are you still there?" I said.

"Yes, I'm here." Vera sounded a little smaller than she usually did. "Maybe we should just discuss this some more soon. Face to face."

"I'm actually in London right now, on business."

"London! How much is this call costing?"

I laughed despite the tense nature of the conversation. "It's worth it."

"We can talk later, when you get back," she offered.

"A few more minutes," I begged.

"Okay, then tell me more."

"This is the best moment in my life, and let me tell you why…"

CHAPTER TWENTY-TWO:
WE WON

I returned to the room. Tess was still asleep, so I lay down next to her. I never truly fell asleep, just drifted in and out, but I felt her moving eventually. I heard her packing, and when I opened my eyes, she sat on a chair, fully dressed, her suitcase packed. She was deep in thought and didn't notice me stirring, so I lay there spying on her motionless form. The sheet smelled of her, and I took a deep breath of her perfume.

She looked up. "We should talk."

She must have noticed my movements, or perhaps she was talking to herself—speaking out her thoughts. I didn't say anything but went to the bathroom to wash up. I felt the night was an inevitable conclusion to our story. We had choices to make, and if we'd taken the wrong path of succumbing to our emotions, then all would have been lost. There would be no salvation on that path. We wanted each other, but we were brave enough to stop, even in the height of our passion. If nothing else, I was at least proud of that fact. Now, the difficult part was the next step.

I walked out of the bathroom feeling resolute and prepared. Tess still sat in the same position, erect and deep in thought, with her suitcase standing next to the chair like an obedient dog. As soon as she felt my presence in the room, she stood up sharply and touched the suitcase as though telling it to get ready.

I stepped forward and kissed her on the cheek. "Did you sleep well?"

I felt the need for establishing some normalcy, but the kiss and the question caught her off guard. It took her a moment to shake the puzzlement from her face. I took a step back as she had visibly stiffened.

"Tess—"

"Could you please help with the suitcase?"

I wanted to clean the slate, but it seemed she was still grappling with the unknown that the night before had introduced. She reached down to pick up the suitcase herself, but I grabbed her hand and pulled her into my arms.

"We'll be okay," I said, meaning to reassure her.

She pulled away and asked me again to take her suitcase down. There was nothing else to do. She was not ready to talk. She was overly polite, and it seemed all the little actions that up until the night before were normal and routine were now filled with profound innuendos.

I took her suitcase downstairs and hailed a cab, but she wouldn't let me accompany her to the airport. She opened the cab door and said goodbye, and I thanked her for her help. She smiled but didn't say anything for a moment.

"I should go," she said.

But she didn't move, so I leaned closer to kiss her goodbye. Even that little action felt wrong, so I pulled back abruptly.

"Tess...I don't know—"

"Just don't," she said.

"But—"

"Let's just say our goodbyes." She leaned close and hugged me. "I love you, but we can never talk about last night."

From her tone I knew that it would have been futile to pursue it even for a moment. There was nothing to say; I could only agree with her decision.

She boarded the taxi without looking back, but as it was about to leave the curb, I stopped it and leaned through the large window, holding onto the frame.

"Tess..."

She waited, but I couldn't think of anything to say. We had made a mistake.

Tess didn't say anything either. She looked at me, and I looked back at her. She was lovely.

I leaned in and kissed her. I knew it was our last kiss.

She pulled back and said, "Let go of the cab, Donte."

The cab drove off, and she did not look back.

I came home a week later but didn't try to contact her or Herman. I called Vera, and we met for an hour without a single word of recrimination. We met again a week after that, and it seemed we were ready to start putting our past behind us.

After a few weeks I gathered enough courage to call Tess. She seemed normal, but I felt the remoteness in her voice. We chatted for a short time, but she said Herman wanted to talk to me. I thought he knew. My heart skipped a beat when I heard his voice over the receiver, but my fear was unfounded; Herman was unchanged. We talked for a moment, but I couldn't handle it, so I said I needed to hang up.

It took me another week to see them, and although the contact was unsettling at first, the meeting went well. Tess was more like herself. I think I was, too, but I knew that it would take more than a few weeks for us to fully expel London from our minds. I didn't want to, at least not for a while longer. We could never have that moment back. With our last kiss, a part of us died as well.

AUTUMN 1981

CHAPTER TWENTY-THREE:
LOS ANGELES

The plane glided over the stark topography that had come to be known as the City of Angels. We sped past the wooden houses below us as the pilot lowered the aircraft into its approach to the airport. A thick canopy of smog covered the vast view on the horizon while millions of cars inched their way toward it.

The airplane hit the tarmac hard, and the passengers were jolted forward. Twenty minutes later I walked out of the terminal. A blast of heat hit my body as the loud sounds of Los Angeles assaulted my ears. This is normal in Los Angeles. The air was thick, and the sidewalk was dirty from the millions of passengers passing through LAX.

Charlotte's lunch with Vera had helped smooth the way between Vera and me, and after months of tiptoeing around each other, we managed to rekindle a semblance of a closer friendship. She had her life and I had mine, and occasionally we crossed paths, enjoying each other's company, friends but not too friendly.

A few days earlier she had called to tell me she was in Los Angeles. Without any preamble she told me that she was sitting on the patio of the Wilshire Boulevard Brown Derby, enjoying the warm autumn southern California sun. That's how she put it, and before I could say anything, she told me all about how cobb salad was created at the Brown Derby. She offered a positive evaluation of the salad and then a two-minute criticism of the quality of their wine.

"What are you doing in L.A.?" I asked.

"Los Angeles is great. I don't know why you're always bitching about it. I'm sitting outside on the sidewalk, and the air is so nice. I wonder how miserable it is back in the City."

"Well—"

"You've got to come down. Just go to the airport and fly down now," she said.

"I don't know," I replied, even though I was delighted by the invitation.

"Okay, forget it. Not sure why I asked."

"No, I'm sorry. Believe it or not, I was planning a business trip there for next week, but I can change it and come this week." Then I added, "That is, if what's-his-name isn't with you."

"His name is James. And no, I'm here alone." And then she added, "I'm sorry, I shouldn't have called you. This was a mistake."

"No, Vera. This is good."

"Look, Donte. I was sitting here, and I thought, wouldn't it be nice to have you here next to me—to talk, to watch people. We can never be lovers again, but we can be friends. Can you handle it, or was this a mistake?"

"I can. I promise," I replied.

"I'll pick you up from the airport."

"Sounds great, Vera."

Life is often very complicated, but it could also be that simple.

*   *   *

As I walked out of the arrival gate, Vera honked the horn several times to get my attention and then waved her arms just in case I had not heard. I nodded and walked toward the car, a small red convertible with the top down. She jumped out without opening the door and waved at me. Her skin was well tanned. I saw the sun pass through her creamy linen dress. She sported a short haircut that framed her round face perfectly. She looked gorgeous, and a tinge of envy entered my body and rested in my mind.

"I'm glad you're here." I tried to sound nonchalant, but she could always see through me, even if no one else could.

"I'm happy to see you too," Vera replied. She grabbed my bag and threw it in the back seat. She then jumped over the door and slid down in front of the steering wheel.

I pressed the door handle, but the door was locked. I searched for a mechanism to unlock it myself, and Vera waved her hand to indicate that I should do as she had done.

I lifted one leg and put it over the door but fell over into the car, my head on the floor and my legs up in the air. She laughed, clearly enjoying my predicament.

I cursed under my breath, but Vera heard me and laughed again. I sat upright, and she put the car in gear and sped out of the airport. I heard a cop yelling behind us to slow down, but Vera was not listening.

She drove down Century Boulevard for a while before turning onto the freeway, where she sailed at ninety miles per hour. The howl of the wind was drowning out the radio. And neither the radio nor the forces of the wind stopped Vera from talking nonstop. Occasionally she would turn to face me or move her right arm to emphasize a point, but it was all lost on me. I was busy pressing phantom brakes and bracing myself against the dashboard for dear life.

She looked at me with a bemused smile for a moment, and then, once again, her lips moved soundlessly.

The warm sun relaxed me somewhat, and I loosened up my grip a bit to relieve the cramping around my knuckles. Vera seemed to know her way and took exits without consulting a map. She zoomed on and off of freeways and city streets with the confidence of a native, at a seemingly constant speed of ninety. From 2nd Street she took a sharp right onto Maple and then slammed hard on the brakes, forcing me to grab the dashboard to stop my head from becoming a permanent fixture on the windshield.

She turned the car off, and there was a blessed silence.

"Here we are," she offered, "and without taking a single wrong exit."

She looked happy and confident but also seemed a little nervous; I knew I was. This was a big deal, even though we tried to conceal it under a guise of a routine visit. It was so unlike her to want to drive, let alone drive the way she had.

The jumping in and out of the car without opening the door was new too. She tried to repeat the act again, and at the same time a valet tried to open the door for her, which forced her to perform a very interesting and admirable ballet move in order to avoid crashing into the poor guy.

I fiddled with the lock and managed to exit the vehicle like most people would. The valet stood clear of the car until we were done.

"My meeting isn't here," I shouted at her, my ears still plugged from the wind.

She only gave a knowing glance.

"Vera, did you hear me?"

"I heard you. Your meeting is in the office on the next block, so you can walk over there, or, if you wish, I could drive you there when you're ready to go. For now why don't you just come up and have a cup of coffee at the bar? They have the most wonderful collection of coffees here," she said.

We walked inside and ordered a cup of coffee. Vera insisted that I try some unusual variety, but she only ordered a basic black coffee for herself. It was bitter and pungent, but I drank it anyway. She didn't stop talking about the city and her wonderful rented car.

Time moved very fast, and soon I stood up and said that I needed to leave.

"I'm in room 2301," Vera said. "Just come up when you're done. I'm not leaving the hotel, but if I'm not in the room, you can find me on the roof. They have a pool there."

I walked over to the office, and a young woman directed me to the conference room without saying a single word. She was all smiles.

I walked in the room; everybody had already been seated.

They hated me. The feeling was mutual. They thought my London success had gone to my head.

I am sure they were right.

We talked. We discussed. They wanted certain things. I disagreed. They rallied, but I refused to give in. They appealed to my sense of self-importance, but I was too smart and, perhaps, important. They threatened to involve the boss, so I gave them his direct number. They would never call him, so I gave an inch. They got emboldened, so I re-entrenched.

They despised me.

Lunch was served, and everything came to a crashing halt. Food makes people reasonable. They tried again. I gave in to some more of their demands, not much, just enough to keep the conversation going. I knew how much I could give them in the end. I knew how to play the game.

We ate more.

There were supposed to be more details to cover in the afternoon, but I felt too tired. I had been sent from my office to convey a message, and I had accomplished my task. I gave a final offer, not wanting to prolong this any further. They didn't believe me and started to demand more. I needed to leave, so I walked out while they were still eating and arguing. The silent woman spoke out as I entered the elevator, but I only heard the first part before the door shut her out.

I rode the elevator down, accompanied only by the soothing music of KJazz. The door opened. I walked quickly out of the building and onto the warm, busy street. I stood there for a moment to get my bearings and then dashed quickly back to the hotel, as though an invisible string had pulled me hard toward my destination.

CHAPTER TWENTY-FOUR:
A POOL ON THE ROOF

The doorman tipped his hat and opened the door with a smooth flourish. I hurried toward the elevators and pressed the button several times. Nothing happened. I pressed a few more times and waited impatiently. The door opened, and I heard soft rock. I stepped in and was about to press the floor when I realized that I had forgotten the room number. Twenty something.

I was mad.

The door closed, but I still couldn't remember the rest of the digits. I pressed the open button and walked toward the receptionist, who put on an automatic smile as soon as she saw me.

"May I help you?" she said.

"Yes, you may..." I looked at her nametag, trying to make the impending request personal. "Keesha." I smiled while Keesha held her frozen grin. "I'm meeting my friend here on the twentieth floor, and she told me the room number a few hours ago..."

Keesha nodded, knowing the rest of the story.

"But I can't remember the number now, and I was wondering if you could tell me."

"I'm sorry, sir, I can't give you this information, but I could call your friend for you." She typed on her keyboard as I gave her Vera's information.

She frowned. There was a problem.

Keesha confirmed my prediction: a "do not disturb" instruction from Vera.

I asked her if there was anything else we could do. I said "we" to make it partially her problem as well. She shook her head.

But Vera knew me too well. I gave my name and asked if there was a message for me.

A bit more typing and then a broad smile. "Yes, there is."

She printed the message from Vera and handed it me. It told me all I needed to know.

I waited impatiently by the lobby elevator again and then more impatiently while it climbed twenty-three floors. Room 2301 was at the end of a wide hallway. I knocked gently on the door, but there was no response. I waited a few more seconds and then knocked harder; still no answer. A young maid exited the room next door, pushing her cart into the hallway, and looked at me with puzzled eyes. I motioned that there was no answer.

She smiled and pointed to the doorbell and then offered, "I could also call downstairs for you, sir."

I pushed the doorbell but nothing happened. I felt anxious.

I looked at the maid, but she had moved on already. She had her own life. There were hundreds of rooms to clean.

I felt exhausted, so I leaned against the door and lowered myself to the floor. I sat like a schoolboy at recess. I pounded the back of my head against the door. *Bang. Bang. Bang.*

The maid ignored me. She had seen it all.

Now I had a headache to add to my list of woes, but the banging had cajoled me a bit. I remembered something about the pool and swimming.

I ran toward the elevator and pressed both buttons. Again, the impatient wait. It arrived. The music hadn't changed. A quick glance told me that the pool was on a higher floor. Another slow ride. I was outside on the top floor, and there it was.

The first thing I noticed was the large bar by the entrance. The bartender nodded in greeting. There were many people milling around, all with large glasses of an orange drink. I searched the area, but Vera was not there. The bartender noticed me again and helpfully pointed to the changing room. I ignored him. He and I were the only fully clothed people in the place.

I stepped closer to a small blue pool with colorful tiles. Sunbathers in loungers lined the perimeter. Vera was the only person in the water.

She swam fast and nonstop. She was in form, her head turning after every three strokes, her body streamlined with the surface of the water. She wore black goggles that gave her a sci-fi fifties look. I just stood there looking at her, mesmerized by her movements. I noticed other men were doing the same. I felt tired just watching her swim and decided to lie down on an unoccupied chaise lounge.

Vera continued going back and forth, and the audience, as if watching a tennis match, moved their heads with precise synchronicity.

Finally she stopped at the other end of the pool and grabbed a large orange drink. It must have been the specialty of the bar. She pulled herself up out of the water with one smooth movement and grabbed a large hotel towel. She put on a white bathrobe that was a bit too large for her. It fell around her shoulders. Then she turned around and saw me.

I felt embarrassed for spying, but she produced a broad smile and walked over before I could make a single move.

She walked gracefully even with the large bathrobe and the drink. She came close to me and kissed me on the cheek. I could smell chlorine and the coconut of sunscreen.

"Your nice suit's getting wet," she said. She had dripped all over my dress pants when she leaned in to greet me.

But what was a little water compared to her affection?

"I wasn't expecting you till much later." Her eyes sparkled.

I explained the drama at the office while she slurped the large drink through a couple of small straws.

"Gustavo made it," she said.

"Gustavo?"

"The bartender," she replied matter-of-factly and then handed the large goblet to me. Although it was faint, I could taste the rum. It had been a long time since I had seen Vera drink.

She grabbed the drink back and bowed with an exaggerated display. "I'm glad you're here, sir, but I have to take a shower and settle my bill."

We walked toward the bar, and Gustavo nodded. "Another one?"

"No, I think we're done. I'll just take the check," Vera replied.

"On the house," Gustavo offered. He then looked at me and said, "Vera and I made a bet, and she won."

He called her by name as if he knew her. I was annoyed.

"Gustavo bet that I wouldn't be able to tell what's in the concoction, but of course he was wrong," Vera explained triumphantly.

Gustavo reached across to shake my hand. "Gustavo," he said.

"Donte," I replied.

"Have a seat, Donte, and I'll make another round."

"And you'll put in the good champagne," Vera demanded.

"Of course," Gustavo replied.

Vera then looked at me and said, "He tried to make a variation of an Al Capone, but he used gin instead of whiskey, and he added a bit of champagne—but not a good one—orange, and Grand Marnier. And finally, he left out the bitters."

"And I was impressed that she knew," Gustavo added.

I was getting more annoyed, but before I could say anything, he produced two new glasses and commenced in making the drinks. He then made a show of pouring from a new bottle of champagne.

We sat at the counter, and I took a sip of my drink. It was delicious though a bit sweet.

"Business or pleasure?" Gustavo asked me.

For a second I didn't understand what he meant, but before he could explain, Vera replied, "It depends on how you define intention."

"Oh, so it's complicated?"

"More than you know," I offered.

Vera looked at me and smiled.

Gustavo was about to say something else, but a new customer, an elderly woman, had sat down at the bar, so he left without saying anything.

Vera and I sipped our drinks in silence.

"In my line of work, there's no complication," he continued when he returned, "and there are no seams between business and pleasure. My business is to please people." He smiled, clearly feeling satisfied with himself.

"But life is complicated," I said.

"It sometimes feels that way, but I've been bartending for a long time, and one thing I know for sure, one thing I'm totally certain of, is that life is definitely not complicated."

"As you might have guessed, I've also been a bartender," rejoined Vera, "and as one professional to another, I would say you're full of shit."

"Am I? How many life stories have you heard in your career?" Gustavo asked.

"You know the answer: hundreds. But hundreds of drunken stories of suspect veracity," she said.

"People lie to their doctor and even lie to their priest, but rarely do they lie to their bartender," Gustavo replied.

"Perhaps that's the case in L.A., but where I come from, people lie to everyone," I offered.

Vera bit her lip but didn't say anything.

Gustavo produced two glasses of water and put them in front of us. He was about to push his point when he noticed another customer calling him. "We shall continue." He walked away but came back quickly.

"You may be right that some lie," he said as if there hadn't been a break in the conversation. "But even in their lies there are some truths, don't you agree?"

Vera nodded in agreement, but I stayed stoic.

"Take you, for example," he said and then added quickly, "If I may?"

I nodded again, interested to see what he had to say. I was starting to like him.

"I asked if you were here for business or pleasure. You could have picked either or both, and I'd have believed you. In fact, if you didn't want to chat, you would have just picked one and given me a one-word answer, but you wanted to chat and wanted to be truthful."

"Maybe I don't like to lie, or maybe I just like to chitchat. Maybe I was trying to figure out what you were doing with my friend," I said and again noticed Vera frowning at my comment. And again, she didn't say anything directly to me.

"Yes and no. Business or pleasure pretty much covers everything, so it's not a lie to pick one," he replied, not deigning to respond to my last comment.

"And there are bartenders who don't like to talk. The good ones know when to shut up and when not to. The same goes for the customers," Vera added.

"I'll give you that," I replied.

"Your answer, and I'm paraphrasing, was, 'It's complicated,'" said Gustavo. "And I'm thinking, what could be so complicated for a man who is here with his beautiful wife, who is not only a great swimmer but, best of all, knows her cocktails?"

"He's not my husband," Vera interjected rather harshly.

"I apologize. I didn't mean to pry. I should shut up," Gustavo said.

"Don't be silly," Vera said. "We wanted to chat, and you're an insightful person."

"As I said, it's complicated," I offered.

Vera added, "We're two difficult people, treading through a complex maze. We're going to go downstairs to change, and then we're going out for a drink or two, and, if there's time, dinner—"

Gustavo picked up her line and continued with it. "And you'll be pleasant and friendly with each other, and then you'll go back to San Francisco and say you had fun. You might see each other in a week or two and do the same thing again."

"Is that so bad?" Vera asked.

"It depends on where it goes from there," he said.

"So that's your advice, bartender?" I asked.

"Oh, no. That was my prediction based on what Vera told me earlier and what you just now implied. My advice is to be honest."

"I've been honest with her," I said before Vera had a chance to respond.

"You misunderstood me. You need to be honest with yourself."

"I don't understand," I said.

He opened his mouth to speak, but his other customers were losing their patience with his inattention, and he was forced to tend to them.

He was taking too long to return this time. I looked at Vera and she nodded, so I put some bills on the counter and we left.

It was time to make our decision, I thought. I wondered what Vera was thinking. We'd been talking to each other through the bartender, but it was time to speak directly.

Yet we rode the elevator in silence. Vera started to hum along with the dreadful music.

She opened the door to her room and walked straight to the bathroom, but before closing the door she shouted, "Go ahead and make yourself comfortable. Your bag is in the closet."

I found my bag and changed from the uncomfortable suit into more relaxed slacks and a T-shirt. By the time I was fully dressed, Vera was out of the shower, toweling her short hair dry. She was very efficient.

"Do you want to take a shower?" she asked.

I could have used one, but I thought it would be better if I didn't. She shrugged at my refusal and sat on the bed to comb her hair. I sat on the chair and watched her tidy herself up in silence. She saw me watching her, smiled, and patted the mattress on her side as an indication for me to come sit next to her.

I moved over to the other side of the bed and sat.

"Take off your shoes," she ordered, and I obeyed.

"I feel so exhausted," she said and leaned back against the bed's end board with a long yawn. "I did several laps. Do you mind if we sit here for a while?"

"Not at all. I feel a bit tired too."

"Good. Maybe we can take a little nap before going out."

She pulled the cover back and slid in between the sheets, still wearing the bathrobe. I lay on top of the quilt with my head on the pillow. We faced each other.

She looked lovely with her full lips and sparkling eyes. I stared deep into those eyes, and she returned my stare without blinking.

"It feels right, doesn't it?" she said.

I think I understood what she meant. She meant being happy by just being together, without skewed expectations—being comfortable lying side by side like the old friends we were, without pretense, without trying to impress. She meant that she had forgiven me, or, at least, she was going to forgive me soon. I thought just lying there was wonderful.

"It always did," I replied, but then instantly I knew it was the wrong thing to say.

I expected her to jump up and denounce me, but she just lay there looking at me. I wanted to wipe some of the memories from our brains, but I knew that would never happen.

"Not always," she corrected me but without any traces of judgment, just a simple statement of fact.

I stirred a bit, feeling embarrassed, and I felt my defenses going up.

She reached out and touched my face as an assurance. "But not always," she repeated softly, though I could hear the echoes of resolution deep within. "It feels right at this moment, and that's more important." She again brushed her hand on my cheek.

I was itching to explain myself. She was right, but I didn't think she understood the context. She was still staring at me, penetrating deep within me. She was not the same woman who I had left almost two years ago, not even the same person who I had tried to hurt at Charlotte's party. She had always been strong, but now she seemed to have a sense of balance, a keener understanding of where she was and where she was going.

Before I had chance to speak, Vera said, "Earlier today, when I was driving to the airport to pick you up, the radio was playing Schumann's second symphony. Do you know that piece?"

I nodded.

"The music pulsed with its journey from depression to joy. I felt as though Schumann was speaking to me, and I couldn't help but start to sob and then laugh out loud, like a crazy woman. Yet, listening to that piece cleared my mind. I knew that there was a purpose for having you visit me away from our city. I knew that I must take the opportunity to clear whatever clutter had come between us. It was impossible to do it in San Francisco, where every corner was a reminder of our past."

But what about me? I knew the answer, but I still felt the need to explain it to her. I could see she was sensing my impatience.

I couldn't help myself, so I reached out and said, "Vera—"

She stopped me by putting her finger on my lips. "Let's just lie here for a moment."

CHAPTER TWENTY-FIVE:
THE CONVERSATION

I slept deep and long. When I woke up I was still in the same position as when I had fallen asleep, and I'd left a small pool of drool on the pillow. The left side of my body tingled and cramped, but I was mesmerized by the view from the window. The shades were pulled back, and below me were twinkling lights in a dark pool of night, stretching for miles. For a moment I forgot where I was and stared outside without any comprehension. The room was not lit, either, but a narrow beam of light stretched across from the room next door.

I twisted on the bed and lay on my back, feeling the blood rush to the side of my body with a force that made me ache.

The door opened, and the room was flooded with harsh white light.

Vera entered, fully dressed. "I was scared you might sleep the whole night."

"What time is it?"

"It's seven."

She stood at the bottom of the bed. She had both of her hands on her waist, but her body was partially twisted to the side so that I could only see the fingers of her left hand. She looked like a postmodern glass jar. She had put on some lipstick, but I couldn't tell the color in that light. Her hair was combed straight down. She wore a tight, spaghetti strap black dress that fell above her knees.

"Well?" she asked.

I thought she was asking me to say something about her dress.

"Aren't you going to get up?" she said.

I still couldn't feel the left side of my body, but I dragged myself off the bed, which made me feel better though still groggy.

I walked to the bathroom and took a long, hot shower. I assumed Vera would hound me for wasting time, but she didn't bother me. I was glad to be standing under the shower, letting the hot water wash away some of the grime of the past that was still greedily sticking to me.

When I stepped out of the shower, my old clothes were gone and a new set of evening clothes hung on the door, even a new pair of underwear. I wondered if it was strange for Vera, as my ex, to pick out new clothes for me, to handle my underwear. But it had the same normalcy that I'd felt lying next to her that afternoon and taking a nap; it just felt right.

I brushed my teeth and shaved. Vera had put my toilet bag next to the sink. I walked out of the bathroom refreshed and ready for an adventure.

"Where do you want to go?" I asked.

"What time is your flight back?"

"Late."

"Let's go upstairs for drinks, then."

I was surprised by her offer. I didn't know why, and at the time I couldn't possibly have asked, but after our breakup, she had given up drinking. She completely stopped cold.

She used to be a drinker. She loved her liquor. It wasn't like she was an alcoholic, but she certainly enjoyed it very much. Her drinking picked up a bit when her father passed away. Naturally, his death took its toll on her. He had been a lovely man, and even I missed him. But then she stopped drinking.

So the offer of a drink was surprising—but I welcomed it. I refused to ruin the evening by asking questions and scratching at old wounds.

We took the elevator back to the top floor lounge. It was crowded but not so much that we couldn't get a nice table.

She ordered a glass of cognac, and I felt compelled to do the same.

"I didn't know you drank cognac," I said.

Of course I knew.

"Didn't know I drink cognac or drink, period?" There was a lilt in her voice. "I missed drinking."

"Since when?"

She laughed at my question and mulled it over a bit.

"Not long," she finally said. "Okay, since the lunch with Charlotte," she admitted with a puff of air.

The whole thing felt a bit surreal to me—the call, the drive, the afternoon nap, and then sitting with Vera at the bar. It felt like being a passenger in a fast-moving train, but this time I was not resentful. I was happy to be sharing this ride with her.

The waitress came back with our drinks.

We touched our snifters. I put the huge chalice under my nose and let the aroma take me. I took a little sip, and the powerful taste of oak casks invaded my mouth and throat. Instantly I felt the warmth of the liquid traversing my whole body.

"Has a nice length," Vera said while rolling her tongue in her mouth.

"Length?"

"Oh, it means it has a long bouquet and it's very smooth."

"Yes, it does." I meant to reconfirm her assessment, but it came out sarcastic.

"I just read it in a magazine this morning," she offered quickly. We both knew she was lying, and she laughed dismissively. "I guess I still have it."

"I don't think you ever lost it."

"Yes, I'm drinking again. Why not?"

"I welcome it."

"I'm sure you do."

"What do you mean?" I said.

Sometimes I felt rather awkward with Vera—not in a bad way, but at times I couldn't read her well. This was truer that night as I was trying to rekindle some type of friendship with her.

"Nothing," she dismissed me and then offered, "I feel so centered now. I haven't had an epiphany or anything, but I think I've found my way."

"I wish I could be as certain."

My honesty shocked me, but Vera seemed to understand. She sipped a bit from her drink and moved within whispering distance of me. She licked her lips and smiled, which always accentuated her lovely dimples. She looked at me conspiratorially, which made me lean even closer. I could smell her perfumed hair and feel her breath on my face.

"We never had the chance to talk, not in a civil manner, anyway," she began. I nodded in agreement, though I felt the fear deep within. "I always knew..." she paused and put her hand on my own for assurance—and I thought, *I don't think I am ready for this.* "Rather, I always felt that you had more feelings for Charlotte than you admitted and, as amazing as it may be, even some feelings for Tess. I took all this as simple, far-off romanticism."

My heart pounded so hard that I could see the fabric of my shirt moving up and down.

She said, "But there you were, ready to throw away everything over a fantasy, and then you did."

I was stunned and pulled back hard.

"Please don't," Vera said in an even but forceful tone. "Please let me say what I have to say before you judge. I know you want to jump in and explain, but I think you owe me that much."

I owed her far more, I admitted but only to myself. I was not ready to speak.

"You never asked, and I never told you where I was for those ten days when we broke up," she said.

She looked up at me quizzically, but I couldn't return her glance. I knew where she was for those days, but I forced myself to keep quiet.

"Ironically, I was with Tess. As I said, I suspected but needed to be sure. Tess is so lovely. She's so kind and warm, and I could see how everyone would love her. But she's also so very devoted to her husband, and I knew you were deluding yourself. You were just acting like a selfish, pathetic schoolboy, but Tess couldn't help but defend you. I couldn't figure out if it was just her kindness that prevented her from saying anything negative about you or if there was something deeper."

She took a deep breath and held it for a moment, closing her eyes, thinking. "We had long conversations about you and your friends. It felt like you were all in a soap opera—every one of you going after everybody else with love, lust, and lies. We talked about the past and how we came to where we are, but it was always veiled. Your best friend Herman, as I'm sure you recall, was not so guarded."

I recalled Herman and his unguarded attacks. I felt betrayed by him then, but I was trying very hard to understand him as well.

She shook her head slowly. "I never found the answer to that riddle. Tess is good with keeping secrets. But I don't think it matters anymore, does it?"

I stared out of the window, at the millions of lights shining across the city. I didn't think she needed an answer—that world no longer existed.

Vera reached over and turned my face toward her. "And then you left all those lovely messages. All those beautiful words."

She wiped her cheek, trying to be inconspicuous. She then took a large sip of the brandy, held the liquid in her mouth for a moment, and then let it slide down her throat.

"Those words were so comforting." She closed her eyes and tilted her head to the side. Her body gently rocked like a small boat on a lakeshore. She was far away for a moment. She opened her eyes and was back in the room. She shook her head like a disappointed mother and bit her lower lip as though to stop herself from saying what she needed to say. She opened her mouth and then closed it quickly, but it didn't last long; the truth came out anyway.

"But you didn't say the right words, and, my darling, you simply waited too long."

She spoke without any malice, without any accusation, another statement of fact.

She paused and waited for me to say something, expecting an elaborate defense. But I thought it was too easy to look back and say I should have or I could have, but the fact was that I wasn't ready, and such words wouldn't have helped, nor would they have been sincere.

I heard Vera's proclamation, and it occurred to me that, despite all the angst, we had made the right decision then. I could have done so much more. I certainly could have done it differently—gentler, kinder. I could see it now, but I was not in the right state of mind back then, no matter how I'd glossed it over with words. There was nothing I could say or do that would change the past.

We had finished our drinks, so she signaled the waitress for another round.

When I still hadn't responded to her comments, she said, "I went to the Central Market today."

Grand Central Market is the oldest market in Los Angeles. Vera went there often with her father when she was a little girl.

"How was it?" I asked, happy that we had moved on to the mundane, but everything that night was purposeful.

"I went out for a walk, and although the air was a bit smoggy, I enjoyed the walk. Downtown L.A. has changed since our last visit; it looks much nicer."

"Did you find your place? What was it called?"

"José Chiquito. Yes, I found it."

This was her dad's favorite place in all of Los Angeles. In the couple of trips I had made to L.A. with them, he always made sure we visited José Chiquito.

"It took me a while to locate it, though," Vera continued, "and for a moment I felt a deep sense of disappointment, but then there it was, right in front me, in the same place it had always been. I didn't recognize any of the people behind the counter. Even though it was early, the place was as busy as the way I remembered it. I sat at one of the stalls and ordered my dad's favorite plate."

"Carnitas tacos with a side of black beans and a glass of tamarindo," I said.

Vera laughed loudly. "Yes, exactly," she added. Then she stopped smiling and said, "But every bite of the carnitas reminded me of him, and it only made me miss him even more."

"I miss him too, Vera. He was a great man."

She ignored me or didn't hear me because she continued on with her soliloquy. "I was sitting at the counter feeling melancholy, and then I remembered what my father had once said about Tess. It was a blatant warning that I dismissed and then forgot, but it came to me clearly today."

I knew what was coming, and my heart fell.

"He said, 'Be careful that Tess doesn't steal your husband.' It was a strange thing for him to say, and I dismissed it as that," Vera said.

At the time Vera and I were not married, but that didn't stop her father from believing we were. I had overheard him saying a version of that warning at other times and Vera dismissing it, but clearly she had a motive for bringing it back up.

"Vera," I said, but she shook her head and stopped me.

"I didn't believe my father. I'm not stupid—there was no denying that Tess is a desirable woman, but I never believed that Tess would ever waver from her devotion to Herman."

"Exactly."

"No, not really, Donte. My father was lovely, but he was wrong. Tess didn't steal you away from me. You left on your own."

"Vera, the only thing I can say is that I am utterly sorry for everything. I'm just—"

"We both behaved badly. I should have given you a chance to come to your senses," she offered.

She was being generous, but I shouldn't have been given a pass so easily. That night she chose to tell a story that should have been told long before. Vera would not be distracted by my apology nor allow it to change her version of what had happened between us.

We had finished our second drinks, and she signaled the waitress for the check.

"What time is your flight?" she asked again.

"We still have plenty of time."

"I'll drive you."

"No need. I can grab a cab," I said.

The waiter showed up with our bill. Vera paid for it, dismissing my offer to pay. But we didn't get up to leave.

"I'll drive you." Her tone implied that she didn't want to hear any argument, so I nodded in assent. She asked the waiter if he could call the valet, but he said she had to call him herself. She went to the hostess table to use their phone.

I sat there alone thinking there was so much more to talk about, but clearly, she was dismissing the past and me along with it. She would return in a moment and then drive me to the airport, and I would go home, and she would return from her trip later. And then we might meet again and be civil to each other, like we were today, and she would be generous and kind, as she always has been. But then what?

It occurred to me as I was sitting there, waiting for her to return, that it had always been I who lived in a self-centered bubble of pettiness. And I'd been there before, that state that the drunks call a moment of clarity. But, as with most addicts, this awareness of my own shortcomings was always fleeting. I think Vera saw it in me, and maybe the others did too. And I wondered if, in their private conversations, they pitied me. But then again, even spending the energy to think about their conversations was sad and ironically proved their point; pathetic.

I had been cruel too. I was unkind to Vera when she thought she was pregnant. At the time I didn't see it as a joyful event that would cement our relationship but as a trap. So I did what a heartless man would do: I gave her an ultimatum and saw her crumble and melt away right in front of me. But instead of comforting her, I simply drowned in my own misery. It's so easy to talk about right and wrong when it's someone else's life. But when it's time to do the very right thing that we all preach, the shackle that binds you to your own self can be so heavy and strong that there is no right or wrong. She sobbed softly in the bedroom, and I sat in a trance in the kitchen.

At the end there was no pregnancy, just a false positive, but the price we paid was too much, too taxing for any relationship. I exposed parts of myself to her that should have never been uncovered. In time, when we had no more tears and the wound was replaced by a deep scar and our memories were fogged with other events, we moved back to our routines, but our lives were never the same again. And within a year there was no more us.

I could see Vera across the bar talking to the valet on the phone; she looked up and our eyes connected. She waved and I waved back. She pulled her hair back and smiled broadly.

As I was looking at her, it became unmistakably clear that I loved her as I had never loved anyone. But was that enough to cure us? I had no answers, and even if I thought in the affirmative, I wasn't sure if Vera would agree. But even in that euphoric state, I knew I couldn't trust myself to sustain it. I told myself to slow down and be realistic. I was happy that we had made progress, become more civil toward each other. I could pick up the conversation with her when she returned to San Francisco. I needed more honest conversations, not just with Vera but also with Tess, Charlotte.

I told myself that I needed to move one step at a time. I had neglected them all, and it was time to make amends. It was time to make everything right. It was time for me to decide.

I didn't know that night that none of my angst mattered because within a short few weeks, I would be at a dinner with my future wife, and at that moment in time, she and I would make a decision that would change both our lives forever.

PRESENT DAY

CHAPTER TWENTY-SIX:
AT A CROSSROADS

My grandmother used to say that it's a single moment in your life that defines the path to your future. And every time she said that, my grandfather inevitably would add, "And ours was October 10, 1981, at 10:32 p.m."

But the last time she said it, my grandfather stayed silent. No one in the room took notice of it even though the exchange had been the mainstay of every October 10th party. Perhaps it was her barely above-whisper pronouncement as if she had stopped believing in it; or perhaps my grandfather had become hard of hearing; or perhaps Uncle Nadir's recent death had put an end to them celebrating the single moment they had claimed as the defining event of their lives.

But no matter the reason, each of the guests found an excuse to leave early, and then came the opportunity for me to hear a different version of my grandparents' often told story. I had filled dozens of pages by the time my grandfather reached the part of the story where he confessed to neglecting his friends and the need to make a decision.

He looked up, and I could see he was tired. It was very late, but I could tell he was worn down by the struggle of recalling painful memories from the depths of his past. He had been talking for hours in his haphazard way, speaking somberly of his days in high school one minute and then, almost mid-sentence, digressing to speak with the exuberance of a teenager about times with his friends years later.

Like most old people, he had vivid memories of decades earlier but hazy ones about the recent past. He would look up in excitement when he would recall a little nugget from a long-ago event. Other times, when he was uncertain, he would look intently at his hands like an infant who had just discovered parts of his body that didn't exist to him before.

I would worry that the moment would pass and that he would forget the newfound memory, but each time he would look up and tell the episode as if it was a movie playing right in front of him. Other times, when he would recall a difficult moment, he would stare at the wall across the room. I would try hard to penetrate through his guarded emotions and could see that he was debating whether to share or not. At those times I would walk over and touch his head or kiss him on the cheek to bring him back and then return and sit at my desk, and he would tell the story without looking at me, haltingly at first but then with gusto and no apologies.

After several hours of conversation, my grandfather went up to say goodnight to my grandmother, which gave me an opportunity to quickly scan what I had on the pad of paper. I certainly didn't have enough, and it was clear that we would need more of these sessions before I could even make an outline of their story. Even what I had was full of holes, missing parts, and at times contradictory stories— fifty years of memory is a lot to store. I also needed to work on my penmanship or remember to bring my dictation pad.

When he came back, he told me about his visit to Los Angeles and his conversation with Vera. He paused when he said he needed to have an honest conversation with the three women who had helped define his life.

"Are you going to finish?" I asked when the silence lingered.

"No."

"What do you mean, 'no'? You promised to tell me everything."

"Did I? Well, I'm tired now," he said and then added, as if confirming it to himself, "I'm not young anymore."

"I'm sorry. Should I come tomorrow, then?"

He pondered my question for a moment, and I could read regret on his face. I could see he was still debating if he should tell me everything.

"No. Not tomorrow," he replied.

"Day after?"

"No. I think I've told you enough for this year."

"Please. Come on—"

"I'll tell you more at our next party," he offered with a little smile.

"What? You want me to wait a whole year? That's not fair, Grandpa. You can't tease me like this. You're being cruel."

"Perhaps. I'm too tired to be anything at this point."

And with that he stood up, leaned over and kissed me on my forehead, and told me to lock up the house before leaving. Then he walked out of the room at his painfully slow pace.

I came back the day after, pretending to have left something at their house. But he saw through me and would not entertain even a short conversation. My grandmother smiled at our maneuvering but didn't say anything. I had promised to keep his story from her, not that she inquired about it. She made me a ham sandwich and put it in front of me even though I told her I wasn't hungry. She then forced me to eat it as a way of changing the subject.

"Everything is going to be fine," she offered as a parting gift, but I left their house feeling defeated.

I tried several more times as days and weeks passed. He became older and weaker. It's strange how in our old age each day carries more weight than the next. We don't see the impact of time when we are young; the days are mingled together. It seems it's our age that defines time and not the other way around.

After several weeks of attempts, my grandfather relented and told me a bit more, and then some more weeks after that, and by the time we reached the end of the summer and were nearing their annual party, he told me the real story of his October 10th dinner with my grandmother.

We were in his study, and he had just finished telling me about his time with Tess in London. He had remembered more, and, without any sense of self-consciousness, he told me every detail of his encounter with her. When he was finished, he asked me to make him a gin and tonic and gave me detailed instructions of how he wanted it. When I came back with his drink, he was deep in thought and didn't notice my presence, and I stood there in awe of his power of concentration.

Several minutes passed, and I could hear the old-fashioned clock counting each second of the night. When he looked up, I could tell he was finally ready to tell me about it. He took the gin and tonic from me and sipped gingerly from the tall glass, and then he told me to sit at his desk. I obeyed like a little child, ready to record and take notes when he was ready.

He stared at the far wall and then told me the final chapter without looking at me and without pausing.

It took me several minutes to understand, and he waited patiently until I looked up. He smiled meekly, quickly averted his eyes, and stood up.

This was the most detailed of his many stories, perhaps because there were only two of them, and only he held the truth. Finally I understood why he had insisted on making me promise to with-hold it from my grandmother. Still, I had learned that each of his stories needed several tellings to make sure it contained the truth that he really believed in, even if the years had eroded the facts. I needed him to tell this one again, even if it was very painful for him.

"Could you tell me more tomorrow?" I asked as he stood staring at the far wall.

"No. Let's wait until after the party like we did last year."

"It's several weeks away."

"You've waited this long, so I'm sure you can wait a bit longer. I'm not going anywhere, at least not yet."

Of course, he was wrong.

*   *   *

I was on my way to Washington, D.C. for a hard-sought interview that was scheduled for the following day. As the plane touched down, I received a message, a simple note from my mother asking me to call her. It could have been nothing, just my mother being my mother as she has always done, making sure that I had landed safely and want-ing to wish me luck with the job interview.

But I knew, without wanting to believe it, that my grandfather had died only a few days shy of October 10th.

I had offered to delay the trip—somehow I knew what was coming, as one sometimes does—but he had laughed it off.

"You'll get another stab at me," he had promised. "Go and do your thing, and we will chat after the party," he had ordered.

"I'm so happy you love your grandparents so much, darling," my mother had offered, "but you need to get on with your life. It's an important interview."

My grandfather didn't seem to be able to recover from Nadir's death, and each day he looked frailer than before. I could feel Death hovering about him, and I was hoping I could be there for him when he needed me the most. I didn't want the news of his passing to be hidden within a cold message. And yet, my first real thought wasn't about him but about the interview. For a fleeting moment, I was more upset about how this would impact the interview than I was about the death of the person who was everything to me—the man who instilled the love of knowledge in me. How cold. I didn't want to think about the job, but my mind, as if not in my control, went back to it. I didn't want to be so heartless, but I guess I was no different from anyone else in this story.

I contacted my mother, and she confirmed it without saying a word, her image on my phone blurry in my eyes. But I still needed to hear it.

"Is it Grandpa or something else?" I asked, wanting to cry.

"He passed away a few hours ago."

There was a pause, each of us digesting the news. We all expected it but perhaps not so soon. For a moment before my mother had answered, I thought perhaps it wasn't him but my grandmother. I didn't want to think about it, but I wondered if I would prefer her dying over him.

He had died as my plane took off from San Francisco. He would have said, *I soared as you did, child.* But in the end he had died alone, in his study with the book on the history of San Francisco atop his lap, as if the book was cursed. It seemed, or at least with my own bit of idealism I hoped, that he had spent his last moments with the memory of his friend.

"Did he suffer?" I asked.

"No. We think he died peacefully."

"I'm glad."

"Yes."

"Let's hang up," I said.

"Okay."

I was still in the airport. There were hundreds of people walking around me, going to a myriad of destinations. I walked to the nearest waiting area and sat down. I couldn't bring myself to leave the airport, as if that action would bring the real world to me. I needed to stay in the make-believe world of the airport.

I didn't really cry. I didn't cry when I sat in the waiting area, nor when I found the courage to leave, nor when I stood waiting for a taxi, nor throughout any part of the trip. The grief was just there, settling heavily in the bottom of my heart, and it never moved. I looked and acted like any other passenger in the Dulles Airport. I wondered how many others were in mourning that very moment in Terminal C. I wondered which of us would break down and cry for our lost love. None of us did. We all went about our business. I wondered how many of us would reach our destination carrying the pain and keeping it forever. I knew I would.

I didn't call my grandmother that day nor during my time in D.C. My mother wanted me to return immediately. She became angry when I refused, unleashing her frustration on me. I stayed and interviewed for the job as I had planned. In the end I didn't get it. I could blame my grandfather's death or my mother's anger for my failure, but that would be dishonest. I wasn't really qualified for the job in the first place. My grandfather had arranged it for me through one of Nadir's friends.

Days went by. No one noticed that October 10th had come and gone. It no longer held the import that it had before. I missed my grandfather's funeral. My mother was furious, but I couldn't find the courage to go. I knew he would understand. I still hadn't cried.

And then, about a month later, I couldn't stop crying.

I cried when I asked my grandmother to tell her side of the story. I cried when she asked me to tell her about my grandfather's version. And I cried when I denied her request.

My grandfather's death was another reminder of the fragility of time, and I became more eager to piece together the final story. I approached the rest of his friends, and to my surprise they were all eager to speak. They also saw the ephemerality of life and wanted to add a touch of their own memories to the story, but none really knew about the dinner that sealed the bond between my grandparents. They were more interested in their own roles in the story than the story itself, as if the more their names were mentioned on the pages, the longer they would live.

It has now been two years since my grandfather's death, and ever since then, I've been struggling to piece together the final scene. I'm not sure how to present the last tale, the one that started it all. I am not sure my grandfather is the right narrator for it. I am not sure if he told me the whole story or even if the parts he did tell were the real truth.

For the most part I have tried not to be an aggressive editor and let my grandfather tell the story as he wished it. But I think the last chapter, the chapter that began their world of October 10th parties, needs a certain impartiality that no matter how much he tried, he could not muster. So I decided to tell the final story, with all its blemishes, my way.

Here is my truth of that night.

OCTOBER 10, 1981

CHAPTER TWENTY-SEVEN:
A DINNER AT 10:32

"Trust me, you'll like the place," she said.

She wanted to go to a new restaurant that she had read about a few days earlier but didn't want to take a cab. They stood next to her car, debating about what to do, when she suggested the restaurant. He was hungry and couldn't think of any alternatives.

They sat in her car, and she set the radio to a jazz station. They drove through the streets as if driving with the rhythm of the music. She searched for the right address. The jazz on the radio was mellow and intoxicating, so they just listened for a while without talking. The music changed, and she started speaking again, picking up with their earlier conversation.

"I know we did the right thing," she said.

He didn't say anything.

"But then we didn't, did we?" she said. She was right, but there was still no reason to reply. "And you know, I can understand most of it and can even accept it, but what about the weeks after? Why didn't you try to come after me? Why did you let me go?"

He finally replied, "I was so confused. The letters..." He tried to recall the content of the dozen or so rambling letters that had only added to his confusion. "The letters, to be honest, didn't help. They were written by a stranger and not by a person I once knew. And to be truthful, I didn't want honesty either. I thought you didn't want me, and I wasn't sure I wanted to see you."

"It was hard, you know, sitting there, going through every minute detail of our lives and seeing no hope," she replied. "We had spent so much of our lives together that when it collapsed, I buckled under it too."

He looked straight ahead, not daring to look at her, but he sensed that she was no longer angry. She was sad, the deep melancholy we feel when we know there is no hope.

She tried a different approach. "I can understand how you might have felt with your perceived love for her." She stressed each word with an undue sense of bitterness. "But you loved a person you couldn't possibly have."

He held his tongue, so she continued, not expecting a response.

"Yet it never materialized," she said. "You didn't fly off with her to some wonderful destination. No! Perhaps because it was more of an infatuation than a real thing. And perhaps even a one-way affection as well."

She looked at him, but he refused to make eye contact, remaining as stoic as possible.

She laughed, though there was no mirth in it. "I'm sorry. I don't mean to be vicious, but you need to hear it now and from me. I think everyone expected you to come to your senses in a few months. Everyone but me, that is. I knew better. They all thought it was a positive sign for us because you weren't dating anyone."

She was right, but at the same time she wasn't. He wanted to tell her about the few months of solitude and then about London, San Francisco, and Los Angeles, but he was afraid to get it wrong again. He knew there was something else besides courage that stopped him from making the wrong choices; it was the knowledge that deep down, there was only one person for him.

She touched his shoulder. "What?" She wanted to know why he kept silent. She wanted a response.

"Oh, just that you're so right."

"Am I? But not really, right? That's what you are thinking. You could have saved everything, but once again you waited too long," she said.

He visibly stiffened, but she ignored him. A moment earlier she had taken an exit, and she needed her full attention to find the right street to turn onto.

He felt frustrated and angry. Why was he there? There was no room for the two of them, and it seemed that he, as she had aptly put it, was late once again.

She found the place she was looking for and pulled into the parking lot. They were greeted by a couple of valets. The doorman graciously opened the front door, and they walked into an ornate lobby decorated with oversized paintings. They had no reservations, but the maître d' was hospitable and accommodating.

They were escorted by two handsomely dressed men and seated at a small corner table. He felt underdressed and said so, but she shrugged her shoulders and said, "You'll be fine," as though that resolved the issue.

The menu was wonderful and almost everything was priced the same, expensively. As soon as they sat down, they were served two small aperitifs that he had never tasted before. He sensed a hint of almond and orange. They sipped the drinks in silence.

Then the waiter showed up and started to recite some specials, but she stopped him and said she was ready. She ordered the duck crespelle with spicy Cremona mustard seeds; pancetta-wrapped pork tenderloin with dried fruit and Marsala; and a bottle of wine.

He was not in a good mood. There was no happy ending to this story. The meal in the fancy restaurant was a slow, torturous path to the inevitable. He couldn't think about food.

He said, "I'll have the same."

"I thought you hated duck," she interjected quickly.

The waiter stopped, holding for a confirmation of the order.

"I like it now," he said.

The waiter understood his clenched teeth perfectly and merely nodded and left.

"Please don't be angry. It has taken me a long time to reach this point." She leaned closer and took his clenched hands into her own. Her hands were small and could barely cover his, but they were soft and warm, which made him relax a bit.

"You owe it to me to listen to my side whether you think it is the truth or not, don't you?" She felt his hands tighten again, so she stroked them gently like one would a wild animal. "You know I'm right, no matter how frustrated you feel right now."

She said it as a matter of fact, as though there was no debate. She was right, of course, but that didn't mean that he wasn't ready to jump up and leave.

She sat back and let the waiter, who had just appeared, pour a small amount of wine for her to taste. He noted that he wasn't asked, but it was obvious who was going to do the tasting first.

She smelled the wine a bit and took a small sip. She twisted her mouth and frowned at the glass. She deliberately put the goblet on the side of the table closer to the waiter. "This will never do."

He expected the waiter to argue, but the waiter simply and without any sarcasm asked, "Would you like to look at the wine menu again, or should I open a new bottle of the same?"

"Definitely the menu," she said.

She studied the menu intensely and decided on a Kistler Pinot Noir that was three times the price of her first choice. The waiter nodded approvingly and left.

"It's wasted on me, and it's pretty expensive," he said. He knew this would provoke her. He wanted her to be angry, so she wouldn't rely on the truth.

"I'm sure it's wasted on you, but I'll enjoy it," she said, and then leaned close again and kissed him on his forehead. "Don't be angry. We're in a great restaurant. We're going to get a nice wine and eat great delicacies. More importantly, we are together, at least for this moment. What else do you want?"

Not to be there, he thought.

He was tired of these momentary respites. He wanted to leave before she could give him the final news. He wanted to leave, but he didn't move. He knew she was right, and perhaps that was the problem.

He said, with a forced smile, "I want you to be happy."

"I am," she replied quickly and without any trace of doubt, and that scared him even more.

And then she was all movement, eating the bread in big chunks, laughing out loud, and savoring the new wine that she quickly approved.

After the first glass they talked like regular people. They discussed the merits of different cities. They compared and contrasted London and Madrid and San Francisco and Los Angeles. They whispered about the old man and his trophy wife two tables away. The first course was tasty, even though he hated the texture of duck. The skin was crispy and the meat tender. The second course was even better than the first, and by the time they finished the bottle of wine, they were right again.

At least for that moment, it felt right sitting there across from her, just the two of them talking about the present, especially after the arduous marathon earlier in the day when she had forced him to face a different reality. He felt as exhausted as if he'd run the real thing while she was like a zealous coach, pushing him to his limit, making sure he challenged himself and accepting nothing but the best.

She refused the offer of a dessert menu, which meant he did, too, but she wanted a glass of cognac. He was a bit nervous about it but didn't want to ruin the good feeling that had returned between them. So he ordered a glass of cognac as well.

She arched her eyebrows but didn't say anything. Then she leaned forward and asked, "Do you remember last year's party and Charlotte's late-night game?" She said it casually.

He thought she was going to make fun of the silly game, so he nodded with a smirk. "Yep. Pretty strange night."

"Remember the roaring fire and the intoxicating scent? It was strange but interesting. We had to put on those blindfolds."

She spoke in a mellow fashion, and he misunderstood the depth of her tone.

"But mine was defective. I could see through it," she said.

"You cheated?"

He was still in a mellow mood; her earlier remark about being angry with him was just a blip in his periphery. He couldn't see what was coming.

"I didn't do it on purpose. It just happened, and everyone was so quiet, as if in a trance, that I didn't want to complain. I could sort of see people stumbling about. I was half expecting one of the boys to cheat, anyway." She frowned at his attempt to look innocent. "Please. It's not that far-fetched. Anyway, as I was saying, everyone looked kind of confused with their hands stretched out in front of them. But the mood changed immediately after everyone was seated on those comfortable cushions. Everyone looked so serene, so peaceful, especially you."

"I think everybody—"

She stopped him. "No. Not really. I'd never seen you that way. You just sat there comfortably and motionless, as though you were waiting for something wonderful but were too afraid to move, in case it would flee from you."

"It was a strange feeling," he said.

"Did you figure out who sat in front of you first? Could you tell each person after you touched them?" she asked.

She tried to sound casual as though it was an easy question, but he could see that her eyes were searching, whether for clues or betrayal.

His mind raced to find a resolution, but now he was torn between what he wanted to say and the truth. He was sure that he could not tell her, but then, why shouldn't he? He didn't think there was anything to hide. So what if he had recognized the first person and no one else? It's better to be honest, but he was sure she would be hurt. She would be angry. It would confirm what she already believed.

Be honest, he told himself.

Think about it. You can't. Don't be honest, he warned himself.

Don't be a fool, be honest.

Honesty's reward is pain and sorrow.

She will never forgive you if you are not honest.

She is looking at you, begging you to tell her what she needs.

She is looking at you, begging you to tell her the truth!

"Funny," he said, even though there was nothing humorous at that moment. "I was sure the first person was you."

He wasn't certain why he gave such an answer or how she would react to it, but the words rolled out of his mouth easily. She was about to say something but stopped. He was surprised by her reaction. She was about to speak but stopped again, as though she had lost the will to speak, afraid of what she might say.

She moistened her lips with her tongue several times, as if they needed the lubricant to allow her to speak. "You are playing with me, right?" Her eyes looked desperate. She needed an answer.

No, she wanted *the* answer.

Another choice.

How would he respond this time? It seemed that he was just an observer, barely existing between her and the voices that came out of his mouth.

Just say it. You know what you must say.

Tell her it was a joke and let it be.

There is no point to this conversation. There is no reason to tell the truth and no reason to lie. The best answer is no answer at all.

No answer at all? You're a coward.

Yes, that is the best way. Avoid any more conflict.

But again, other words came out of his mouth. "No, I'm serious. I was sure it was you."

"What? Are you sure?"

He couldn't tell whether she was hurt or touched.

She was composed again, and her voice was as even as ever. "I was watching you, and, as I said, you were so calm, so patient. You reached out so tentatively, so gently, and you seemed to be lost in your own exploration. I couldn't see your eyes, of course, but I could see your face, your mouth, and your eyebrows. They were all so concentrated, so focused."

She waited for a response, but he was just staring at her. She had prepared herself for many responses, but not the one that was given. She wanted to trust him, but what he had said was too much, so she continued, not knowing what else to do.

"Some people were more guarded, protecting their bodies, but others freely gave their faces. And you were so gentle, your fingers so kind. I could tell you were not sure. I could tell you hadn't discovered the truth. And then ten fingers landed on your face, and instantly there was certainty. There was recognition and, with it, an immense joy and comfort. I saw it clearly on your face. I looked around, but the others seemed to just play on the surface. They were concentrating hard, but to them it was just a childish game. Not to you."

She shook her head. "Not to you. Do you understand?"

He didn't respond, waiting for her to finish.

"And the recognition. I saw it plainly on your face. I'm sure of that. At least I was sure then. You recognized *Tess*, and in an instant I saw tenderness followed by frustration and sadness."

She stopped, breathless. She looked confused. She wanted to believe him, but the images in her mind were too vivid.

He didn't dare to speak. He feared what might come out of his mouth.

"And now you say you thought it was me? Do you seriously want me to believe that all that emotion was for me?"

She was getting angry. Her voice was rising.

He saw that she wanted to believe. She was trying very hard to believe, but her logic was telling her the impossibility of his confession. She was trying to connect the images in her mind with his statement. She was frustrated and couldn't get satisfaction from her own words. She stopped talking and stared at him. Her eyes were pleading.

Amid that chaos, he could hear his own voice calling on him, urging him. He wished that what he had said was the reality. He wished it had been she who had sat in front of him, exploring his face. He wished it so hard that he began to believe that it could have been the truth.

It may be the truth.

Yes, you feel it as if it was the truth.

It could be nothing else but the truth.

He knew it was the truth.

She reached over and took his hand. "Tell me, please. If you ever loved me, tell me the *truth*."

He knew for certain that there could only be one right answer, the only answer. He knew it then as he had known it all those years.

He took her hands into his own and noticed the time on her wristwatch.

It was 10:32.

She looked at him expectedly. She was no longer certain.

It was the moment.

My grandfather took a deep breath and offered my grandmother the truth with all his conviction. "Vera Pacient, it couldn't have been anyone else but you. Whatever you saw on my face, affection or tenderness, could have been only for one person, the person I have always loved, and the person I will always love. The person who is sitting across this table from me, the person whose trembling hands I'm holding in my own, right now, at this moment."